THE VODI

JOHN GERARD BRAINE was born in Bradford, Yorkshire in 1922. He sprang to immediate fame in 1957 with the publication of his first novel, *Room at the Top*, which was a critical success and a major bestseller on both sides of the Atlantic and was adapted for the screen in an Oscar-winning 1959 film starring Simone Signoret and Laurence Harvey. Braine's second novel, *The Vodi* (1959), met with mixed reviews and disappointing sales, but was his favourite of his own works. His next book, *Life at the Top* (1962), a sequel to *Room at the Top*, sold well and was filmed in 1965.

Braine, who was commonly associated with what the British media dubbed the "Angry Young Men" movement of working-class writers disenchanted with the traditional British class system, continued writing until his death in 1986, though at the time of this publication, all his works were out of print. Recently, there has been renewed interest in Braine's work, with Valancourt's reissues of *Room at the Top* and *The Vodi*, and a 2012 BBC miniseries adaptation of *Room at the Top*.

JANINE UTELL is Associate Professor and Chair of English at Widener University, where she teaches 19th and 20th century British literature. She is the author of *James Joyce and the Revolt of Love: Marriage, Adultery, Desire* (Palgrave Macmillan, 2010).

By John Braine

Room at the Top (1957)*

The Vodi (1959)*

Life at the Top (1962)

The Jealous God (1964)

The Crying Game (1968)

Stay With Me Till Morning (1970)

The Queen of a Distant Country (1972)

Writing a Novel (1974)

The Pious Agent (1975)

Waiting for Sheila (1976)

Finger of Fire (1977)

J. B. Priestley (1978)

One and Last Love (1981)

The Two of Us (1984)

These Golden Days (1985)

* Available from Valancourt Books

JOHN BRAINE

THE VODI

With a new introduction by

JANINE UTELL

Kansas City:
VALANCOURT BOOKS
2013

The Vodi by John Braine
First published London: Eyre and Spottiswoode, 1959
Published in the U.S. in 1960 as *From the Hand of the Hunter*
First Valancourt Books edition 2013

Published by Valancourt Books, Kansas City, Missouri
Publisher & Editor: James D. Jenkins
20th Century Series Editor: Simon Stern, University of Toronto
http://www.valancourtbooks.com

Library of Congress Cataloging-in-Publication Data

Braine, John.
The vodi / by John Braine ; with a new introduction by Janine Utell. – First Valancourt Books edition.
pages ; cm. – (20th century series)
ISBN 978-1-939140-40-1 (*alk. paper*)
I. Title.
PR6052.R265V63 2013
823'.914–dc23
2013009347

All Valancourt Books publications are printed on acid free paper that meets all ANSI standards for archival quality paper.

Cover by J. Victoria Terrell
Set in Dante MT 11/13.5

INTRODUCTION

Who are the Vodi?

They are creatures of fortune out to destroy you when you least expect it. Creatures of memory, seen and unseen. They are frightening in the ways they show us how much we are not agents of our own fate, especially just when we think we've got it all. We never see them, but we feel their presence in the world and in our heads. They are figments of childhood, returning to haunt a grown man in the depths of illness and fear.

That man is Dick Corvey. Suffering from advanced, possibly fatal, tuberculosis, he rests in a provincial sanatorium, slipping back and forth between the past and present, between an interior world and the rhythms of the sickroom. The Vodi are beings invented by Dick and a childhood friend when they were young to explain why bad things happen to good people. Dick says to his nurse, Evelyn Mallaton, "Some people do everything that they should. . . . Never do anyone any harm, and they're always unlucky. Everything goes wrong for them. . . . The decent people always get it in the neck. And the real swine, the selfish ones, always have good luck. They're favoured always." As Dick reflects on his life – his dead mother and declining father, the changes wrought on his postwar working-class town in the north of England by those with more power and money, the fiancée he loses when he gets sick, the job where he is little more than an ineffectual clerk – it seems increasingly clear to him that he is a victim of the Vodi. He is one of the unlucky ones who cannot catch a break; and every time he thinks he can regain control over his destiny, he slides back into resignation and despair.

The Vodi, published in 1959, is John Braine's second novel, following the bestseller and classic of the Angry Young Men phenomenon *Room at the Top* (1957). *The Vodi* is something of a departure while still exploring many of the themes and motifs that preoccupied the author throughout his career: masculinity, sex, success and failure, the gritty geography of the working-class North, where Braine was from, and its influence on character. Braine's prose is straightforward, his dialogue echoing everyday speech and slang, his authorial eye clearseeing. In his transparent prose and in his heroes he reminds one of George Orwell, another writer deeply invested in the exploration of class and what it does to character and a man's sense of self and free will. Dick Corvey is an inheritor of Gordon Comstock, the bungling protagonist of *Keep the Aspidistra Flying* (1936) who shilly-shallies about careers and women, who cannot make a decision until one is forced upon him. We might see shades of Dick, too, in Orwell's *Coming Up For Air* (1939), as that novel's main character George Bowling gets lost in the world of his childhood trying to figure out why his middle age turned out the way it did.

But even as Braine espoused a realism of both language and experience, it is used in the service of a kind of strangeness. In talking about his own writing, Braine expressed a commitment to realism; his *Writing a Novel*, published in 1974, is a manifesto for realism, "a vigorous exactitude of presentation" as the only way "the essential strangeness of life can be conveyed." The realistic representation of the familiar in all its detail allows for a sort of hyperreality, a de-familiarization, like looking at something totally quotidian too close up. Later in life, during a 1984 interview, Braine said, "Once you know about reality, revelation starts, intensity starts." One can perceive the unusual because one has learned to look at the world so closely. It is this strangeness that characterizes *The Vodi*, the revelation of a man's inner life, the intensity of memory, perception, desire, and fear; the supernatural that is the logic of the child and the working of the mind of a man whose body is turning against him. All of this makes *The Vodi* a difficult novel to classify.

Much of the narrative emerges through flashbacks focusing on Dick's youth and friendships in his hometown of Silbridge; his family life and employment first in his father's sweet shop, then in a factory that makes radios; his return from wartime service in Burma; his courtship of and engagement to Lois, then the subsequent breakup once he is admitted to the hospital. All of these scenes from the life of a reasonably healthy and completely ordinary young man, a man who doesn't have any particular ambition, likes going to the pub and meeting girls, has a cozy relationship with his parents and siblings, are interwoven with episodes set in the Nedham sanatorium. The thread telling the story of Dick's life pulls us through to the moment of his illness; the scenes of his attempts at a cure at Nedham and his growing attraction to his nurse Evelyn seem then almost to hang, suspended by that narrative thread in time and space. We are in limbo with Dick, waiting to see if, like his mother who died a slow, painful death of stomach cancer, he will be taken by the Vodi – or if he will wrest some control back over his own life and future.

Part of the strangeness of the novel, then, too, comes from its representation of the world of illness. Braine himself, at the age of 30, went into a sanatorium in the Yorkshire town of Grassington with tuberculosis; he stayed there for two years trying to recover. (He attributed the resurgence of the disease, diagnosed during the war in 1943, to working so strenuously on early, and unsuccessful, drafts of *Room at the Top*.) One of the strengths of *The Vodi* is its exploration of what it means for the mind and body to be lingering in a state of illness, to be subject to "the Bug." Nothing much happens in *The Vodi* as Dick can do very little but explore the recesses of his own mind and memory, thinking about his vulnerability and mortality. His consciousness becomes more and more attuned to the world of the hospital and of illness as they shape his desires and needs. Braine describes a night from Dick's perspective early in the novel; he is trying to sleep after reading the newspaper, and even the listings of the evening's events, everyday pleasures like the cinema and dances, make him feel bitter and isolated because he cannot participate: "Night had settled over the hospital; soon all the lights in the wards and cubicles would be turned off. At nine the radio would be turned off; should he listen to it now or should he not try to evade what was going to come to him? . . . Not being able to sleep, one had to think." The position of being a patient prompts reflection, anger, resignation, feebleness, self-pity, dark humor. Small events are magnified, time seems to stop, perceptions are heightened, slights are felt more deeply.

The realistic details of life in a provincial town, life in a hospital, the drinks, the slang, the medicines and procedures, the cut of a woman's dress (almost always a little too revealing to the protagonist's eyes): this is what John Braine does so well, as many reviewers noted of *The Vodi*, even if it wasn't as well-received or as commercially successful as *Room at the Top* had been two years earlier. Richard Hoggart, author of *The Uses of Literacy*, a groundbreaking sociological study of the working classes which came out in 1957 (the same year as *Room at the Top*), was one of Braine's most astute readers. Coming from the same background as Braine, Hoggart recognized what the novelist was trying to do in capturing that world. In his review for the *Guardian*, Hoggart wrote that Braine was a "gifted and skilled writer" whose prose is "extremely vivid." He noted that what Braine does best is to get at "some kinds of raw and direct awareness; the verbal and intellectual pugnacity of lower-middle class lads in their inevitable pains." Where *Room at the Top* took as its hero – or possibly anti-hero – a "lad" of intense masculinity and sexual prowess, *The Vodi* gives us a more complex protagonist, more pain and less pugnacity, less Angry Young Man but rather a figure almost Romantic (consumption being, of course, a significant trope for the Romantics, embodied in the figure of poet John Keats).

This tortured and damaged masculinity, with a dash of the poetic, is what makes Dick attractive, at least at first, to Evelyn Mallaton. While much of the novel is told from the point of view of Dick, Evelyn gets some scenes of her own as the omniscient narrator occasionally slides into her perspective and experience. The first time this happens is when she is shaving Dick; she notices that he has a certain appeal, and it's a key moment where pity becomes empathy, and the potential for sexual desire emerges. The use of shaving in the scene is important: it's a masculine activity, but because Evelyn has to help Dick her appreciation of his masculinity is tempered with pity. Braine writes, "As she put aside the razor to lather his face again, [she] felt the stab of pity again. It hurt even more this time; to her disgust she found herself welcoming the pain. And then she saw a picture in her mind: she was holding his head between her breasts, she was giving him comfort like mother's milk." The complicated relationship between desire and pity, between compassion and lust, is examined rather brilliantly by Braine in *The Vodi*, and he doesn't shy away from the less appealing ways desire manifests itself. Dick makes himself pathetic; Evelyn hates herself for wanting her more virile and obscenely healthy boyfriend Harry and then withholding sex from him unless marriage is on the table. She is drawn to Dick one moment for his firm mouth, sensitive hands, and unabashed admiration for her figure, and repulsed by him the next for his illness, the way it diminishes his manhood, and his utter ineligibility as a marriage partner. Bodily need, bodily weakness, and the connections men and women seek to feel less alone and less ashamed of vulnerability are key themes for Braine, and the unflinching sensitivity with which he addresses them in *The Vodi* makes this a remarkable novel.

Despite, or perhaps because of, Dick's frailty, the reader develops a deep sympathy for this flawed man. The world he lives in, peopled with vibrantly drawn secondary characters more real than the Vodi who plague him, is intensely imagined. Finally, we root for Dick to leave the inner world of his mind and memory, to get well again and get on the bus that will take him far away from Nedham. We want to believe he can claim a piece of that vibrant and vivid world for himself.

Janine Utell
Widener University

May 24, 2013

THE VODI

FOR
PAT, ANTHONY
AND POPPA

FROM his concrete dugout a general was watching the attempts of a raiding-party to capture a strongly defended hill. Through his binoculars he saw a figure detach itself from the mêlée and come running across to the dugout.

A few moments later a small private threw himself down the steps, sat on an ammunition-box, and lit a Woodbine.

"Well, my man," the general said, impatiently, "what message have you got for me?"

"I haven't any message," the private said.

"No message? Then what are you doing here?" He pointed towards the hill. "Return there immediately. That's where the fighting is."

"Fighting be damned," the private said. "They're *killing* each other."

I

THIS morning – cold and fresh with a pale sun reluctantly administering sudden jabs of heat – Dick felt the whole burden of his illness like an enemy triumphantly straddling his chest. He looked at Rock and Percy and Peter through half-closed eyes; wishing that they would go away. They were free of the outside world or, at least, they were free to walk as far as the South Pines a quarter of a mile away; and whilst he had no desire to go there, he didn't want to be reminded of its existence. His country was his cubicle with its waxed floor, its clothes locker, bedside locker in white-enamelled steel, its steel and blue leather visitors' chair and its silver-painted radiator.

He closed his eyes, then opened them again. It wasn't any good; he didn't feel awake in any true sense of the word and yet he couldn't sleep. The pill Doctor Redroe had given him last night had bludgeoned him into oblivion efficiently enough but now he felt thwarted of rest; eight hours of real sleep had been filched from him and would never be returned.

Peter pulled a letter from his pocket and started to read it, his lips moving. The envelope was pink and unstamped and when he took out the thick sheaf of paper there was a smell of perfume. It wasn't very good perfume – a factory chemist's rough sketch of the piercing freshness of lilies-of-the-valley – but, for a second, it enabled Dick to forget the taste of blood in the mouth. He looked at Peter, rapt in his private dream, with a derisive yet pitying fraternity: his black polo-neck sweater, a full size too large for him, made his peaked little face with its black lemur-staring eyes seem even younger and more defenceless.

Suddenly Percy snatched the letter. Holding it high above Peter's head he pretended to read from it. "Dearest, sweetest Peterkins, when I lie awake in my little narrow bed how I wish you were with me. You are so thin that there would be plenty of room for us both. . . ."

Peter leapt at him but Percy easily held him off, one big hand clutching the slack of the sweater like the scruff of a kitten. "Of course, Peterkins, we wouldn't get much sleep——"

"Give it back to me, you rotten devil," Peter shouted. "You know damn well it doesn't say that. I'll kick your big fat belly, I swear I will."

Percy pushed him away, then put Dick's bedside locker between them. "There's worse to come," he said. "Oh my, I daren't read this bit out . . ."

Tears came to Peter's eyes, abruptly he turned his back.

"Here you are, you clot," Percy said. "I was only joking."

"I'm fed up with your lousy jokes," Peter said. He walked out of the cubicle, his narrow shoulders shaking.

"Why the hell can't you leave the kid alone?" Rock said. "He's only sixteen."

"I told you, man, I was only having him on."

"Bloody well lay off him in future."

Percy scowled. "Don't you bloody well tell me what to do, chum."

"For God's sake, shut up," Dick said, peevishly. "If you want to fight, go outside."

The hard angles of Rock's body relaxed.

"We couldn't fight anyway," he said. "Not with our PPs. Mind you, it'd break the monotony . . ." He looked gloomily around the cubicle. "I hate the mornings," he said. "Think I'll retire to my cubicle. Got anything to read, Dick?"

"You can have those Penguins in the bottom of the clothes locker," Dick said.

"They're new," Rock said. "Have you read them all?"

"I don't want to read them."

"Please yourself," Rock said, "I'll bring them back."

"Don't bring them back."

"That's silly," Rock said. "Why don't you want to read them? You used to be keen on reading—"

"Jesus God, shut up!" Dick shouted, then started to cough.

Sister Lardress bustled in, round-cheeked and small and bouncing. "Shoo!" she said, "let him have some rest. *You* should know better by now, Rock."

"I'm borrowing some books," Rock said.

"You do that," she said. "Take them and go away. It's a lovely spring morning – off with you quicksticks and do a dozen Circles before lunch. What are you waiting for?"

They trailed out sheepishly.

Sister Lardress straightened Dick's pillows and pushed back his bedside locker.

"You mustn't mind them," she said gently. "Time hangs very heavy on their hands."

"I'm drama, I expect," Dick said. "They're waiting for me to die. I give their drab lives a bit of colour."

At the word 'die' Sister Lardress's face drew as stern and disapproving as if he had uttered an obscenity.

"Don't be so *ridiculous*!" she said, sharply. "You'll live till you're a hundred."

"What for?"

"There's a thousand things to live for. You rest now. I've got work to do."

Looking at her stiffly corseted back as she whisked out, Dick was suddenly and affectionately reminded of the wooden figures in the Noah's Ark his father had made him for his fourth birthday. Her skirts were so stiff that she gave the impression of being carved in one solid piece from waist to hem-line, like Mrs. Noah. But it was no wooden figure which had seemed to be with him all the time he'd had his last haemorrhage, her healthy rosiness smudged with fatigue. How old would she be? Forty, perhaps. Not much more; in her plum-coloured topcoat and high-heeled shoes walking down the drive on her evening off to catch the Nedham bus, she looked considerably younger. Idly, he considered her possibilities as a woman. He was sitting in the Grey Lion with her on a fine summer's evening. They'd finished their drinks; he was putting his hand on hers. That was enough; without saying anything they were outside, walking along the narrow path which led from the back door of the pub to Kellogg's Woods. He could smell the rankness of the elderbushes beside the path, then the deader, blacker rankness of the stagnant pond at the entrance to the woods.

They were breasting the hillock past the pond now and were descending into a grove of oak trees. On the right, the hill rose steeply, pitted by hollows. The hollows were oddly uniform in shape and size, rectangular with steep sides, like graves for giants.

One of them had been a grave for Sheila Simmerton, too. They'd hanged Walter Perdwick for it twelve years ago at Tanbury Jail; he remembered Walter, shambling and gentle, his fair hair plastered straight down with a centre parting always at least forty-five degrees out of true. Walter wouldn't have been hanged, everyone said, if only he'd been married to Sheila; he was crazy about her, but she'd never be content with any one man.

He remembered her coming into the shop one day when he was serving. His voice was breaking then; he began his 'good-afternoon' in treble and finished it in bass.

She was wearing a blue flowered dress with pink frilled petticoat showing at the hem; that was the fashion then, though even if it hadn't been, it was the sort of fashion Sheila would have liked. She wasn't good-looking – her mouth was too big, her skin too dark, her breasts too small and her hips too wide – but she was always lively, she crackled with femininity.

Walter, of course, wasn't the man for her; she said as much one evening in the Grey Lion. He was a keen motorist; cars were indeed his only topic of conversation.

"Walter's high-powered," she said, "but he has a crash gearbox."

It had filtered through to Dick; it leapt to his mind that morning she came into the shop. The picture the phrase evoked was so disturbing that he gave her a packet of St. Bruno instead of the twenty Capstan she'd asked for.

"You know I don't smoke a pipe," she said, putting her face forward so that he could smell the cachous on her breath. "Are you in love, Dickie?"

He blushed, her staring brown eyes upon him. He knew that she was measuring him up, if not for use at that very moment, then for some time in the future. He gave her the Capstan and nothing ever came of that moment of communication. A month later she lay strangled in Kellogg's Woods.

With an effort he took his mind back to Sister Lardress. She'd be wearing high-heeled shoes and would stumble over a tree-root. Ursula – her name was Ursula – Ursula would stumble and he'd take her arm – and then he dismissed her from his mind, made her a Noah's Ark figure again. It wasn't the thought of taking a woman through Kellogg's Woods which interested him; it was the thought of Kellogg's Woods.

He remembered Tom's excitement when Sheila's murder was discovered. Tom was of course one of the first to know.

"The Vodi's killed Sheila Simmerton!" he shouted. "She's stark dead in Kellogg's Woods!"

"They're always killing people," Dick said. He'd taken it as a joke; though the Vodi was, he knew, responsible for all murders and, indeed, for all crime, murder wasn't a real thing to him.

"They found her this morning," Tom said, "Just by the entrance to the North-West Passage. The place is swarming with coppers and they've roped the whole woods off."

"You're kidding," he said. Then he looked at Tom more closely and knew that he was serious. Tom was usually inclined towards dandyism; that morning his tie was half under his ear and he'd fastened all three buttons of his blazer, pulling it out of shape. And his bony, tough face which normally had an adult composure was disarranged too: he looked like a rather frightened little boy.

"I'm not kidding," Tom said, taking a comb from his pocket and restoring his hair to its normal smoothness with the aid of the Chocolat Menier mirror. "All the Tanbury coppers are here, too. Old Relentless Rupert thinks he's died and gone to heaven. He's investigating like mad."

"He's been sacked for not turning in the Chief Constable's share of the cocaine profits."

"He's been reinstated," Tom said without a moment's hesitation. "Nelly started to like him again after he'd had Phil Hawkins beaten up. It wasn't just that they ruptured the poor little devil – he didn't even start the fight. He was trying to separate them."

"That isn't what I'd heard," Dick had said.

"Naturally. But it's what happened."

"But is Sheila really dead?"

"Stark naked and clawed to pieces."

She hadn't been, actually; apart from the marks on her throat, and presumably the navy-blue tinge of her face, she looked as if she'd fallen asleep; and she was fully clothed, her limbs arranged with touching decency. Or so Ray Tomkins, the farm labourer who'd found her, said at the trial. But Tom and Dick decided that Ray, like everyone else at the trial, was under orders and what had happened was that the Vodi had tortured Sheila to death and then carried her body from the Kasbah to the hollow by the entrance to the North-West Passage.

"Who are they going to hang for it?" he asked Tom.

"Probably the Vicar. They know that the last thing he'd do would be to be mixed up with a howwid *woman*."

"Someone'll swear they saw him staggering out of the woods wild-eyed and covered with blood," Dick said. "Want an orangeade? It's Saturday."

On Saturday and no other day, Dick was allowed to issue hospitality to the extent of six soft drinks.

"Pineapple," Tom said. Dick served him the drink, which he took standing up. There were no chairs by the soda-fountain; Dick's father said that he sold drinks and not seating accommodation.

Dick thought of the shop as it was then with a bitter melancholy: it had been redecorated in pillar-box red and white, the chequered black-and-white lino was still shiny, the chrome hadn't begun to peel from the soda-fountain and there were a hundred different kinds of sweets which you never saw now – Duncan's Vita-Milks, Callard and Bowser's Raspberry Noyeau, Nestlé's White Chocolate . . .

Tom, taking a meditative mouthful of pineappleade, said: "I'd hate to swear some poor devil's life away. Even if he *had* done it."

"It's not a question of them liking the job," Dick said.

Tom knew as well as he did that the witnesses for the prosecution all had the choice between either obeying the police's orders or at some future date being hanged themselves. The police had the same choice too; everyone was acting under orders. It explained a lot of things, Dick thought bitterly.

Walter ran away – or rather drove away – in his black-and-cream

S.S. Jaguar as soon as he saw the police car go past his house. He didn't go very far; they picked him up in a bar in Wakefield, pouring double brandies down his throat and shaking uncontrollably.

He let himself be arrested without any fuss; all that he said was: "Let me finish my drink."

"You see what I mean?" Tom said to Dick on the Sunday evening as they were walking down the High Street. "He never even tried to get away. He knew the coppers'd have a description of his car and he knew they'd pin the murder on him the moment he scarpered. He's condemned himself to death, that's what."

"Maybe they'll acquit him," Dick said. "Can't imagine poor old Walter harming anyone."

He looked gloomily at the display of sports shirts in the Co-op window. It had been a fine day, but after all it was Sunday, with the sad bells ringing and the swings chained up in the Park. And Silbridge looked even worse in summer – flaccid under the sun, drably naked in its embrace, without a shred of darkness to conceal or to dignify its scarred hills and low-browed houses and the smoking pyramids of its slag-heaps. He turned away from the window, surprised by the intensity of his hatred for the place.

"They'll only acquit him if he's guilty and it's a really clever murder," Tom said. "And then Nelly'll look after him for the rest of his life. But poor old Walter's just the sort of chap that Nelly doesn't like."

"They'll acquit poor old Walter," Dick feebly insisted; but Tom was fitting together the pieces of the jigsaw – or, perhaps, Dick thought, the jigsaw was assembling itself.

"They've measured and weighed Walter already," Tom continued with relish. "And the chaplain's been round to do his stuff because he's due for his annual booze-up the day before the execution and he doesn't want to profane so solemn an occasion with hiccups or diarrhœa. Mind you, he'll send him a postcard – 'THINKING OF YOU. GOD IS LOVE. CYRIL.' That'll sustain Walter at the dreadful moment when they say: *Perdwick, the time has come to be very brave.*"

"That's what they say in France, you clot."

"They say it in England, too. Nelly thinks it's more classy."

It had been a child's game; and like most child's games it had been rigidly formalised. That Sunday they'd worked out everything that would happen. The summing-up had been taken out of the Home Office files – there were a hundred thousand there, with blank spaces left for names and dates and places, each representing a murder which Nelly intended to commit. They had been compiled in consultation with Nelly, who'd driven to London at a steady hundred, doubling the year's road casualties in a single day; her Bugatti Royale was a wonderful car but, as its designer said, it was made to go and not to stop.

"Poor old Sheila," Dick said. "She was a cutie, she really was. Led Walter the hell of a dance, though. You know that new barman at the Grey Lion? Pale chap with a little black moustache? Last week she took a fancy to him and sat there showing all she'd got. Walter kept hissing to her to pull her skirts down, but she wouldn't take a blind bit of notice."

"Hell, that's when he'd have killed her if he were that kind of chap."

"I wish there were something to do in this dump on a Sunday," Dick said.

"Walter'd change places with you this minute."

"It's a pity," Dick said, "but he's unlucky. Just the sort that Nelly doesn't like."

He remembered saying that in Silbridge High Street as plainly as if he were there, walking past the Town Hall and the Fire Station and the melancholy little municipal park. Walter, unlucky, shambling Walter, whose mistress was unfaithful to him and whose wife wouldn't sleep with him because she hated all men, had gone meekly to his death, food for the hangman's dog these twelve years.

There was nothing left in Tanbury to remember Walter by; and no-one to remember him but Dick. He'd had a son, Harold, the consequence, it was whispered, of his getting roaring drunk one night and raping his wife. Harold was pale and shambling like his father. He used to come into the shop for sweets, generally with an entourage; not many eight-year-olds had as much pocket-money as Harold; nor as many expensive toys. Dick remembered him coming in with Sam Tranmere, whose father had been out of work for two years.

"My daddy's bought me a FROG," he said to Sam.

"That's nothing," Sam said, "I've got one."

"*Mine's* a Puss Moth. I'm getting a Hawker Fury, too, Daddy said. And I've got a Meccano car set – the big one. You come to my house for tea and I'll show it working."

Sam wouldn't ever have received that invitation to tea, of course. Walter's wife had few visitors and none at all after the execution. She was rather good-looking, as plump and fair as Sheila was dark and thin. She read a lot; Dick often used to see her going into the Golden Circle Library with a pile of books under her arm and Harold trotting beside her. He remembered Harold trying to take her hand once; she slapped it away.

And now they were both dead. But the death of Harold's mother had been a miscalculation. She was exactly the sort of person the Vodi liked, because she so obviously didn't like anyone at all. Except her friend Jacqueline, some ten years older than herself, blonde and plump also, but giggling and ebullient in a rather frightening way; you somehow felt that what she was laughing at wasn't very pleasant.

Sheila, now, may have been a whore, but she made no bones about it. And there was a sort of generosity about her which had nothing to do with sex. She had been generous even with Moustache Maurice the barman; he was sure, looking back, that it hadn't been so much a question of her wanting something from Maurice but of her wanting to give Maurice something.

It was that impulse to give which had doomed her. And Harold, too, ugly, sly Harold with his watering blue eyes and sallow face, Harold, who carried his money in a leather purse and counted it out in front of children whose parents were unemployed and who never had more than a halfpenny in their pockets – Harold was doomed the moment he tried to take his mother's hand. The Vodi didn't in the least mind Harold possessing four and sixpence, a Frog Puss Moth and a Meccano car set; and he could have been given a real Hawker Fury for all they cared. What those beady eyes among the crowd on the opposite pavement noted was Harold's hand reaching out for his mother's; the weak, unguarded impulse, the split-second message from the brain to the tendons of the hand, filled Harold's lungs with coal gas a year afterwards. The postman had found Harold and his mother. Harold had been wearing blue striped pyjamas; his mother had a pink wool dressing-gown with rayon lapels over a black rayon nightgown. He remembered the dressing-gown because Mrs. Hadley next door but one had sold it to Harold's mother through the Clothing Club and now, she said, she was eighteen-and-sixpence out and didn't know what to do.

He and Tom, some three months after, had broken into Walter's house one foggy night. To say that they broke in was an overstatement; it had been a fluke, a matter of one of a bunch of old keys fitting against all expectation. Before they went into the house, they put old socks over their shoes; moving slowly and flat-footedly as a hundred thrillers had taught them. But they needn't have taken the trouble: the fog muffled all sound.

Standing on the frayed lino of the kitchen, Tom whispered: "Here Harold choked slowly to death. The Vodi laughed, its eyes gleaming in the darkness."

"His mother held his head in the gas oven," Dick said. "The Vodi promised her eight draws on the Treble Chance so she could go and live in Capri with Jacqueline."

"Harold's sweaty feet were drumming on the floor," Tom said. "*Mummy, help me!* he shouted. Then his feet stopped drumming and she let him drop." He played the tiny beam of his pocket torch over the room.

"Nelly was in the corner there," he said, "laughing fit to bust. She turned to Harold's mother and said: *Well done. A neat job, Sophie. Now I'll keep my word and you and Jacqueline can sin in the sun the rest of your lives.* And then Harold's mother looked at Harold in his blue striped pyjamas and she started to cry. So Nelly lost her temper and the Vodi moved in."

They went out of the kitchen into the living-room. Dick took out a five packet of Woodbines; they lit up solemnly and ritually. The room had been heated by a gas fire; it was still there but the pipe had recently been cut and sealed off.

They moved into the hall. "Pink roses again," Tom said, flashing his little Ever-Ready pencil torch along the walls. "Walter got a dozen rolls cheap."

Dick was beginning to feel frightened. The house seemed on the verge of some statement spoken in words of mouldering brick and worn linoleum and damp plaster, which wouldn't, when it came, be pleasant to hear. He kept hearing faint rustling noises, sometimes rising to a sigh; it was as if a gag were working loose. "I don't want to go upstairs," he said.

"Don't be so bloody soft, man," Tom said.

"I don't want to go."

"You're mardy. You're dead mardy. I duff you. Go on. I duff you."

Dick looked at the steep, narrow stairway with its banister covered in with cream plywood. There were the marks of grubby hands on the plywood. Tom swung his torch upwards to the door on the first landing; it was flush-panelled in the same shade of cream with a red bakelite push-handle. There were the same marks beside the handle.

"I don't care if you do duff me," Dick said. "I wish I'd never come." At home, he thought, they'd be listening to Band Wagon now; the fire in the big, old-fashioned range (Dentdale Suprema, Jno. Hebble, Birmingham, 1901, it said in fantastically decorated lettering on the oven door) would be the only light in the room, because his father believed you should listen to the wireless single-mindedly. Joyce would be in her room reading or taking a bath or washing her hair; since leaving Tanbury High, she always seemed to be in a blue kimono with her hair loose and shining and the bathroom was always full of the smell of scented soap and shampoo and all over the house there were stockings and brightly coloured skimpy underwear. Sam would be at the Tech; at about nine-fifteen they'd hear his motor-bike, it being a Thursday and not a Friday. Fridays he'd go to the Seven Dancers after the Tech. Friday night was Sam's talking night when, his tongue loosened by three or four pints of mild ("Bitter's poison, Our Kid; a headache in every gill.") he'd go into great detail about his future plans. The living-room would smell of newly-baked bread and the newly-ironed linen and his father's St. Bruno flake. He wanted to be there, or in bed with a hot-water bottle at his feet, reading *The Exploits of Brigadier Gerard*, the little bronze-painted gas fire muttering cheerfully to itself, and Sam in the other bed scowling over some highly technical book on radio or electricity. Simply by being in Walter's house he was turning away from that snug, warm world. It had seemed to him earlier that evening when Tom had called, when the magic, evocative phrase 'Going Out' had been spoken, stuffy and boring – it didn't seem so now.

"Come on," Tom said, impatiently. "They might have left some money behind. Ray Watson found half-a-crown in Jacksons' old house last week."

Dick had a vision of the coin, heavy and mill-edged, six visits to the Electric Palace or that Lockheed Vega kit or the roller-skates for which he somehow never saved up enough. For a moment the house had a veneer of treasure-island glamour; then he was left with the feeling of grubby melancholy. "I don't want the damned money," he said.

But he followed Tom upstairs; it had now become a question of prestige, there was even a certain exhilaration in doing the very thing all his instincts told him not to do. There was nothing upstairs but four bare rooms; in the smallest, the bathroom, there was an empty disinfectant bottle. And that was all. There wasn't even a halfpenny to reward their search. It was even more cold and damp upstairs than it had been downstairs; one didn't need any great amount of imagination to see fungi on the walls and skeletons piled up like firewood on the naked floorboards.

The most frightening room was at the other end of the landing from the bathroom. There was barely sufficient space in it for a single bed and a chest-of-drawers. The ceiling was deep blue dusted with silver spangles, and on the walls blue and red rabbits and penguins and elephants danced in procession past black toadstools and pine trees, led on by gnomes with fiddles and trumpets and harps.

"Harold's room," Tom said. "He'd be lying here, crying for his Daddy and then his mother would come in, very quietly. *Come with me, darling*, she'd say. *I've got a lovely surprise for you . . .*"

Dick shivered. "God, it's cold here."

"The Vodi was here last night. Nelly's made this one of her branch offices. It's always cold wherever Nelly has been."

"I want to go home," Dick said. He was appalled to find a childish, almost tearful whine in his voice.

Tom put the flashlight into his open mouth and gibbered at Dick, his face momentarily a Hallowe'en lantern. "Spreadeagle Sara and her mate are off early tonight," he said. "Let's bring 'em here."

"They wouldn't come."

"Not much they wouldn't. They were with Herbert Barker's gang in the Old Mill last week."

Dick heard a rustling noise from downstairs; it was a shade too emphatic for any explicable synonym in its sound range. It couldn't possibly be a mouse or a piece of plywood suddenly deckling with damp or an unnailed hinge on the verge of creaking in a gust of cold night air; it could only be the sound of a gag being finally spat out, the voice becoming intelligible at last, about to appeal for help. He jumped across the room to Tom, almost landing in his arms like a frightened child, then stopped himself, his body a fraction away from contact.

Tom's limbs were rigid; his face didn't belong to a schoolboy of 1938 but to the corpse of a knight butchered at Richmond or Flodden. His Elfrida hair-oil conveyed the authentic tang of some battlefield embalming fluid, a long-ago violence and writhing and screaming frozen in the light of candles. And the smell of violets didn't only remind him of death and battlefields; it reminded him also of Sheila, who, everyone said, you could smell before you saw her.

The hard lines of Tom's face broke up into laughter. "Wait for the footsteps," he said, "the little pattering steps of the Vodi and then Nelly, thump, thump, THUMP!"

For a moment Dick wanted to hit Tom, to take the superior smile off his face. Then he started to laugh too. "It's mice," he said, "the Vodi feeds them."

"No," Tom said, "it's rats. Big black rats. The hangman feeds them. They're just finishing Walter."

They walked slowly out of the room, treading on the ball of the foot and the heel, as they had learned from a thousand thrillers. They didn't run; but they were out of the house and into the High Street within ninety seconds, breathing hard. They stopped beside a lamp-post and Dick said wistfully: "If it had been the Saint there'd have been a smashing bare tart and a million pounds in bullion there."

"That's kids' stuff," Tom said. "He strolled into the Vodi H.Q., nonchalant and nicotine stained as usual and started to tell Nelly she was an evil, fat excrescence. Nelly just spat at him and he shrivelled up and died."

The smell of liver and onions from the kitchen grew stronger, coarse and cheerful and faintly boozy. He was suddenly assailed by a fierce thirst. But it wasn't beer he wanted; he had a gin-and-tonic, whisky-on-the-rocks longing, he wanted to be in the cocktail bar of the Tanbury Roynton, nibbling cheese biscuits and crisps, listening to the businessmen talking about their new Jag or Sunbeam-Talbot or Zodiac and their last trip on the Skymaster. He wanted to be with Lois in his clerical grey suit and his chukka boots, lolling back in one of the Roynton's dove-grey arm-chairs with the whole evening before him. There'd be a crumb of biscuit on Lois's lower lip but he wouldn't have to tell her about it; her pink tongue would dart out like a cat's and take it away. He'd noticed that trick of hers time and time again; on all of those many evenings, in fact, when life had so indisputably opened up for him. But, unknown to him, in a page-boy's or porter's or commissionaire's uniform or through peepholes in the wall, the Vodi had been watching. Lois, from the time she'd first possessed breasts, at the age of fifteen, had been fond of showing all she dare of them; she wasn't exactly shameless, it was just that her dresses and blouses and jumpers were always low-cut. The watchers would have noted this; they would have noted also, with a dry, snickering approval, his eyes focusing under her chin and above her waist whenever she leaned forward. That they would understand; what they wouldn't understand, what they were ordered to hate, was his look of unguarded tenderness whenever he looked into her eyes, her large warm eyes, clear and grey and childish.

But he didn't want to remember the bitch. He didn't want to remember those large warm eyes, those big breasts which seemed subcutaneously waxed like a film star's but which weren't, which were as real and good and as springy as her yellow hair and her smile with the one-sided dimple. He didn't want to remember anything about her; he didn't even want to remember her imperfections, the ankles which were a little too strong, so that her legs were only passable in sheer stockings and high-heeled shoes, her hands which were white and well-kept, but plump and stubby-fingered with irregular nails. He thought of the hands, the not far from ugly hands, as he'd felt them often, soft and caressing and gratuitously shameless, and his mouth became still dryer, but not with thirst.

He heard the meal-trolley rattling over the uneven concrete passage which connected the ward and the kitchen. He didn't bother to look up when it was pushed into his cubicle; he would see her face soon enough, and it would be a face he'd seen many times before.

"Good afternoon, Mr. Corvey. Are you ready for your delicious lunch?"

It was an agreeable voice, low and soft and clear; it was a voice which wasn't putting on any sort of act.

"I'm Nurse Mallaton," she said, as she helped him to a sitting position and pulled forward the bed-table.

"I haven't seen you before," he said.

"I've been on the Women's Ward." He looked at her rosy face and shining fair hair with a detached interest; after he'd seen her a few more times, she'd merge into the background. He'd no more notice her than the white coolie-hat lampshade hanging from the ceiling or the white-enamelled locker containing the clothes which he'd never wear again.

"You can feed yourself now, you lucky man," she said. "But just ring if you need help."

He looked at her unsmilingly.

"I can manage," he said. He was suddenly angry: she was altogether too cheerful, the colour in her cheeks was too even and clear, she even smelled too good, too clean, too feminine. And she moved so freely that there wasn't any question of what she was like under the dress; she was tall too, with her head set nicely on her shoulders, and a straight back—but straight was the wrong word. It was shaped as it should be, her youth and health and pride in herself held her body in the springing delicate bow, not corsets and will-power. She had good teeth too and a full mouth – red without benefit of lipstick, because she was so damned healthy. It was rather too large but so were her features. Her arms were rather too muscular – but he was crying sour grapes. And these grapes were totally and hopelessly out of reach – there was no point in longing for them when in fact he spent so much of his time in longing for the bunch labelled Lois, the bunch he knew very well tasted good.

He started to pick at the liver and onions she'd put on the bed-table for him but after a few mouthfuls laid down his knife and fork.

"You'll never get better if you don't eat your dinner," she said.

"This was terrible to begin with," he said, petulantly. "But they've fried it in axle-grease. I couldn't eat it if I were well."

"If you keep it quiet, I'll bring you some chicken. They sent over too much for Mr. Rentier."

"Rudy? I don't want Rudy's leftovers."

"He hasn't touched it. It's still in the serving-dish." It had become important to her that Dick should eat, that he should attempt to survive; looking at him, his mousy hair tangled and his face thin and petulant, she felt the beginnings of tenderness and also an immense impatience – she wanted to pull him out of bed and blow strength into his sick lungs from her sound ones.

"I'll try some then," Dick said.

"Promise to eat some of the vegetables if I bring you the chicken?"

"We'll see," he said. He smiled unexpectedly, showing white, even teeth which gave his haggard face a death's-head look.

When she brought back his plate the liver and onions had been replaced by chicken. He began to eat without a word as she left the cubicle. She opened her mouth to say something, then thought better of it. She served the other lunches mechanically and a little resentfully; after all, she had, at some trouble to herself, broken a regulation. A sanatorium wasn't a restaurant; there was nothing wrong with Dick's stomach, anyway. He might, at least, have thanked her – but she was being childish. You couldn't expect a man whose lungs were being slowly turned to a material of the consistency and colour of Gruyère cheese to be thrilled about a piece of chicken. And it didn't matter to her; she'd done her duty when she'd brought him his lunch. Nevertheless she couldn't restrain a feeling of triumph when she discovered that he'd cleared his plate. Then she looked at him suspiciously. "You've not thrown it out, have you?"

"How could I? I'm not allowed to get up."

"Not being allowed to and not being able to aren't always the same thing."

"They are for me," he said. "There's nothing to get up for."

"Don't be so moronic!" she snapped.

To her surprise, he grinned. "That's a fine word, Nurse. Name of a liner?"

She took away his empty plate and gave him his stewed apples and ice-cream. "You know it's stupid to talk like that," she said.

She found herself so angry that she could hardly keep her voice steady. He'd withdrawn to some point outside life and was sneering not only at her but the rest of the world.

He put his spoon into the ice-cream, his large brown eyes upon her. "You know, Nurse, my father keeps a sweet-shop. It used to keep him, but now he keeps the shop. Before the War, if he'd sold muck like this, he'd have been out of business in a week. It's cornflour and water with a dash of vanilla, that's all."

She took a deep breath and reminded herself that he was nothing to her – a patient, no more, no less. "You look much better now, anyway," she said. "You *must* have eaten it all."

He put a spoonful of stewed apple in his mouth. "I bet Stevie's heart is broken," he said. "He smelled that spare chicken as soon as it came into the kitchen. I only ate it to spite him – my God, here he is."

Stevie shuffled into the cubicle. He was wearing an overcoat in place of a dressing-gown; it reached nearly to his ankles and was a chocolate brown with large red checks and a strange fuzzy texture. He looked at them suspiciously from small black eyes. "More?" he said. "Is more?"

"No more," Nurse Mallaton said.

"Is more."

"Mr. Kidanski, you've already had three helpings. There just isn't any left."

"Me no understand."

He turned and shuffled off, his cropped bullet-head drooping sadly.

"He'd understand if I said I'd give him a pound-note," Dick said. "The greedy Ukrainian clot!" He began to cough.

"Eat some ice-cream," she said.

He spooned it up quickly; it numbed his throat and stopped the cough. "You can take it away now," he said. "I've had enough."

Watching her wheel the trolley out he reflected that she'd be a better companion for a walk through Kellogg's Woods than Ursula. She wouldn't stumble, either. She'd be more likely to help him when he stumbled. You're a fool, he said to himself; she's only been on the ward a day and now you're doing what they all do – weaving fantasies round the pretty nursie, building up a relationship, a wonderful, improbable relationship. It was a year now since he'd been alone with a girl – the three tusslings he'd had with Lois in this very cubicle hardly counted. He had little pleasure in remembering them; afterwards he had always felt himself a little degraded. It was as if there were no trust: to prove that love existed between you, your hand had to be permitted to go there and there, her hand here – you wanted it desperately at the time, if only to prove to the others that you weren't quite defeated, that you weren't just another consumptive. But afterwards you were left unsatisfied and unhappy and the bright and good impulse to touch the loved flesh became in retrospect merely a physical need not very far from squalid. It hadn't always been like that; there had been the evening when he and Lois had been alone together in her parents' sitting-room, her parents having gone to the theatre or, to be more accurate, to a musical comedy produced by the Tanbury Amateur Operatic Society. It had all been in fear and trembling; a neighbour might drop in, her parents might return unexpectedly. So there wasn't as much pleasure as there should have been from the revelation of her white body in the firelight against the background of plum-coloured Axminster and the dropsical olive-green moquette suite and the dark sad oils of Yorkshire beauty spots on the walls. There never had been any pleasure with Lois that wasn't flawed. But, flawed or not, he couldn't help being grateful; he heard her whisper again – *You can open your eyes now* – he saw again the large circular mirror over the sideboard with the gilt filigree frame, he saw the gleam of the firelight reflected red in the dark mahogany of the side-board and yellow from the big picture of Bolton Abbey opposite; he saw at last Lois standing by the fire, her white, stubby hands flying from her face to her breasts, then to her groin.

Even now, even hating her more than he'd ever thought it possible to hate anyone, his mind at odd moments working out crazily detailed plans of sneaking out of the sanatorium after dark, hiring a car at Silbridge and somehow killing her and himself, he couldn't stifle the feeling of wild delight at what he'd seen. *All things bright and beautiful, All creatures great and small* – she'd sung that, jerkily, under her breath, lying on a heap of cushions by the fire; it shocked him a little at the time, but it had, he admitted now, been entirely appropriate.

And then hatred and longing and jealousy combined again to take possession of him. Who would she be with tonight, what gorgeous hunk of tubercle-free man, dancer and footballer and tennis-player, holder of a good job with prospects, on the point of buying a car? Or he'd actually own a car, like Tom. Triumph Razor-Edge Tom. Back-seat cuddler Tom. Successful, energetic, healthy Tom. Was she with Tom now, cosy and snug in some back lane with Tom's bony fingers exploring her body?

"It isn't him," she'd said. "It's not anybody. It's all in your mind."

"You've been out with him. You said so. You've been out with my good friend Tom."

She'd run out weeping; but how long had her tears lasted? The anodynes – drink, lovemaking, dancing, the cinema and theatre – were there for her when she returned home; but there was nothing for him. Only this bed, this cubicle, the white cotton sheets and the red day-blanket which he'd never use again, only the faces and voices of the people who were paid to look after him, only the faces and voices of his fellow-consumptives, who were glad that he was dying because it emphasised the fact that they were not.

And he had Nelly. And the Vodi. That was something to hang on to, not because it did him any ascertainable physical or spiritual good, but because it enabled him to make sense of what had happened to him. Logically it all worked out perfectly: it explained why he was here and told him what to expect in the future. If he could only accept the idea of Nelly and the Vodi completely, he'd be saved. He wouldn't be any happier and he'd die just as quickly, probably with cancer or Bright's Disease as a bonus. But he'd be able to accept everything, to stop fighting and stop torturing himself.

The bell for the afternoon rest rang, and he slid down on his back automatically, pushing the pillow away. The noises of the sanatorium diminished; the Round was empty except for a solitary Stage A man, swinging his stick and, against the rules, smoking a pipe. He'd be out of here within the month and in the world again. He's welcome, Dick thought; Nelly rules that world too.

2

SILBRIDGE was large enough for people living cheek by jowl all their lives to be strangers. Tom Coverack lived only a mile away from Dick; but he didn't know him to speak to until his first day at Tanbury High.

It was in the quadrangle, a huge asphalt barrack-ground just off the main road, that they met. Later, he knew it as the Egg: it took its name from the initials E.G. for Exercise Ground. For Tanbury High was built in much the same style as Tanbury Gaol, plain and massive, with rows of mean little round-headed windows. The walls of the school were rather lower and there wasn't a watch-tower; otherwise, they were uncannily alike. The legend was that the same architect had designed them both, intending the school to be the prison and vice versa. On that first morning he would have believed the story without any question; if that grimy, red-brick building had anything to say to its inmates, it was simply that they were all sinners who would in the very near future be condignly punished. Even the gymnasium, Dick reflected, had the appearance of an execution shed. Later, of course, he grew used to the place, which was to say he ceased to see it. All his five years at Tanbury High he never quite rid himself of the feeling of being about to suffer for breaking some law which he never knew to exist; but never again were the sensations of fear and guilt so strong as on that first day. Tom seemed part of Tanbury High, too, when he lounged across in his brand-new school uniform, the pale-blue cap with its silver and scarlet and black badge set rakishly over his right eye.

"Hey, kid," he said. "You from Minden Street?"

Dick found himself blushing. The quadrangle was so crammed with strangers – none of whom, he felt, intended any good towards him – that even to be identified by the street in which he lived, to be singled out, seemed not only embarrassing but dangerous.

"My father has a shop there," he said.

"We go to the Cut-Price Stores," Tom said. He hit Dick playfully in the ribs. "I say, kid, which would you rather have – a bun on the table or a tart on the floor?"

It had rather shocked Dick at the time. "A bun on the table," he said, primly.

Tom exploded into laughter, showing long white teeth. "That's the right answer," he said. "It's uncomfortable to eat from the floor."

They'd both been eleven then; Dick was actually two days older than Tom. But from the first Tom had taken charge; even at eleven he was the wise one, the self-assured one, the clever one always inboard. It was he who already knew all the Masters' nicknames, it was he who already knew all Tanbury High's unwritten rules (not that there were many, it being a day school), it was he who always knew where and when to report. And it was he, towards the end of their first year at Tanbury High, who discovered the Short Cut. It was only about five miles as the crow flies from Silbridge to

Tanbury but, there being no direct service between the two places, it was necessary to change trams at South Tanbury Terminus. The Short Cut took one, in twenty minutes' brisk walk, straight to South Tanbury Terminus at a saving of a penny. "See, kid, it cuts off the corner," Tom said. "I was looking through Phillips' South-West Yorkshire at the library and it was instantly evident to my giant brain. One ten-minute tram ride and you're home."

"There'll be some snag," Dick said. "We'll have to climb a barbed-wire fence or swim through a sewer or something. You've not looked at the map properly."

"I always do things properly. Hundred per cent efficient, that's me." They were standing by the Catholic Church opposite the school, a new brick building with large rectangular windows, modern in a half-hearted sort of way. It seemed to be looking askance at the big Victorian buildings around it; it seemed so fragile beside their sheer bulk of black sandstone that Dick wouldn't have been at all surprised to find it one morning reduced to a heap of rubble, with the big stone houses still in the same places. But among the pulverized brick and glass there'd be a few traces of stone dust and on the sides of the big Victorian buildings a few traces of brick dust like blood. And when you looked more closely you'd see the outlines of the buildings on the pavement, just a narrow grey line, and you'd know that they hadn't returned to exactly the same places as before.

"I still think there's a catch in it," he said. "Besides, it might rain."

Tom snorted. "You're dead tinny, Corvey," he said. "I'll go by myself." He stalked off angrily down the road. Dick hesitated for a moment, then followed him. There was, after all, something very pleasant about the idea of walking instead of standing in the tram; and the Short Cut was a new experience, in the category of an exploration. "O.K. Coverack," he said, "we'll attempt the North-West Passage."

"It's South-East," Tom said, "but never mind, your geography was always lousy."

They turned right by the Methodist Chapel, monument, with its spire and stained-glass windows, of the days of the wool boom, and along a ruler-straight road of terrace houses.

"Might as well go by tram," Dick said. "How long does this go on for?"

"Don't be impatient," Tom said. "We cross the road here, sharp right and go through this snicket." The path led to a patch of bare rocky land surrounded by red brick terrace houses. The ground sloped downwards so sharply that it was difficult to avoid running. They descended a steep flight of stone stairs and crossed a broad road lined with trees and found the path again, this time smoothly tarmac'd, with grass verges and big houses behind the high walls at either side. Outside one of the houses a young man in black leggings was polishing a plum-coloured Rolls-Royce.

"Must be about twenty rooms there," Dick said.

"Dead right, kid. That's Frank Wadden's house. Eight thousand quid's worth. All from coal."

As they walked on down the hill the houses became smaller and the path turned to a rocky track which brought them out on the main road. They crossed the road and turned down Nightingale Street, narrow and cobbled and winding, then threaded their way through a maze of alleys and courts, past dark lowering tenement houses and dingy little shops which seemed to have little else in their windows but faded dummy cigarette packets and jars of boiled sweets. This was, officially, the Nightingale Green area; and he and Tom used its proper name then. It wasn't until much later, after seeing *Pepe le Moko*, that they christened it the Kasbah. It was a quarter dominated by the canal and the railway and the municipal abattoir and the gaol, pre-eminently the sort of place in which nothing pleasant ever had happened or ever could possibly happen. It was always a relief to emerge from it to take the path on the western fringe of Kellogg's Woods.

Looking back, it seemed as if the Vodi had been discovered at the same time as the North-West Passage. It was difficult to remember a time when there wasn't a Vodi. But, he was pretty sure, it was after they'd been using the North-West Passage for about a year that Tom, one wet autumn evening in Kellogg's Woods, suddenly stopped. "Look!" he said, pointing to a gap in the silver birches high on the hillside. "Look, you fool!"

"I can't see anything," he said.

"Just over there, scuttling towards the wall. No good – he's gone now."

"There's nothing there but dead leaves."

"It's the Vodi."

The word was frightening, sharp-edged and sinister and smooth as the gutta-percha on a hangman's rope. And that, Dick thought, had been another moment of choice. He only had had to say, "Bloody nonsense" or "Kid's stuff, Coverack" and close his ears to Tom. But he had listened, and he had gone on listening in the two years which followed and he'd made his own contribution to the legend.

"There's an entrance to General HQ in the Kasbah here," Tom said. "It's so well-hidden that no-one'll ever find it. There's hundreds of others. There's a network of tunnels leading to the Kasbah."

"People are always finding things they're not supposed to find. What if someone discovers one of the entrances?"

"They'll be sorry," said Tom. "All the tunnels are lined with booby traps, one every twenty yards. You've got to say the right password every twenty yards. If you don't the floor falls away and you're impaled on a nest of spikes. They're painted red so as not to show the blood. Old Lammer designed it, it all works by infra-red rays. Nelly sometimes changes the passwords without warning too. She says it sharpens their wits and teaches them to take nothing for granted."

Nelly; you hadn't to forget Nelly, huge and fat and old, always laughing. She had only four teeth: they were long and filed to sharp points. Nelly was a person, an individual; the Vodi were all alike, small and ferret-faced and ragged with no more identity than amoebae. There wasn't really such a thing as a Vodi; there was only *the* Vodi.

But that evening they hadn't worked out the legend to that extent; in fact, Dick didn't even bother to ask who Nelly was. He wanted to be volunteered the information and not to have to ask Tom humbly for it. Tom, he felt then, was nice enough, but a great deal too bossy, too much the born leader.

They walked along the rocky path, scuffing their feet in the dead leaves. They came to a rise; from the top the valley could be seen spread out before them, the pithead wheel of Rosemary Colliery to the left. The spire of Silbridge Church was just visible on the right and in the distance, colouring the puddles in the sad flat fields, bull's-blood and silver, the leaping flames of the coke-ovens.

"You playing full-back again?" he asked Tom.

"Yuh."

"They didn't give me a chance again," Dick said.

"Didn't expect it, did you?" Tom said. "You're lousy and that's praising you, Dick. You play football with your head instead of your feet."

"You know it all," Dick said.

" 'Course I do." Tom found a big stone and kicked it down the hill, then broke into a run.

"The tram's coming!" he shouted, and pointed to the road below. Dick followed him and they went running out of the darkening woods into the harsh glow of the street lamps.

3

"Who told you about the Vodi?" he asked Tom the next day as they were walking up the North-West Passage in the teeth of a bitter wind.

"Jack Lensholt."

"He's dead."

"I know." Tom wrapped his scarf more tightly round his neck. "Jack was a damned good rider. The bike was brand new. It was a fine day. How do you think that lorry came to be there? The driver had his orders."

"The driver cried."

"You'd bloody well cry if you saw a chap's guts steaming in a pile on the road and you knew you'd done it."

"I expect Jack knew too much," Dick said.

"Vous avez raison, mon cher. He used to go to Kellogg's Woods bug-hunting. Proper old B.O.P. type, was Jack. He'd just caught a Scarlet Rupture or whatever they call them and he saw a light. The Vodi had left an entrance open."

"It must have been the visitors' entrance," Dick said. "The one which doesn't have any booby traps."

"That's right," Tom said, not entirely with approval, Dick felt. "Nelly was holding a meeting. All the Vodi were there, their little red eyes glittering. They'd just finished framing Tommy Wander for that smash-and-grab job in Dufton. Jack was a knight in shining armour and said Nelly was evil and he was going to stamp her out. So Nelly said: *I* am *evil and I'm going to stamp* you *out*. And that was that."

Dick opened his mouth to speak, then closed it as the wind threw a handful of sleet in his face. When they were in the shelter of the Kasbah, he said: "It's not worth it to save a penny."

"What's not worth it?"

"This damned short cut, of course. We'll be soaked to the skin."

"Rot! Race you to the top."

They set off as if for the hundred yards sprint and at first on the level ground it seemed as if they were flying, flying past the tall tenements and mean little shops, twisting through alleys and courtyards and muddy paths by henhouses and allotments. Then as the ground grew steeper and muddier they were forced to slacken their pace.

"It's a damned sight quicker going down than going up," Dick said. "This isn't one of your brightest ideas, mon ami."

Tom grunted and walked more quickly, swinging his arms high with his elbows tucked up into his sides.

"We'll have to get moving if we're not going to be late," he said. "Quit bellyaching, will you?"

They reached the entrance of the High just as the nine o'clock bell was about to ring. They ran across the Egg and into the vestibule, where George Gilverton, the history master, stood at the door, florid and scowling. There was a speck of blood on his stiff white collar. He was always in a hurry; but his impatience was quick and efficient, never the flurried or frightened kind. He wasn't much taller than Tom or Dick but you never really noticed it.

When he saw Tom and Dick his scowl increased until his eyes were almost slits. "Corvey and Coverack!" he shouted, "Rascals and rogues and scoundrels! Fiends and traitors and turncoats!

Thirty seconds to divest yourselves of your sordid stinking mackintoshes!" He aimed a cuff at Tom, who dodged it, and another at Dick, whose head it left ringing as he scuttled with Tom into the cloakroom. Panting, they took their places in the Assembly Hall. From under the portrait of Lord Rammerby, the Chairman of the Board of Governors in 1921, who had out of the proceeds of selling coal endowed the school library and also presented most of the busts which stood in niches in the oak-panelled corridor outside, he saw their form master, Screaming Sid, looking thoughtfully at them. If Sid had been on duty, Dick reflected gratefully, he'd have stuck to the letter of the law, which stated that you had to be in Assembly at five minutes to the hour. So there'd have been a hundred lines or an hour's detention or three on the left hand awaiting them both now, according to Sid's mood.

Dick and Tom's form, Upper Three, was placed halfway down the hall; as you went up in the school, so you moved away from the Headmaster, who stood on a dais in front of the Assembly Hall. It was, Tom often said, one of the few advantages of seniority; Kempett was a moist speaker, who deluged everyone in the first three rows when in full spate.

This morning Kempett, all throughout the hymn and the prayers, was absurdly straining at the leash. As soon as the music master had left the piano to take his place with his form, Kempett strode to the dais. He looked round the hall, slowly, deliberately and theatrically.

"There are some amongst you," he said, "who have hurt me unbearably."

He passed his hand over his pale, smooth face, as if to shape it into a proper severity.

"The majority of you, I have no doubt, are normal, happy lads. Absorbed in your work and your games though no doubt" – he permitted himself a small, gold-glittering smile – "rather more absorbed in your games than in your work, your minds are clean and fresh from taint. Mischievous you may be – even wild" – he permitted himself a slightly wider smile – "but *bad* you are not. Filthy, you are not. But, some there are amongst you, some who I pray represent only a tiny minority, whose minds are middens, cloacas of a filth which destroys mind and body alike. Some there are amongst you who are centres of corruption." He dropped his voice to a whisper. "I shall not rest until I *stamp* them out. I shall scourge these sinners, for that is my duty . . ."

Dick wanted to run out of the Assembly Hall, away from the busts of Calvin and Caesar and Hadrian, away from the green curtains, away from the oak panelling and the bare floor sprung for dancing, away from that voice which didn't seem as if it would ever stop. On his other side was Cyril Bardett, a boy from, oddly enough, the Kasbah. For some reason, Bartlett always smelled strongly of fish; and his clothes, even when new, seemed worn and greasy. He had a pale, long face with eyes not unlike Kempett's; it was wearing an expression of absolute boredom as it always did except during the Chemistry period.

Tom was listening as if in rapt attention, his bony face mediaeval in a shaft of light. Dick tasted again the fried bread and bacon he'd had for breakfast, greasy and rancid. Suddenly, he was gripped by a dull fear, an actual grinding pain in his bowels. It's me he wants, he thought in panic, remembering the story he'd told about the convent and the candle factory to Rayden of the Lower Third at break on Thursday; I always knew Rayden was a rat.

Kempett's voice went on remorselessly; it was as if there were a tiger padding round the boys, stopping to sniff here and there and then continuing, patient and unhurried. "Some amongst you, some standing here now" – he paused and appeared to look straight at Dick – "do not wish to take the trouble to repay their parents – and, I may add, the Council – for the sacrifices which have been made on their behalf. These sacrifices cannot, of course, be measured purely in terms of money. They are to be measured in terms of decency, in terms of hard work, in terms of" – his voice rose to a shout – "LOVE!" He scowled at his audience, as if daring them to contradict him.

Dick had a wild longing to shout obscenities at him, to leap out to the dais and punch the tall skinny body on which one almost expected to see, so far removed from normality and so caught up in power as it was at this moment, a bird's head, like Thoth the Destroyer in the book about Ancient Egypt he'd just borrowed from the County Library. But, even as the thought came to him, he rejected it. It was blasphemy, as unthinkable as an attack upon a god.

"But there are boys to whom words like decency and work and gratitude and love are meaningless. These young gentlemen" – Kempett spat the word out – "are interested only in the precocious pursuit of adult pleasures, if so they may be termed. To smoke, to drink, to pursue giggling girls, to collect filthy, obscene, soul-destroying pictures – these are the preoccupations of some of our scholars. I shall not permit it. I shall not permit it for their own sakes." There was a last flurry of hail on the windows and then the sun came out, filling the hall with light, glittering on the gold signet ring on Kempett's left hand. "Let sharp physical pain be their medicine," he said. He snapped his fingers and the school porter, Hangman Harry, shambled in from the corridor with the cane.

Dick was dizzy with relief. It couldn't be him, the most he'd done was to smoke and he'd been too careful for Kempett to find him out. The relief was immediately replaced by another emotion; it was exactly the same emotion he experienced in reading the chapter in *The Black Tulip* where the De Witt brothers were torn to pieces by the angry mob. He hated that chapter, but he kept returning to it, he almost knew it by heart. If he had been free to leave the Hall now, he wouldn't have done. He was excited, feverishly excited. The big feature was about to begin.

Kempett left the dais, swishing the cane gently in the air. "Robert Palworth, come here! John Kisham, come here!"

It couldn't, of course, have been anyone else. Palworth and Kisham had a reputation for that sort of thing. Particularly Kisham, a stocky fifteen, who shaved every day. Palworth, thinner and far less self-assured, was the faithful friend, the one who made up the party of four so that it could be separated into twos. Palworth dragged his feet as he walked up to Kempett; he had a small Cupid's-bow mouth, too pretty for a boy's, which was pursed into an odd primness. His large brown eyes were staring. Kisham walked jauntily with a faint smile on his face. His back was very straight.

"Robert Palworth, hold out your hand." Palworth's hand was

shaking; Dick noticed that the smile had left Kisham's face. It was as red as Palworth's face was white. The cane came down six times on the outstretched hand, a sound like the crack of a whip. "Your other," Kempett barked. "Your other hand, boy." Palworth put out his right hand very slowly. At the third stroke his body began to shake and Dick could see the glint of tears in his eyes.

"Go back to your place," Kempett said. Palworth didn't seem to hear him but remained where he was, one extended hand under the other. "That's all," Kempett said, loudly. "And let this be a lesson to you." Palworth slowly let his hands fall to his sides and returned to his form. Dick noticed his swollen hand as he passed and realised – somehow there was a vicarious triumph in the realisation – that what had turned Kisham's face red was not fear or shame but anger.

Kisham's left hand was extended now; the smile had returned to his face. He might, if the cane hadn't been there, have been expecting a large tip from a kindly uncle. He had a heavy face with a straight nose and heavy chin; his jowls were already a little fleshy. At that moment he looked older than Kempett who, as he brought the cane down for the first stroke, had now an air of being a schoolboy in masquerade; his thin body was vibrating with rage, his face had lost control of itself. With the sixth stroke, the sound of which set up a faint echo, it was evident that he hadn't been putting his full strength into the caning of Palworth.

Kisham drew his left hand back to change over to the right. Kempett frowned. "Keep your hand there," he said in a whisper like a lover's. Kisham put his hand back; his smile grew broader. At the eighth stroke the colour left his cheeks except for a patch on each cheekbone. At the ninth stroke the smile became indistinguishable from a snarl, the lips baring on the teeth.

As Kempett stepped back to raise his arm for the tenth stroke, his foot slipped on the parquet floor; he recovered himself and stood still for a moment, his hand flying to his chest. In the silence which followed, his harsh panting filled the hall. Then, suddenly Gilverton was beside him, whispering in his ear. Kempett's mouth worked as if he were about to speak; then, without a word, he handed the cane back to Hangman Harry and swirled out of the Hall.

Kisham's eyes were now half-closed and he was almost imperceptibly swaying. His hand was still extended, the grin still fixed. Gilverton put his hand on Kisham's sleeve. Kisham's eyes snapped open and his hands dropped. Gilverton smiled at him. "Crime and punishment, John, crime and punishment," he said. "Go to the cloakroom." Kisham walked down the Hall, moving heavily as if suddenly aged, the grin now having the appearance of some congenital deformity, a new variety of wryneck.

Gilverton folded his arms, a small spruce figure in brown worsted, gleaming light tan shoes and a beige silk tie. "You will all bear in mind," he said, "the words of the Headmaster. I fully agree with them. Starting with Lower One you will now proceed to your classrooms. QUICK MARCH!"

At break Dick said to Tom: "What the hell had they done?" Tom, leaning against the wall, pulled out what appeared to be a packet of cigarettes and handed one to Dick. Dick bit into the sweetmeat and asked again, "Just what *did* they do?"

"Don't eat it, you fool," Tom said. "Keep it in your mouth. The Screamer can see us from the staff room window. I want to be unjustly accused and rehabilitated."

"You'll only get a hundred lines for childish impertinence," Dick said. "Like Parton did. What did Kisham and Palworth get flogged for?"

"They went to Rumbold Fair," Tom said.

"They were canned," Ron Liphook drawled.

Dick looked at him coldly. He didn't like Liphook; he didn't know whether it was because of his drawl, his unnatural neatness, his way of always pleasing those in authority or because of his meanness, a meanness which seemed to extend to his face, which would have been pleasant and open if only there'd been, particularly at the mouth, a milligram more of flesh.

"I was asking Tom," Dick said.

"Tom doesn't know," Liphook said, "else you wouldn't have to ask him."

"I know they went to Rumbold Tide," Tom said.

"You heard that from Jacko Brown. They didn't get done for

going to the Tide though. They were drunk as lords, both of 'em. Kisham's people went out and it was the maid's night off. Old Palworth called for Kisham and Kisham was showing him all the different kinds of booze they've got. So they sampled the wine that was opened and then they tried some Benedictine."

"I've had some in chocolate liqueurs," Dick said. "It's smashing."

"It wasn't little chocolate bottles they drank it from, though," Liphook said. "It's strong stuff, kid. Anyway, they were absolutely sozzled. So they thought they'd clear their heads if they went to the Tide."

"How were they found out?" Tom asked.

"The Screamer was there. Says he was walking through the park and spotted two boys in school uniform behaving queerly."

"The dirty man," Tom said. "He'd be trying to pick someone up. Or looking at the girls' knickers in the Fun House."

"They'd picked up two tarts there," Liphook said. "They had their arms around them and Kisham was practically undressing his."

Dick felt a keen spasm of lust and envy. "They wouldn't dare in public," he said.

"I don't suppose Palworth would," Liphook said, "but Kisham would, particularly if he was full of sherry and port and Benedictine. Then Palworth tried to do the swallow and started spewing. Enter the Screamer."

"You didn't mention the best part," Tom said. "The Screamer went to school early yesterday morning and searched their desks. There was a packet of Woodbines in Kisham's desk and a bundle of dirty photos in Palworth's. My God, they scooped the jackpot between 'em."

Dick remembered the details of the flogging and felt sick with anger. "They should sue that old devil, Kempett," he said. "He nearly killed Kisham."

"My dear boy," Liphook said, "who's *they*?"

"Their parents. Palworth's and Kisham's."

"It was their parents who asked Kempett to flog 'em. They were spotted by a copper on their way out. He knew the Screamer and he helped him take Palworth and Kisham to the Screamer's car."

"Bet he reported it just the same," Tom said.

"'Course he did. But the police aren't prosecuting. They said they'd let it go for the sake of the school if the Slaverer'd flog them."

"The swine," Dick said.

"You're dozy," Liphook said. "They were damned decent, really. So was the Slaverer. He could easy have expelled them."

"Bet you the Slaverer's looking over those pictures with the Screamer now," Tom said. He mimicked Kempett's unctuous voice. "Pass the magnifying glass, my dear Terence, so that I may examine this young lady's nipples more closely. Oh my, how revolting, how obscene and soul-destroying. Let me have that lingeries study too, old man. It's one's sacred duty to look into these things . . ."

"Did you see Gilverton, though?" Dick said. "He stopped the Slaverer from killing Kisham."

"Like the entry of the Marines," Liphook said. "Our gallant Georgie galloping to the rescue on his white steed."

"He runs the school really," Tom said. "The Slaverer's only a figure-head. George didn't care if the Slaverer did kill Kisham, but he knew damned well that Kisham would have killed the Slaverer in another moment. Didn't you see his face turning blue? He's got a wonky ticker."

"Hope the old pig dies this morning," Dick said.

"That's no way to talk," Tom said. "He hated flogging those wicked boys. It hurt him more than it did them. Didn't you know that?"

Kisham, his swagger returned, went past on his way from the sweetshop, chewing noisily. His swollen left hand, dark red and blue, hung limply at his side. He didn't speak to Tom and Dick and Liphook – they were only Third Formers – but he winked at Tom as he passed.

"Where's Palworth?" Tom asked.

Kisham stopped and frowned, as if deciding whether or not Tom were worth answering. The colour had come back to his cheeks; in his barathea blazer and bright grey gabardine trousers sharply creased, his new shoes dazzlingly polished, his cap on the back of his head to reveal well-brushed chestnut hair with the hint of a wave in it, he looked healthy, normal and undefeated; as he looked at him Dick's feelings of pity and hatred were replaced by something warmer, by a feeling which was mixed up with the picture of a hand unbuttoning a blouse under flaring yellow lights in a fairground; it made him happy in a way he couldn't precisely analyse.

"He's blubbing on Gilverton's shoulder," Kisham said in his harsh booming voice. "Hell, he's got nothing to blub about. The Slaverer only stroked him." He swaggered on towards the group of Sixth Formers at the far end of the quadrangle; they opened their ranks to receive him like a guard of honour.

4

PALWORTH was innocent, of course. Kisham wasn't, and normally would have escaped scot-free but for the fact of his having cheeked Nelly. He'd seen her run a crippled child down with her Bugatti and said it was a rotten shame. That had been five years ago, but Nelly never forgot an insult. Not that, Tom said, Nelly could ever make Kisham really suffer.

"Why not?" Dick asked, as they were going down the North-West Passage that evening. "He's human, isn't he?"

"Glad you think so," Tom said. "You looked at him as if he were a superman. He's human all right. But Nelly can't do anything really bad to old Kisham."

"Why?"

"I don't know," Tom said. "She just can't, that's all."

They were entering the Kasbah; in the grey of the winter's afternoon the tenement houses seemed taller than ever. It was quiet now, at the hour before the husbands returned from work; so quiet that it was frightening. It was as if the whole district were awaiting some colossal and irretrievable disaster.

They turned to the left past the junk-yard crammed with cars, prams, mangles, rusting boilers and metal bedsteads. The ground rose sharply above the junk-yard to a small field, the only patch of green in the Kasbah, where a tethered goat was grazing. In the centre of the field a large metal hoarding stated in red letters on a bright green background that Suco Soap Soothes the Skin. The depressing effect of the hoarding was, for Dick, heightened by the fact that the company, a local one, had gone bankrupt some five years ago: that was one of the reasons for the Kasbah being so poverty-stricken.

The junk-yard, too, always depressed him. Because of the smoke coming from the chimney of the little wooden hut by the entrance, he knew that somebody – Charles Listock it said in straggling letters on the notice above the door – owned the yard. And the battered old Fordson lorry permanently parked outside the office was evidence that business was being done there, but never once in the three years that he and Tom used the North-West Passage, did they see anyone either going into the yard or leaving it. On the day of the flogging there had been a new addition to the cars, a Cord roadster with a long bonnet and a two-seater body. The yellow enamel was scratched and chipped, the upholstery ripped to reveal the stuffing, the yellowing glass of the windscreen broken; it looked as if it had been there for years, but it could only have been delivered that day.

"How did it get there?" Dick asked.

"Listock drove it there."

"You couldn't drive it in that condition."

"It's one of Nelly's old cars. She got fifty quid for it. Listock had a buyer for it and he'd been promised seventy quid from Randy Widden. Randy collects cars like other people collect stamps. Listock thought he was sure of twenty clear profit but when he drove it to the yard the Vodi was waiting. They slashed the upholstery and kicked the engine to bits and put a bomb in the gearbox. Now it's not worth ten bob. Nelly says that Listock's too keen on money and must be shown that there are higher values."

They turned into a narrow alley between two blocks of four-storey tenements. Both the opposing walls were devoid of windows; passing between their black, cold blankness, Dick was always assailed by claustrophobia. They emerged into a cobbled courtyard and left it through an arched passageway. As they reached the main road a small figure scuttled through the passageway in the direction of the alley.

"It's the Vodi," Tom said. "Did you see that ferrety little face and those luminous eyes? He's followed us all the way." He sniffed. "He's left his trail behind. Incense and rosewater and sweaty feet."

It was a pleasure to be out of the Kasbah that evening; outside the courtyard began the normal civilised world of the cinema and the dance-hall and the roller-skating rink and the Maypole and Boots and Freeman, Hardy and Willis. Once out of the Kasbah the shops became real, brightly lit and clean and prosperous. They'd only visited one Kasbah shop; it was an off-licence, very cool and smelling both earthy and antiseptic, with overtones of stale beer and tobacco. A fat young woman in a blindingly white overall had served them. She reeked of perfume and sweat and when she leaned over the counter it was evident that she wore nothing beneath the overall.

That had been last summer; they called back to the shop often, but never saw her there again; they were served instead by a middle-aged man and a younger one, obviously father and son. It was easy to work out what had happened; her husband and father-in-law had kept her hidden in the cellar and then one day they'd drunk too much bottled beer. So she'd been forced to attend to the shop; the twenty-four-hour-a-day Vodi patrol had spotted her and now she was a Bride of the Vodi.

Thinking of her now, Dick said to Tom: "Sometimes I wish I were in the Vodi."

"It's too tough a life for you."

"I'm as tough as you are."

"No, you're not. *Absolument pas.* You're always expecting everything to be perfect. Hell, I watched you this morning – you were nearly blubbing. I'm damned sure it didn't hurt old Kempett more than it hurt Palworth and Kisham, but I'm not so sure that it didn't hurt you nearly as much."

Dick felt tears prickling his eyes. "The old devil," he said, "the cruel old devil."

Tom laughed; looking at him Dick felt that suddenly the Kasbah had extended its boundaries.

The cough began as a tickling in the back of the throat. He

poured himself a glass of water from the covered pitcher at his side and sipped it slowly, but the tickle became a rasp which grew more and more intense until it convulsed his whole chest with pain. There was the familiar sickly sweet, sweetly salty taste of blood in his mouth; he rang the bell and then lay back.

"Staining?" Nurse Mallaton asked him in what seemed to be the next second.

He nodded.

"Don't worry," she said. "The doctor's on his way."

His mouth was full of blood; he spat into the sputum cup, her arm around his shoulders. When he saw the bright frothy blood he had to fight to keep his hold upon consciousness.

"All right," he said. "This must be it."

"Don't talk any more than you have to," she said.

"There's a sound like the sea. Like the sea in a seashell."

He saw the faint flicker of a smile on her face. "You're not little Dombey," she said. "Now be quiet."

Then there was ice in his mouth and the green cloth screens were around the bed and Doctor Redroe was leaning over him. His white coat was unbuttoned, revealing a cream silk shirt, fawn cavalry twill slacks and light brown suède shoes. His tie was of bright yellow silk with a pattern of green locomotives and veteran cars.

"Button your coat, Doctor," Dick heard himself saying thickly, "your tie's hurting my eyes."

Redroe, his finger on Dick's pulse, grinned. "You'll live," he said. "Long enough to give me cheek and spoil my afternoon tea." He took a hypodermic syringe from the tray which the probationer, Laggons, had just brought in. Laggons was small and plain and cheerful with a loud Barnsley voice; she was now looking at Dick with round shocked eyes. Normally, he liked Laggons; she bounced round the ward like a friendly puppy. But he hated her for that look of pity – it made him feel naked and defeated.

"I'll quieten you down, my lad," Redroe said. Dick felt Nurse Mallaton's cool hands upon his sleeve and he closed his eyes. Then he felt the stinging cold of surgical spirits on his wrist and opened them again to intercept a look between Redroe and Nurse

Mallaton. Redroe's round chubby face with the small twinkling eyes and scrubby red moustache was for a second sad and pleading; hers was provocative and at the same time cold.

He turned to Dick again.

"There we are, Dick," he said. "Not enough to make you an addict, but enough to stop you getting excited. Snuggle up to your hot-water bottle and there'll be a hot drink too in a minute."

"When am I going to get some brandy?" Dick asked.

"Never," Redroe said. "Ah've supped it all, lad. Didn't know I could talk Yorkshire, did you?"

"I'll report you to the Friends of Nedham," Dick said.

"You can't," Redroe said. "They're all in the racket with me."

He sat down beside the bed.

"Now, stop yattering, old boy. Just relax." He took Dick's pulse again. "Don't worry. I've seen men worse than you live till a hundred."

Dick noticed that Nurse Mallaton's eyes were unusually large and widely spaced; when he looked at her the fear and loneliness left him entirely. Or was it the drug already at work, planing the rough edges of pain? He smiled drowsily at her. "I never liked that silly little Paul," he said.

When he awoke, she was still there. "What time is it?" he asked.

"Past seven," she said. "You've missed supper, but you're to have something now."

"What was it for supper?"

"Rissoles and chips. Smashing."

"It wasn't worth waking up for."

"You're not having that. It's too good for you."

She brought in chicken broth and toast, and fruit salad with, inevitably, ice-cream. There was a cup of tea, which he drank greedily before he touched anything else. He found that he was hungry; he cleared his plate and then asked for another cup of tea. The sun was setting now; the wind blew cold on his face. Nurse Mallaton had put on his cardigan for him, and as he sat up in bed drinking the hot tea and feeling the warmth of the refilled hot-water bottle in the crook of his knee, seeing in the distance the lights springing up in the valley and hearing the sound of cars from the road to Nedham village, he experienced something which was somehow related to happiness. It was ridiculous to think so, he must be going out of his senses to dare to imagine it; but he had a premonition of something good in store for him, the future was going to be what it had been for him only two years ago, a cupboard crammed with new pleasures, new excitements, unguessable splendours. It was even possible to hope that he wouldn't always be alone.

Nurse Mallaton brought in the *Tanbury Gazette.* She looked at him lying back on the pillows, his hands folded and his face thin and white, and felt a curious sensation, like a contraction of the womb, which was almost a pain. She recognised it: pity. He wasn't much to look at, only about an inch taller than she, with a body which even before the Bug had gnawed it could have been at best what they call wiry. He spoke quite well, not too broadly or sloppily, and he wasn't semi-illiterate. But he had unmistakably the Silbridge accent, the accent which she herself had taken twenty-one years to get rid of. He wasn't what they call a gentleman and he wasn't rich. And he was full of bacilli. It was stupid of her to think of him as other than the raw material of her job; pity was fatal. Once you let pity in, then you were ruined. That's what your seniors always told you and of course they were right.

Dick had a firm mouth, not too thin and not too loose and slobbery. And he had marvellous teeth. His hands were white with long tapering fingers; the filbert-shaped nails were a little clubbed, but less than one would have expected. They were too pretty for a man's: hers were square red hunks of flesh in comparison. But otherwise he was just the sort of man you'd be introduced to at a party and never give a moment's thought to again. There wasn't anything about him worth remembering. There never had been any drive or energy; he was a failure. He was unlucky too, which was even worse: he was one of the few who were allergic to antibiotics. No miracle cure for Dick; that would have been too easy, too normal. She'd seen a lot of people die this past eight years; mostly they died very well, either making an honourable surrender or fighting to the last gasp. Dick would die badly, he'd drift into death, he'd accept it, he'd say, with a shrug: *I can't be bothered to live.*

And he was already, looking at the evening paper, in a world of his own. His eyes scanned the paper, but she knew that he wasn't reading it. The real Dick Corvey was somewhere else; and wherever he was, he wasn't enjoying himself.

Back in the kitchen looking over the diet charts, she wondered drearily why she'd come to Nedham in the first place. She'd wanted to be nearer her parents in Tanbury, she'd wanted more experience, and, of course, she'd wanted to get away from Rawminster right from the moment when it first became evident that Rupert Hicknall had no intention of marrying her. And it wasn't just that; there was something about the way in which his friend Trenton looked at her – excitedly, sniggeringly, a little contemptuously – which made it plain that Hicknall had been boasting of his conquest – *A piece of cake, old boy, we couldn't get on the job quick enough . . .*

But at the time he'd talked, vaguely but convincingly, of love and children and marriage; and it was a warm August night and she wasn't wearing much and there was a penetrating smell of grass and wild mint. At the age of twenty-seven she should have known better; though at least she'd been wise enough afterwards not to talk about marriage again with him, or to repeat her stupidity.

What made her dislike him all the more, what made her leave Rawminster so quickly was, strangely enough, the fact that he was a very good doctor, cheerful and conscientious and tender. That rather smudgy face with the dark complexion and the motor-car salesman's moustache and the loose mouth and turned-up nose seemed to acquire adult planes, even an unselfconscious nobility, when he was on the wards. He lived to a code in the hospital; but once outside it, if you wore skirts and had the usual protuberances and the usual feminine instincts, you were fair game, you didn't count as a human being. And your instincts, your damned feminine instincts, actually welcomed that masculine arrogance and insensitivity, particularly after living in the Nurses' Home, where nothing was ever secret, where everyone understood everyone else twenty-four hours a day. And at the back of her mind had been the idea that him making love to her did really mean making love, that he wanted to give her a baby and work to keep it and her.

And now there was Harry, who wasn't quite as skilful a seducer as Hicknall but who, to judge by their last tussle in his car, would like to be. She'd been going around with him for four months now and he hadn't even talked about marriage. He was, she recognised, much the same type as Hicknall, bulky and hearty and hard-driving and, so it would seem, not the marrying kind. The marrying kind were like Teddy, the librarian she'd met when she was at Warley Hospital a long time ago: they made you feel like a princess, they even wrote poetry for you, they wanted children and a home, but they didn't love you enough to go to the effort of saving and planning. She'd have married Teddy if only, after six months of courtship, he'd shown any signs of cutting down his bachelor pleasures, if only he'd made any attempt to save, if only he'd not been so irredeemably ineffectual.

She thought of Dick Corvey again and remembered the moment of warmth there'd been between them when he picked up her allusion. He'd been grown-up then, laughing at himself: there had been a living man behind that smile. She brushed the memory away impatiently; Dick was no use to her or any other woman. The bell rang, and she looked at the indicator. As she went to answer it, she noted with surprise and annoyance that she was disappointed it wasn't Dick's number.

Dick put down the paper; even the small advertisements made him feel bitter. The Tanbury Rugby Club was holding a Gala Ball, the Film Society was showing *Les Enfants du Paradis*, the Operatic Society was staging *Showboat*. To hell with them. Let the dance hall floor collapse, the film projector break down, the showboat sink. The world should have stopped when my life stopped . . .

Night had settled over the hospital; soon all the lights in the wards and cubicles would be turned off. At nine the radio would be turned off; should he listen to it now or should he not try to evade what was going to come to him? At this time there'd be some pop tunes; they weren't always reliable drugs, but they could sometimes induce a vapid cheerfulness, or at the very least stop one from thinking. But when the drug had begun to work, when one was an inhabitant of a June and moon, Dallas and palace nirvana, the radio was turned off; and, not being able to sleep, one had to think. And his thoughts always boiled down to this: it wasn't fair. He'd worked as hard as anyone else, if not a damned sight harder, he'd served in Burma if not with distinction at least to the best of his ability; and he'd always been honest. He could have made a fortune just after the war when cigarettes were in short supply; particularly if he'd taken Ben Longtaft's hint and let him know that delivery van's route. But he wasn't a thief any more than he was a drunkard or a lecher. He couldn't, like his dear friend Tom, put it away night after night (and now that he was a big business man, presumably lunchtime after lunchtime, too) and unlike Tom he didn't steal other men's women. All that he'd ever wanted had been to settle down with Lois; all that he'd ever wanted had been to love her. And now the roof had fallen in on him. The first shock was over, the dust had settled and he could now see that his whole life was *kaputt*. And he was the last person to whom this should have happened; why, in real life, did the fire and brimstone never hit the equivalents of Sodom and Gomorrah? Why was it never people like Tom who got it in the neck? You were the person you were born to be and you might as well accept it. He wasn't a Tom Coverack – he was born unlucky, the Bobby Quedgeley type.

Bobby Quedgeley was the French master at Tanbury High, a bachelor who lived with his sister. He was a small man, with thin hands always looking uncomfortably dry with chalk-dust and a pale face as blank as one of the numbered drawings in keys to group portraits. He always wore the same tie – dark blue with stripes of a paler blue in a polka-dot arrangement as if they hadn't the courage to make a solid contrast. It was symbolic of his general inoffensiveness; he must have chosen it on the grounds that it couldn't possibly give distress to anyone. He ran a Morris Minor two-seater which was some ten years old but was so well-maintained as to be indistinguishable from new. He was the neat, old-maidish type of bachelor as opposed to the boozy roarer; his neatness was, in fact, obsessive, as was the number of times a day he washed his hands.

He lived on Boggart Moor, south of Silbridge, which, together with Kellogg's Woods, was the only open country in Silbridge. Tom and Dick and Ron Liphook, who for some reason had attached himself to them at that time – it would be about their fourth year at Tanbury High – went for a walk there one cold spring afternoon, an afternoon on which Sunday and sunlessness and the presence of Liphook had combined to induce in both Dick and Tom a ferocious melancholy.

To reach Boggart Moor you left the main Barnsley road and walked up a narrow winding side-road; Dick wondered how Quedgeley could bear to risk the springs of his precious car on it; the surface was tarmac, but subsidence from old mine-workings had so pitted and rutted it that it was little better than a cart-track.

The houses – all back-to-back with low alleyways ending in a view of w.c.'s and coalsheds – suddenly gave way to the moors. The air wasn't much cleaner – even the grass seemed black rather than dark green – but it was colder and the wind had a keener edge. The moors, like the village green at the top of the hill, weren't likely to be photographed in *Country Life*, to say the least of it; but they were better than nothing. On the skyline to the left were the slag-heaps and pitheads of Barnsley; to the right the chimneys of Tanbury and Morley and Wakefield; but there was at least some thirty square miles of moorland, there was at least the village green with the seventeenth-century yeomen's houses and labourers' cottages around it and in the centre the old Saxon cross.

Outside a cottage at the far end of the green stood a grey Morris Minor two-seater. The cottage had a fussy trellis-work porch and mullioned windows; cut into the blackened stone over the porch they could discern the figures 1798.

"Quedgeley's," Liphook said.

"I know," Tom said.

"They say his sister's barmy and that's why he doesn't marry."

"They say a lot of things," Tom said.

A gramophone record was put on in the cottage. It was a boys' choir singing; the words were Latin. It was plainsong, Tom supposed; there was no accompaniment, only the high sexless voices which made music without effort, which, at their highest notes, seemed not to have stopped at any limit of the human thorax or vocal chords, but to have continued into a pitch beyond his ability to hear. There was in the song – if song was the term

– a sensual appeal which was out of his experience. *Dies irae, dies illa, solvet saeculum in favilla* – there was no ache, no throb, only an ordered ecstasy in which no heads were lost, no clothing torn. He felt lonely; the voices were talking, almost arrogantly, of a cold and superior world of which he could never be part.

"Mark you," Liphook said, pointing his forefinger at Tom, "she's not mad. Neither of them wants to marry. They don't need to."

Dick, out of earshot of the music now, heard Liphook's sneering voice. "What are you driving at?"

"She's nice," Liphook said, and giggled. "Remember her dress at Sports Day?"

It had rained on the last Sports Day and Myra Quedgeley had worn a transparent green mackintosh and hood over a flowered green dress. The mackintosh had held the dress tightly over her chest; but when she took it off at tea, there had been far too much of her small but pleasant breasts on view. What had made it unforgivable was that it wasn't intentional. The dress was of expensive material, but badly cut; and her brassière didn't fit. She had been a target of male desire, but then so had Kempett's daughter, Marie, a plump and ready-for-marriage nineteen in a V-necked white dress under which, the boys noted when she stood against the light, she wore no petticoat. Liphook sniggered when talking about Marie too, but there'd been a note of respect in his voice; Marie had known very well what she was doing, Myra Quedgeley hadn't.

Myra was one of those people who'd always do the wrong thing; Liphook, Dick thought, was one of those people who'd always, socially at any rate, do the right thing. And that was why he liked Myra and why he didn't like Liphook.

"I know what you mean," he said, "and it's not true."

"It's true about the dress," Liphook said. "Ask Tom."

"You weren't talking about that. I say you're a bloody liar."

"Then my mother and father are liars, too. I heard them talking about it. Bobby and Myra used to live with their parents down South but they threw them out. Their parents did, I mean."

Dick remembered the dress again and the valley between her breasts. Something disturbing and rank was entering the afternoon, saying No hoarsely to the cold and the smoke from the power station and the Special Offer of Two Pounds of Our Best Sugar for the Price of One outside the grocer's window at the other side of the green.

"I don't care," he said. "Someone made it up."

"You're sweet on her," Liphook said.

"Hell, no," Dick said. "She's old enough to be my mother." As he said it, he felt an enormous pity. She'd been enjoying herself so much that afternoon; she'd been so pleased not only with her dress, but with her raincoat and hood, that at moments she'd seemed younger than Marie Kempett. Marie's face was only flesh; you could understand it as far as you ever understood girls. But there was something behind Myra Quedgeley's face with its thin almost hollow cheeks and big mouth with too much lipstick and the big brown short-sighted eyes, that he could no more understand than he could understand the plainsong. There had been a big splash of mud on her left calf, too; he thought of that jarring note with anger and sorrow.

They walked on past the village green; it was all open country now, with no protection from the biting wind. The road dipped steeply and the pitheads and chimneys were out of sight; then it rose again and the illusion of a country walk was gone.

"It's a beastly hole," Dick said. "Lousy, rotten old Silbridge."

"You've got to live here," Liphook said. "Make the best of it, kid."

"Dick's right," Tom said. "The damned place should be blown up. Hope they bomb it all to bits. Tanbury too. Old Kempett going up sky-high like a rocket, then Paunchy, then Screamer, then Gusto, then Gallipoli, the gallant old swine. I'd watch 'em all die and laugh."

"It might be *you* they'd watch," Dick said.

"No," Tom said. "It's a special bomb I've invented. The Schoolmaster-Killer Mark One."

"If there's a war, what are you going to be in?" Liphook asked.

"The Government, I hope," Tom said. "Touring the lines in an armoured car, my great belly shaking like a jelly. Hey, did you hear that? That's poetry!" He broke into a little jig.

"I'm going in the Air Force," Liphook said. "Flying Hawker Furies. Whoooom!"

"Whoom into the ground, you silly devil," Tom said. "People get killed in those things."

"You're one of those who wouldn't fight," Liphook said. "My Dad's in the Territorials. He says we'll all have to fight for our country when Der Tag comes. That's German for the Day."

"Fancy that," Tom said. "I'd never have known if you hadn't told me. Well, Rubykins, I'd fight, really I would. In the War Cabinet, sending you out against hopeless odds."

"Don't call me Rubykins."

"Liphook, Lips, Ruby Lips, Rubykins," Tom said. "It's logical. In the grim chess game of war, as old Gallipoli would say, you'll be a pawn swept early off the board. Frizzled alive like that chap who crashed at Yeadon. And I shall wipe away my tears and continue with my labours."

Liphook looked puzzled. Then his face cleared. "You're cynical, that's what you are, Coverack. Cynical."

"I think you're both daft," Dick said. "Anyway, I want to get back and finish my homework. Lets go back the way we came; it's about a million miles longer by the Moor road."

"Ah, thou wantest to see the fair Myra Francesca," Liphook said heavily. "So be it. Rightabout turn!" He did the turn smartly as, no doubt, his father had taught him; the other two, their hands in their pockets, slouched behind.

Soon after that the Vodi turned its attention to Quedgeley.

"They're blackmailing him," Tom said to Dick as they walked through Kellogg's Woods one evening.

"I expected it," Dick said.

"You know what for."

"Mind you, I don't care what that stinky old Liphook says. I don't believe it."

"Neither do I. When Nelly told him – she had the Vodi take him to the Kasbah – he ran amok. Tried to strangle her. So they beat him up with rubber truncheons. The marks don't show."

It was nearly the end of March, but there seemed to be no green anywhere they looked. The grey sky and the black trees seemed to say that they had no business to be there, that there wasn't going to be any Spring and the world belonged to winter.

"They'll take all his money before they finish with him," Tom said. "And his china too." They knew that Quedgeley had a fine collection of china from a recent article in the *Tanbury Gazette*, which showed Quedgeley and Myra, open-mouthed as if having both been notified of some great personal misfortune, with an expert from a London museum, a small bald man still in his coat and gloves, scowling at them as if he entirely approved of that misfortune.

"The poor devil," Dick said. "Why does Nelly always pick on the decent ones? Why doesn't she have a go at old Kempett?"

"Kempett's just the sort of man she likes. He's one of her husbands. That's why he goes on so much about things being obscene and filthy and soul-destroying. He's got to sleep with Nelly every other Wednesday. Turns him up a bit."

"Only four teeth, thirty stone and smells of musk and incense. Golly, it's enough to put him off sex for life."

The vision of Nelly and the Vodi was far too real. He could see the fat laughing face of Nelly; when she laughed her whole body quivered in its light shot-silk dress, all colours of the spectrum and decorated with human teeth. Very small, very white ones, forming the letter N over her left breast, if that was the proper name for those two monstrous accumulations of flesh beneath her collar-bone. The light from the fire played over the wall-paintings commissioned from Gusto Dulleagles, the Tanbury High art-master. The paintings represented all the things you wanted to do but had never and would never do; he saw himself and a woman on the far wall high up; he closed his eyes but could still see it, and could still see the Vodi dancing widdershins round Nelly. They were singing in their hoarse childish voices: he couldn't catch the words, but knew that their message was one of hatred and contempt for the whole world. Now he was in the centre of the circle and he could smell their bodies – like unwashed children's, metallic and yet moist, rusty iron after the rain.

And then he was asleep, thrown into nothingness; he awoke

suddenly and completely, his mind clear and his body possessed by a febrile parody of energy. It was one in the morning by his luminous wrist-watch. The watch Lois had given him when they were engaged; the gift which was evidence, some eleven months ago, that she really loved him. The official gift, the love-token, wafer-thin with a black face; it was never more than two seconds fast or slow and everyone who saw it admired it. If it came to that, everyone who saw Lois admired her. She wouldn't be seen here again though, she wouldn't come into this cubicle next visiting day and smother him with kisses and say she couldn't live without him. The world wasn't run in that way – though he had hoped once that she would come back, that she'd make the gloriously silly romantic gesture. And then he realised that all sane people are governed by common sense; they have to survive, they can't afford to be too weak. Marriage was a partnership, they'd often said. So if he caught T.B. he couldn't pull their full weight and most likely would never be able to. The marriage couldn't then be a partnership; so Lois gracefully bowed out. One really couldn't blame her, the cold-hearted fornicating bitch . . .

He pushed the bell-button at his side. Nurse Dinston, a skinny man of sixty with a permanent stoop to the right, shuffled into the cubicle. Dinston had been at the sanatorium since its earlier days; he was one of the first patients to undergo, and survive, a thoracoplasty. He had a room in the Nurses' Home in which, during the winter, he spent most of his time, the gas fire full on, listening to opera records and smoking black shag. He'd never married or taken any interest in any of the female nurses, but every month he drove off in his bright red Morgan three-wheeler with the outside Anzani engine, spruce and shaved in a grey-blue Harris tweed suit and a checked blue cloth cap which he never wore at any other time.

Wherever he went, he certainly went with a honeymoon smile on his face and returned still spruce and shaved, but without the smile. Dick wasn't quite sure whether he liked him or not; he was always cheerful, always agreeable, always good at his job, but there was an air of non-attachment about him, as if some great force had begun to suck him dry and had been interrupted before it had finished.

"What dusta want, lad?"

"I'm thirsty," Dick said. "I can't sleep."

Dinston winked at him. "Dusta fancy a bottle of ale? So do I. But neither on us can ha' one. Lemonade's poor stuff and milk's for bairns. How about some tea?"

"Fine." He wanted Dinston to keep on talking, he wanted another voice to keep away the loneliness. "Bring me a woman, too. A clean plump virgin about eighteen."

Dinston chuckled. "Tha's getting better, tha' mucky devil." He put his finger to his mouth. "Sitha, hasta heard this one?"

Dick had, during the war: it was the one about the girl who asked the chemist for a packet of corvettes. But he laughed at the pay-off line so as not to hurt Dinston's feelings; and hearing the story again made him remember fleetingly the time he'd been first told it by an A.T.S. in a Pompey bar. Dinston told him two more in rapid succession which this time he hadn't heard, then shuffled off down the corridor.

Dick lay back contentedly. The night would be shortened now; there'd be a wait for the tea and then the drinking of the tea – he'd be keeping awake for a purpose.

He heard footsteps and the voice of the Night Sister. He closed his eyes as she approached his cubicle. A torch played briefly over his face. "Is he all right, Nurse?" he heard her say in a whisper. "Sleeping like a babby," Dinston said and their voices and the smell of Lux toilet soap on the Sister – he knew it was Sister Waimer by her impeccable County accent, sad and lost two hundred miles away from home – and the smell of Lifebuoy and shag tobacco from Dinston passed on. But he was even grateful for that, that once again there'd been some contact with real life. It would have been more pleasant if it had been Nurse Mallaton in Sister Waimer's place; he'd nothing against Sister Waimer, but with her square plum-red face and stocky fifty-year-old body she wasn't exactly the type to drive you mad with desire. But it was wonderful to hear voices and to see the narrow white beam of the torch contradict the darkness; if he had his way he'd have a million soldiers march through the hospital all night bearing torches and singing to light up the black, sad, cold valley.

His eyes began to close: incredulously he abandoned himself to sleep, then felt a hand on his shoulder.

"Hey, lad," Nurse Dinston said. "Get this into you." He helped Dick to sit up in the bed. "It's in mi own mug. Tha can't taste it in an eggcup. And here's a dripping sandwich. Get it down thee, there's all t'good of t'meat in it."

"Has she gone?" Dick asked, biting into the dripping sandwich.

"Aye. Sorely disappointed. Tha wanted a woman – there she was. But she didn't want to disturb thee."

"I said a young virgin," Dick said.

"She'd be better for thee than any silly young lass. And far more grateful. But eat the bread-and-dripping and drink the tea and build up tha vital energies. And there's a bottle for thee, to save my legs. My God, tha never wor so well looked after in all tha life. Leave t'cup and t'plate on t'bedside table when tha's finished."

He went away before Dick could properly thank him. The dripping was beef with a proper admixture of jelly, heavily peppered and salted. He was tasting it for the first time since his mother had died, since he and his father never bothered to cook a joint on Sundays.

The hot, sweet strong tea accumulated heat in his stomach which sent up messages of comfort to his feet and fingers and stomach and even to his chest. He put the mug and plate on the bedside table and was ready for sleep when he remembered something Rock said to him in his early days on Ward Seven-A: "Dinston's a stickler for the rules, but he'll always give a chap tea if he thinks he's not got long to go. And if he's absolutely sure, he'll give 'em something to eat, too."

Dick felt something near to anger – be damned to his charity, the lovable old character who can tell who's going to crease it before even the doctors do. Then sleep took over, this time a gentler sleep which allowed him a moment's grateful reminiscence of the food and drink, and the thought, even if only hazily formulated, that perhaps Dinston wasn't always right.

5

He awoke to see Nurse Mallaton standing over him, a steaming bowl of water on the trolley. It was a cold morning again, but the cold had warmth at its centre, the sun was reflected back from the hoar-frost so that the ground glittered as if decorated for a gala. For a second he had an intimation that already on its way was some event likely to make him permanently happy, then decided not to be taken in by the confidence trick. He knew how it worked: he was softened up by eating something he enjoyed and by six hours of dreamless sleep. Then the first approaches were made by the sun, the dry healthy coldness, the sparkling ground; and then Nurse Mallaton's clear eyes and unblemished skin and slender ankles finished off the job, painlessly extracted from him his one possession of real value, the knowledge that he was finished. *Kaputt.* Don't forget that, Corvey, *kaputt.* He closed his eyes.

"Wake up," she said. "Wash and shave to make you handsome, Mr. Corvey."

He grunted. "Why can't you let me sleep?"

"You sleep too much, Mr. Corvey. Come on, you'll feel much better. I'll give you a shilling for each time I cut you."

She propped him up in a sitting position and then, assisted by Nurse Laggons, put up the screens. They were – for he really didn't count Laggons – alone in a cool green world. And once again the proximity of her healthy femininity made him almost happy; then, after she'd taken off his pyjama jacket, he caught sight of his own arms, reduced almost to concentration-camp dimensions, the veins blue and obscenely swollen against the white skin, and he let himself drift away from reality.

"I can see you've slept well," she said. "You'll be able to shave yourself soon." The razor swept smoothly over his face; he knew by the way in which she handled it that she wasn't in any danger of losing her bet.

"You do it better than I would. I like to be looked after."

"You're lazy," she said, and then as she put aside the razor to lather his face again, felt the stab of pity again. It hurt even more this time; to her disgust she found herself welcoming the pain. And then she saw a picture in her mind: she was holding his head between her breasts, she was giving him comfort like mother's milk. She could hardly bear to look at those large brown eyes, those thin hands – then again she reminded herself that she never felt like this about women patients; she did pity them because it wouldn't be human not to have compassion for some of them, particularly young girls like Rosie Tamby, nineteen years old, five stones in weight, being fattened up for the thora that might save her life but would almost certainly put paid to her chances of marriage.

She erased the picture with one firm act of will. Better to submit to Harry's importunities in the back seat of the Ford, better still to hold out for marriage. Better any man than Dick, even if he did have big brown eyes and a good mouth and beautiful hands.

"You haven't any idea of the results of my last X-ray, have you?" he asked her suddenly.

"You know the rules, Mr. Corvey," she said.

"I can guess," he said. "Prognosis: hopeless."

"No case is hopeless," she said, firmly. "I've seen people who were far more ill than you. Much, much more ill. And within months they were up and walking."

He laughed. "I won't walk again, darling."

"You mustn't call me darling," she said.

"Yes, Nurse. Just as you say, Nurse darling."

She rinsed the soap from his face and dried it. He ran his hand over his face. "Not bad at all," he said. "Pity I'm not going anywhere."

"Do you use after-shave lotion or talcum?" she asked.

"I told you," he said. "I'm not going anywhere."

She had seen a bottle of Yardley's lavender lotion and a matching tin of talcum in his sponge-bag and had asked him because she knew from experience that most men were shy of admitting that they used them; she hadn't wanted him to be denied that small pleasure. The small pleasures were important when a man lay in bed for twenty-four hours a day; or, for that matter, to a woman. Rosie Tamby made up her face elaborately every day and was always experimenting with new hair-styles; but the difference was that Rosie didn't want to die.

"Just as you like," she said. "I haven't any shares in the firm."

She cleaned the razor-blade but did not dry it, and cleaned and dried the razor. The smell of the shaving-soap from the opened bowl reminded her of the times when as a little girl she'd watch her father shaving. She'd liked watching the process at every stage from lathering the dark stubble which made his prim face strangely piratical to rinsing his face in cold water with great huffings and puffings with his face pink and shiny. There was a beautiful smell about him – shaving-soap and toothpaste and toilet soap and masculinity; and he looked so nice in his long-sleeved Wolsey vest with the braces dangling, that she smiled happily at the memory. How tired she was of living in places where no man ever set foot, where there wasn't even a shirt or a pair of trousers to remind one of the existence of men and children and family meals. . . . She'd once known a Sister, a spinster of the 1914 generation, who kept a bowl of shaving-soap in her room to sniff at on the evenings the atmosphere of collective femininity grew too much to bear; it wasn't really a bad idea . . .

"Breakfast soon," she said to Dick. "See that you eat it all this morning."

Mick Rorler popped his head into the cubicle, the screens now having been restored to place by Nurse Laggons. He wore a glaringly blue woollen dressing-gown with a gilt cord; round his neck was slung a red towel.

"Good morning, good morning, GOOD MORNING!" he shouted. He advanced towards Nurse Mallaton. "Give us a kiss, miss! Good morning, Dick, don't look so glum, chum. I'll swap places with you any day."

Dick looked at him sourly. "Sometimes I wish you were back on Silence," he said.

"He *will* be back on Silence if he keeps straining his voice like that," Nurse Mallaton said. "Move your carcase, Mr. Rorler, you're blocking the gangway."

"Not until you give me a kiss," said Rorler.

She smiled into his round face with the fuzz of stiff black hair on top of it. The small black eyes twinkled at her. Rorler was Ward M2's licensed clown, sixteen stones stripped and putting on weight every day, an ex-commercial traveller with a wife as fat and cheerful and black-haired as himself who came chugging up the drive to see him every week in an old W. D. Hillman shooting-brake.

"No kiss?" he said. "Then I'll give you something instead." He pulled four apples from his pocket and threw one to each of them. He took out one himself and started to eat it noisily. "Laxative and toothbrush combined," he said between mouthfuls. "Finest fruit in the world. Get it eaten, Dicky boy." He walked out whistling, swinging his sponge-bag like a sabretache.

Dick scowled. "He's so bloody cheerful that I could kill him," he said. "First thing in the morning, too."

"You've got up on the wrong side of the bed this morning," she said.

"Got up? I wish to God I could." His face clouded. "No, no I don't. I'll lie here and rot. This is the best place."

But she'd gone, throwing a casual goodbye over her shoulder, and he was left waiting for breakfast, which from the smell floating through the ward from the kitchen could only be fishcakes.

There's nothing you can do about it if Nelly doesn't like you, he said to himself. With the smell of fishcakes came the smell of porridge, rankly insipid. Nelly likes Rorler – six months ago he couldn't speak, and look at him now. She likes Rock and Percy and Basil and Peter, she likes all of the people who were here when I first came in; or at least nearly all of them. But not me. I'm the Quedgeley type all right. It was coming back to him now; he derived a mean pleasure from recalling the precise details of Quedgeley's persecution. It wasn't merely a question of taking his money; there was never a moment when he wouldn't be aware of little beady eyes watching him, of grubby hands arranging for everything to go wrong – the leaking teapot, the stalled engine, the missing examination papers, the hole in the trouser seat or crotch, the breaking shoelace, the error in the timetable.

Finally he went to Nelly and said: "I can't stand this any longer. I haven't done what you accuse me of, but I might just as well give myself up. At least I'll get a little peace in prison."

"I shouldn't do that if I were you," Nelly said. "Who the hell do you think runs the prisons?" She looked at him and licked her lips. "Tell you what. Sign over all your best furniture and china and your car and half your earnings and I'll never bother you again."

He signed the agreement gladly and the Vodi took away his possessions that very night. The next day the persecution started again with redoubled force. He went to Nelly in tears and offered her anything she wanted if only she'd leave him alone. "I've given you my Royal Worcestershire and my Wedgwood sets and my Ming vases and my Persian carpets and my jade figurines and my car; you've taken all my money and half my earnings. And still you won't leave me alone. What is there I can do to stop this persecution? Whatever have I ever done wrong to you? I'll do whatever you like. I'll give you absolutely everything I have, if only you'll leave me alone."

Nelly looked at the small weeping man thoughtfully. "It's a great shame for you," she said. "You've never done me any harm. That's absolutely true. I don't think you've ever done anybody any harm." She put a huge cigar into her mouth and made an obscene joke about it which turned Quedgeley's face a dull red. She snapped her fingers and a Vodi ran forward with a match. When he'd lit it he slipped in a pool of blood and tore the skirt of her green silk dress with his foot. Nelly's face darkened and she kicked him in the ribs. Quedgeley heard the bone crack and saw blood redden, the Vodi's tattered shirt; two other Vodi leaped forward and dragged him out screaming.

"Yes, my dear Bobby," she said, reflectively. "It would be difficult to find a more harmless man than you. Even if it were in your power to harm me, you wouldn't. As you say, I now possess nearly everything you own and it hasn't done you a scrap of good. That piece of paper I signed meant nothing, of course. I could suggest a use for it" – the assembled Vodi broke into howls of laughter – "and that, believe me, is its only possible use." She put out a huge hand and brought Quedgeley's face close to her; he could feel the heat from her cigar. "I have most of your possessions; I shall have them all. I have half your salary; I shall have it all. And I shall never leave you alone. I shall always make your life a misery. You'll never have a happy moment again."

"Why? Why? Why? It's not fair, I've never done any harm to you or to anyone. I didn't even know you existed. Please, please tell me why!"

"I don't have to give reasons for not liking you. I just don't like you, that's all."

She puffed a great cloud of cigar smoke in his face. "There's nothing you can do about it if Nelly doesn't like you."

It was then that Quedgeley once again ran amok. He even succeeded in hitting her. That was, Tom said, the reason for his car being returned to him. (They automatically rejected the explanation of it having been taken to a garage for an overhaul; that was too easy.)

"But Nelly had him beaten up the first time he attacked her," he objected to Tom.

"*Tu es fou, mon copain.* The first time he didn't hit her. The second time he hit her on the chest. That's a rotten place to hit any woman in, even Nelly. So there might be some hope for him."

But there was no hope for Quedgeley. Nelly was merely biding her time. Six months later, in the middle of the Remove's music lesson Quedgeley threw his chalk through the window and walked out of the room muttering to himself. He was never seen at the school again. The official explanation was a complete nervous breakdown, but Tom and Dick weren't taken in, any more than they were taken in when Myra left the cottage.

"He's supposed to be in a private nursing home in the South," Tom said one evening as they were walking through the Kasbah. "But he's here." He pointed downwards. "And Myra too. Right underneath us."

"That's what drove him barmy," Dick said. "Nelly wanted Myra as a Bride of the Vodi. She'd had everything else he'd got, so she had to have that." He mimicked Quedgeley's precise reedy voice. "*Poor Myra, poor Myra. O what shall we do? Poor Myra, poor Myra, who'll help poor Myra?* But there wasn't anything he could do but obey orders and go to the Kasbah . . ."

There wasn't anything Quedgeley could do about it. He and

Myra would be slaves of the Vodi for ever; or until Nelly lost her temper with them for being so miserable and unlucky and defeated. There was nothing you could do about it if Nelly didn't like you: that summed it all up.

6

HE was trying to wash away the taste of fishcake with sips of Tizer when Dr. Hinstock, the Superintendent, stormed in, accompanied by Redroe and Sister Lardress.

Hinstock was a tall, jerky-gestured man who, Rock once said, walked as if his braces were tied to his ankles. He had three children and a pretty dark-haired wife, and his big Victorian house – the Dower House of the Nedham estate – always seemed gay with music and children's voices. But he seemed to be lonely; not sadly or arrogantly or worriedly or even of choice, but because his position made loneliness the correct attitude. He wore the loneliness as he wore his black broadcloth suit and stiff white collar, without thought. And, Dick thought, that was why he always felt a twinge of apprehension whenever he saw the man. He couldn't understand Hinstock's world; it wasn't one in which emotion seemed to enter.

Sister Lardress passed Hinstock the dossier. He flipped through the films.

"Have a look at this, Redroe," he said in his sharp, decisive voice, which still at certain words had a trace of Lancashire burr. "Some possibility of fibrosis here," he said. "Mark you, I only say possibility. Depends entirely upon this chap here." He glared at Dick from under shaggy eyebrows which were the only untidy details on his smoothly-shaved tight-lipped face. "You'll have to put some weight on, Mr. Corvey. You know that, don't you?"

He turned, strode the length of the cubicle and said to Dick: "How are you, eh?"

"I wish I knew, Doctor," Dick said.

Hinstock came to Dick's side.

"It was a rhetorical question, Mr. Corvey. I know how you are.

You could be better, but you could be a great deal worse. You had a spread, in *here* of all places" – his voice was accusing – "but now if only we can fatten you up, the surgeon can do something to help you. But you'll have to help yourself. Sister here tells me you're not eating." He pointed a bony finger at Dick. "It won't do, Mr. Corvey, it won't do! Replace those concavities by convexities. Build yourself up and we'll soon have you better. Goodbye now!"

He whirled out of the room, closely followed by Redroe and Sister Lardress.

Dick was left sick and trembling; so they wanted to fatten him for the knife. They'd tried strep. and P.A.S., they'd tried I.N.H. soon after they'd dropped the pretence of tonic pills. Maybe they'd try the P.P. first; but it would be just his luck to have adhesions, just as it had been his luck to have been allergic to the damned miracle drugs. He couldn't take any more needles; they always said it was only a pinprick, but it was as far as he was concerned a savage, crunching pain; even a blood test nearly made him weep. Morphine, now, he didn't object to; there was a generous dose of oblivion in compensation for the pain; but morphine was the one thing they wouldn't give you enough of as long as they thought there was a faint chance of your survival.

Sam, now, would say that he was bloody soft. Soft was exactly what he was, but that wasn't his fault. He'd been beaten soft, like a piece of steak. Tenderised, that was the word, tenderised to provide a tasty nourishing meal for Nelly. He looked at the photo which had been enclosed in Sam's letter: Sam was standing with his wife and two-year-old son in front of a white painted wooden house. Sam was much fatter than the last time he saw him, too fat to wear a striped T-shirt and jeans. He was smiling at his wife, a small girl with big dark eyes; she had one eye on the child, bright and lively with a T-shirt and jeans like Sam's. I'd like to see Sam again, he thought, and my nephew. But I won't; by the time he's saved up enough to visit England again, the Steak Corvey will already have been eaten.

That was another mistake: he should have gone to Canada with Sam.

"Silbridge stinks," Sam said to Dick soon after the war. "So does this bloody country. Hell, we've won the war, but no-one'd think it. I'm clearing out as soon as I can. You should too, Our Kid, if you've any sense."

But he hadn't any sense; and Sam had gone to Canada by himself. And now Sam had a job as manager of a radio components factory at twelve thousand dollars a year, and a wife, a son, a house and a new Chevrolet. And Dick had four suits of pyjamas, a tartan dressing-gown, some clothes which he'd never wear again, and the Vodi.

If he'd gone to Canada there probably wouldn't have been any Lois or any T.B. Now it was too late. Canada, like every other country, wouldn't admit you once you'd contracted T.B. (Or, rather, *committed* T.B.; he remembered that bastard of a councillor at Silbridge grumbling about the scandal – yes, the scandal, of tubercular D.P.s being allowed to enter this country.) He missed Sam now; which was odd, since they'd never been very close.

He'd never understood about the Vodi either. He'd been told about it once; Dick casually let slip a few words. Rather to his surprise, Sam was shocked and indignant. "Never heard anything so bloody daft in all my life, Our Kid! You want your heads examining. Morbid, that's what you are, you silly little devil!"

Sam was the only other person who'd been let into the secret or, now, ever would be. Not that it really mattered; for not very long afterwards, Hellfire Ron annihilated the Vodi with one sermon.

Hellfire Ron was the guest preacher at Lupmore Street Chapel one Sunday evening in 1938. He had something of a vogue at that time; there'd been quite a lot about him in the papers, he broadcast frequently, he'd written a best-selling book he'd made some conversions and several women – though not he – claimed that he'd cured them of various illness, including rheumatism and stomach ulcers. Generally someone leapt up to bear witness at one of his meetings, though he never asked them to do so.

Tom and Dick hadn't been to the Lupmore Street Ebenezer Chapel since they were children; there were generally other fish to fry on a Sunday evening, the fish being the Monkey Run at Tanbury. But their two pick-ups of the Sunday night before had said they were going to Lupmore Street tonight; the girls seemed to be of a generous disposition and Hellfire Ron – the Reverend Ronald Dalmose, to give him his proper name – promised at least to be good for a few laughs.

The chapel was crowded that evening. Lupmore Street, just off Lupmore Park, was one of the few pleasant streets in Silbridge, a street of solid Edwardian villas, lined with cypresses. The chapel – it was now to be closed down, Dick thought with a sharp regret – was a compact red-brick building with large round-headed windows, topped rather incongruously by a tower with an onion-shaped dome; it was as if one of the older men crowding it tonight had topped his Sunday best of navy-blue or black serge and stiff white collar with a fez or a turban.

It was July and the air which came into the crowded chapel was laden with dust and the smell of melting tar; there was a faint smell of trees and grass and water from the park, but it seemed as if the trees and grass were on the point of burning and that the water would soon boil away.

Most of the men were sweating profusely; only the women, in every kind of summer dress from the sodden grey and dried-blood red cotton of the minister's wife to the tightly clinging scarlet and yellow rayon of Bernice Rimpett (one of the reasons for Dick and Tom being there at all) looked cool.

There was, when Dalmose mounted the pulpit, an anticipatory stir as in the theatre when the star enters. He stood in silence for a few seconds, his eyes closed. He was a short, tubby man with a pink complexion and sandy hair and an expression of determinedly cheerful normality. Looking at him Dick found it difficult to believe all that he'd heard about him.

Dalmose opened his eyes, rested his hands on the lectern and began to speak in a low, gentle voice; he didn't seem to worry whether anyone could hear him or not, though, Dick realised, every syllable came to him with absolute clarity in his seat at the back of the gallery.

"My friends, for so I hope I may call you, it affords enormous happiness to me to be amongst you here tonight, to speak to you as a member of the same great family. I come to you from another town, a town which you in your sturdy local patriotism may well count as foreign parts" – there was a snicker of laughter – "but I am no stranger. In reality my town is very near, in fact it is *your* town; for we are all members, dear brothers and sisters in Christ, of the same great circuit. Tonight my own family will be listening, in a church very like this, to the minister preaching the word of God in South London. They are in a sense here in this chapel in Yorkshire just as we, dear brothers and sisters in Christ, are in theirs.

"Now, brethren, I'm your guest. So for a moment I'm going to make small talk. I'm going to talk about the weather. Because no matter how much the clever ones may sneer, we're all interested in the weather. I'm going to say: *What a beautiful summer we're having.* For we are having a beautiful summer; and it's not over yet." He paused and shot out his right hand at the congregation. "But *am* I making small talk? Aren't I making *big* talk? For summer's well worth thinking about. How grateful we ought to be for God's gift of the Seasons!

"It's not just that it's good to see the sun and the blue sky and the grass and the flowers, but it's good to see, too, God's children in the bright and gay summer attire which they've bought by the sweat of their brows, by the winter's hard labour. And how right and proper it is! For is not man entitled to innocent relaxation, and woman too?" He flashed a white-toothed smile round the packed chapel. "Here are the lads in their clean shirts and their dazzling ties and well-polished shoes – so well-polished, brethren, that it hurts my eyes. They've made an effort because, first of all, they've come to God's house and it's natural when you're meeting so very special, so very important a person, to want to look your best. And the other reason – I'm speaking for the bachelors – is the girls in their gay and charming dresses, just like a garden of flowers."

He stopped to wipe the sweat from his brow with a large white handkerchief.

"And here are the married folk, the fathers and mothers, to each of whom the other will, I am sure, seem as young and beautiful as on the day they first met. And here we have," his voice took on a cooing note, "the little children, the innocents. These have no idea in their heads of courting or of marriage. The little boys play Cowboys and Indians and aren't very enthusiastic about washing behind their ears and think that the little girls are soppy. They're just not interested. And the little girls play with their dolls and talk deep feminine secrets and they think that the boys are rough and ignorant and extremely silly."

His smile, showing white regular teeth, testimony of a childhood of orange-juice and milk and bi-yearly visits to an expensive dentist's, flashed over the audience again. "And so we males generally are, let's face it. The ladies are much, much nicer than the gentlemen." There was a restrained collective laugh, expressing itself in a rustle of starched linen and newly-ironed cotton and a smell of talcum and scent competing with the chapel's atmosphere of varnished pine, floor polish and old velvet. "And yet those little children will grow up. The little boys will lose their interest in Cowboys and Indians, the little girls will find out that the boys are not so bad after all. And for many of them one day will come when life seems to take on a new splendour, a new glory . . ."

Dick looked at Bernice's fair, almost white hair, and felt his stomach constrict with excitement. They'd go to Kellogg's Woods; it wasn't far. Her hair was very fine and soft and she wore it long, over her shoulders. He only needed to put his hand out and he could stroke it. She had childishly thin arms; he felt warmly protective towards her, he wanted to give her something; what exactly he didn't know.

Dalmose's voice continued, the tone fuller and richer now, the *vox humana* note. "How fortunate we are, dear brethren! What happiness there is, what innocent wholesome happiness here and now upon this earth, God's good earth! Should we not be happy, should we not magnify and glorify Him? Yes, we should, we should indeed, we should thank God every waking moment. For each of us the cup is full and runneth over. And this evening, this fine evening, my cup is pressed down and running over. I rejoice to see your bright happy faces both young and old. Particularly I rejoice to see the young people standing bright-eyed at the threshold of maturity. Dear brothers and sisters in Christ, I love you all. It is my duty to love you all. And because I love you all, I must tell you one thing" – his voice was a whisper now – "one terribly important thing. I must warn you for the love that I bear you." He paused for ten seconds and let the silence accumulate until it had abolished even the tiniest sound in the chapel.

"All of you are within a hairsbreadth of Hell!"

He was shouting at the top of his voice, his smooth rosy face was suffused with dark red, a vein on his temple was throbbing. It was as if he'd discovered that the building was on fire and there was only a minute in which to escape – his raising his voice didn't seem calculated, but a painful necessary abandonment of dignity, like a modest woman taking off her dress to bandage a hurt child.

"Within a hundred years we shall all be dead. And for some of us Death may come far sooner. Are we prepared for judgment, for the day of wrath? Day of wrath, O dreadful day – for most of us that day is always tomorrow, never today. But today is here! The day of wrath is here! Hell is real, hell is no myth, hell is not symbolic! Hell is torment and suffering for all eternity!"

When, a full half-hour later, they left the chapel hard on the heels of Bernice and her friend, Rhoda Verwood, he had the same sense of release as when going home from school on a Friday afternoon; Dalmose, particularly when he'd gone into such fire-and-brimstone detail, had been too much of a good thing. He took four Quality Street from his pocket – he'd put aside the wrapped ones – and handed them to Bernice. "Give two to Rhoda," he said.

"Ta," she said. "Oo, these look real good."

Even her broad accent and her slopping singsong intonation didn't affect his feeling of wonder as he gazed at her face in which the angularity of childhood was still visible and her blue, slightly oblique eyes, innocent and expectant. She smelt of orris-root and scented soap and, now that he was near her, he could smell, very faintly, her sweat. He glanced at Rhoda walking beside Tom; she was plumper than Bernice and looked far more mature, but he was glad that he'd not chosen her – she was too bold-eyed, too self-possessed.

"Where are we going, handsome?" Rhoda asked Tom.

"Please yourself," Tom said. "I don't care." His voice was surly; Dick looked at him in surprise; they'd long since agreed that the treat-'em-rough technique was O.K. for Cagney and Bogart but not them.

"We're going for a drink first," he said. "The sermon's made me thirsty."

Tom looked at Dick coldly. "I've not done those trig. problems," he said. "I should be home . . ." His voice trailed off as he looked at Rhoda, who was impatiently tapping her foot. "O.K.," he said. "But I've got to be in early."

"We'd better get moving, then."

Tom didn't speak until they were sitting in the Park Café, drinking ice-cream sodas. "Tastes like soapy water," he said, his eyes darting uneasily around the chocolate-and-green room and the glass-topped tables.

"You should rejoice in God's gift of ice-cream soda," Dick said. "Old Hellfire Ron was good, wasn't he? By God, I nearly jumped out of my skin when he started shouting."

"It's an old trick," Tom said. "Old Kempett does it sometimes. Dalmose'll know that sermon by heart."

Dick assumed an Oxford accent. "It's *naht* old-fashioned, dear brethren, to think of Hell in the language of fire and brimstone. For *that* is the Word of Gahd. Depaht from me, ye accursed ones, to burn in EVERLASTING hell-fiah. Aim afraid, dear brethren, that the fact is theah. If you go to Hell, you will *BURN BURN BURN*." The girls giggled delightedly.

"You ought to be on the stage," Rhoda said without irony.

"Damn well shut up," Tom said gruffly. Dick realised, with a sense of triumph, that Tom had broken a rule: he was losing his temper. He wasn't in charge of the evening in the way that he usually was: Dick was the centre of attention now. "I thought you knew how he did it," he said patronisingly. "Surely you're not taken in?"

"I know how old Kempett flogs people, but it hurts just the same."

"All right," Dick said, smiling. "You'll go to Heaven. *You're* saved, my dear brother."

'There might be something in it," Tom said, slowly. "How do you know there isn't?"

"You're swotting too hard," Dick said. "All that baloney about going upstairs to play a harp or downstairs to roast – it's just for kids."

"It's not what he said. It's just that he seemed so damned bothered about it."

"It's his living," Dick said.

"Yes, but it didn't have to be his living. It said in the *Gazette* that his father has bags of money."

Dick felt angry; Tom was stepping out of character.

"You need a dose of castor-oil," he said. "It's all nonsense."

"Yes," Bernice said unexpectedly. "Why *do* you want to talk about things like that, Tom? It's too nice to think about those silly old sermons. I think he's daft, don't you, Rhoda?"

Rhoda said nothing but stifled a yawn. Tom ordered another round of ice-cream sodas and told a joke or two, trying to manœuvre himself back into his usual dominance. But it was to no avail: Dick was in charge, Dick had defeated him, it was Dick's evening.

For Dick had been right: in that café on an August evening drinking ice-cream soda, eternity had been all nonsense. What was real was the taste of the ice-cream soda and the feeling of triumph when they entered the café with Bernice and Rhoda; the vanilla drink tasted like champagne, he was an irresistible dandy, a resplendent Casanova in a royal blue sports jacket with pleated pockets and a half-belt and one of those woollen shirts with a fastener at the throat – cruising shirts they called them.

Tom, in a light grey suit and a white Aertex shirt and a red tie, had looked far better dressed and far cooler than Dick, but Dick didn't think so then, and neither did Tom. Tom wanted to wear what everyone else was wearing; he'd have given a great deal to be in Dick's shoes – and shirt and jacket and trousers. The knowledge rather pleased Dick though he didn't admire himself for it.

All the Tanbury trams were replaced by 'buses before 1938; the South Tanbury route was the last one to change over. The tram they took to Kellogg's Woods was tall and old with open-fronted top deck; sitting in front with the breeze in his face Dick was cool for the first time that day.

Bernice's hair was streaming behind her and her profile which would in ten years' time be wizened or blurred was now as sharp and delicate as a new penny. They were all singing together – *Moon at Sea* and *The Merry-Go-Round Broke Down* and *September in the Rain* – and even though the tram rode anything but smoothly, rolling alarmingly at each corner, it was a ride which couldn't have been better, an effortless swoop through the summer night.

It was rather strange, too, that they should be walking with girls through Kellogg's Woods. Dick felt somehow provident, squirreling up at least one good event to remember in the winter when Tanbury High would dominate the whole of the North-West Passage.

They left the main path and crashed their way through the bracken ahead of the girls. The bracken opened out into a grassy clearing. It was very quiet except for the buzzing of midges and, far away, the boom of traffic.

He pulled out a packet of Woodbines and gave one to Tom. They lit up solemnly; they'd just learned to smoke then. They didn't inhale and he remembered now the thick sweetish taste of the tobacco. That was a good thing to remember: when you were new to tobacco there was not only the fundamental pleasure of making an illicit entry into the adult world but a new physical pleasure, a new taste and a new way of enjoying taste.

And it was good to remember what Bernice said, for when you were fifteen and had just discovered that girls were miracles, everything that they did and said was miraculous; it was like seeing the unmistakable glimmer of gold through a plain tissue wrapping.

"Your spice were lovely," she said. "Have you any more?" Rhoda giggled. "You are awful, Bernice."

He held out the bag of Quality Street. "Can Rhoda have one?" she asked.

"Of course."

She took the bag from him. "We'll keep them 'cos you're smoking. You shouldn't be smoking at your age."

"I shouldn't be doing a lot of things, but I do."

"If they catch you smoking at your school, they'll cane you," Rhoda said.

Dick gave her a resentful look; he hated to be reminded that he was still a schoolboy.

"They won't catch us," Tom said. "We're too clever." He made three perfect smoke rings; the evening was so still that they seemed to hang motionless for a full sixty seconds before they finally dissolved.

"Come closer," Dick said to Bernice. Tom had now put his arm round Rhoda's waist and was whispering in her ear. Bernice remained still out of his grasp.

"What'll you give me if I do come nearer?" she asked.

"You can have all the sweets."

"I've got them already."

"Then I haven't anything else."

"Will you buy me some ice-cream?"

"If you're a good girl."

She mimicked a lisp. "I don't weally know wevver I'm a good girl," she said, and then came closer to him. "I've been baking today," she said. "Mum lets me bake on Sunday. I'm good at baking, she says." He stroked her hand. The fingernails were short and badly trimmed, but it was a woman's hand, soft and smooth and small-boned.

"We had mutton for dinner today with roast potatoes and green peas," she said. "Next Sunday Mum's going to let me cook the whole dinner."

He took off his jacket. "You'll be marking your dress if you're not careful," he said. "Sit on this."

"It's warm," she said. "Have you noticed how nice it feels when you have the warmth from something of someone else's? Even though it's warm already, the weather, I mean?"

Tom and Rhoda were kissing now, Tom's bony hand running purposefully up and down Rhoda's back.

"Aren't they naughty?" Bernice said. She looked steadily at him. Her mouth wasn't smiling but her eyes were; suddenly she seemed much older than fifteen and certainly much older than Dick; it occurred to him that he wasn't amusing himself with her but she with him. He took her other hand and kissed her. This is it, he thought, this is what a woman's mouth tastes like. He drew her down beside him; after five minutes he glanced round the clearing and saw that Tom and Rhoda weren't there any longer.

The next morning he said to Tom:

"Are we going to take out those dames again?"

"We'd better not."

"Why?"

"They're elementary school types. They want a husband. They're after a man as soon as they can walk."

"Go on, man. They're only kids. You're talking daft."

"I know what I'm talking about," Tom said. "I don't live in a trance like you. I told you what Rhoda let me do, didn't I? She'd do anything to get a husband."

"Bernice only let me kiss her."

"You didn't go about it the right way," Tom said.

"You're clever, aren't you?"

Tom kicked a stone viciously. "It's just as well you didn't," he said. "Wish I hadn't now."

He didn't speak again until they were passing Tom Waddon's house and then he said: "And I haven't done my bloody homework either."

"Did you see the paper this morning?" Dick said in an attempt to cheer him up. "There's a vicar in trouble in Dufton for messing about with a choirboy. Bet he never went near the little devil. Old Nelly's at it again."

"There isn't a Vodi any more," Tom said. "Nelly's been converted."

And that was the end of the Vodi; three words annihilated a whole world. It didn't end immediately, though. Nelly, who never did a job by halves, set up an English Inquisition, and a thousand notorious evil-livers and atheists were burned or hanged, drawn and quartered in Silbridge Market Square.

But within a month of Dalmose's sermon the Vodi was never again mentioned by either Dick or Tom. Was it really the sermon, Dick wondered idly, or was it simply that they were both growing up, that they felt themselves too old to play a kid's game? Or had the fantasy become too real, too demanding? Tom had invented

– or, rather discovered – the Vodi; Tom abolished it. Or had he? Dick started to laugh and then stopped for lack of breath. It's easy enough, he thought, to call up spirits; but not so easy to dismiss them. Tom would be protected by his own toughness and good luck, and always had been; but for Dick there was no protection. He was waiting, completely alone and defenceless, for Nelly to claim him. He started to laugh again.

7

He stopped himself sharply, remembering the D.P. who'd been taken away to the Hemmerby Homes from the cubicle next door. The D.P. was a fat, broad-shouldered little man who always wore a round astrakhan cap and a bright blue lumber-jacket; before Redroe could give him the needle he'd pulled his bed to pieces, broken six window-panes, torn the door of his clothes-locker off its hinges and knocked Nurse Kanley out cold, which wasn't bad, considering that Kanley was twice his size and an ex-regimental boxing champion. It had begun with the D.P. laughing to himself, then talking to himself, then screaming; and now Rorler, who always knew everything, said that they'd given him a prefrontal lobotomy and had transferred him to another sanatorium. "He won't bust any more noses now," Rorler said. "He'll just shamble round with a silly little smile on his face. They know how to tame them at the Hemmerby. My cousin says—"

They wouldn't, of course; for one thing, he couldn't bust anyone's nose – he wasn't even able to get out of this damned bed. But that didn't mean that they couldn't send him to the Hemmerby, that he couldn't finish off his sentence in the equivalent of chains, like those poor devils of matelots he saw once at Chatham.

He took another drink of Tizer and tried to remember a period when the Vodi hadn't entered into his personal scheme of things. He didn't, it was true, think about it during the war, but there wasn't time in Burma to think about any other subject than survival and demob. That was it: first of all the demob leave period of late '45, when your pockets were full of money, you were glad to be alive and even Silbridge seemed beautiful, and there was no need to worry about the future because it would arrange itself into a pattern both gorgeous and sensible. Then there was the whole year afterwards, before everyone started to take exams and wives, before the war was finally over; the shop was still enjoying a wartime boom and his father was glad enough both to let him use the Ford shooting-brake whenever he wanted and to let him live free in return for helping in the shop occasionally. Dick not only had come back from the war in one piece but, unlike Sam, he'd no intention of leaving home.

His job at Larton's didn't pay very well – eight pounds a week before the Government got at it – but it was, after all, ample for pocket money. There was always enough petrol because of the cigarette shortage; there was always enough to drink because they always had enough petrol to discover the pubs which hadn't run dry. Together he and Tom toured the whole of the West Riding that year – it was a good year to remember, a confused but happy succession of pubs and dancehalls and racetracks and cinemas and theatres.

There was a feeling of triumph in the air too; it wasn't simply that he and his friends were victorious soldiers but – it seemed strange now to look back – *their* Government was in power. They'd got their own back; when the Tory Member of Tanbury, after fifteen years of easy victories, lost his seat to Labour, they took a malicious glee in his defeat, though they had no particular love for the Labour candidate, a fat old Trade Unionist whom everyone called John the Dastard (that, in connection with every offence from robbery with violence to returning library books overdue, being his favourite term of abuse). John was as surprised as his opponent when he won the seat; Tom, who was home in time to see the General Election, said afterwards: "You could see he really didn't believe what had happened. He'd have had his usual speech ready about the increased Labour vote showing which way the tide was turning blah blah blah and next time he was confident that blah blah blah and then he found out that the tide *had* turned. He didn't know what to do, the old moron. He must have said it had been a good clean fight at least a dozen times before he realised he needn't bother about any of that mullarkey again. Old

Briller was shaken to the core too. He'd expected to be awarded the seat by divine right, the smug old bastard."

It must have been in 1946 that Tom told them this; late September or early October, he wasn't quite sure which. He was sure that there were still some leaves on the trees and that the sun didn't set until about eight o'clock; and he distinctly remembered a big fire somewhere which they were all glad of. There was a field at the back of the room with short sheep-nibbled grass, sloping sharply upwards; behind it was a smoking slag-heap and, green against the black, a grove of rather depressed-looking trees. Rimelby, of course; they must have been in the lounge of the Frumenty. That would have been the evening when Noll Mainton and Jack Uplyme came along with them; it wasn't the last evening they came, either, until they both got jobs with big shiny cars and expense accounts. He'd not seen Tom for seven months and wouldn't ever see him again now. He wouldn't see Noll and Jack again, either – Noll and Jack, his old school-friends, who always waited until the end of the evening to offer to pay their whack of the petrol, because they knew that by then he'd be uproariously generous and have no small change anyway.

But that evening they were all good friends, the war was over, their demob pay hadn't all been spent and the Frumenty was comfortable and spotlessly clean. There didn't seem much danger of the beer running out either. Rimelby was some ten miles out of Silbridge and it took two hours and three buses to get there. As a village it had a few remnants of prettiness if you disregarded the slag-heaps on the horizon; there were a few trees and fields, and even a small colony of expensive privately-built houses, which was rare for a place for which the raison d'être now was Rimelby Main.

Sitting there with a pint of what was unquestionably well-kept bitter in his hand Dick was full of contentment; he felt tolerant even towards John the Dastard.

"John's not bad," he said. "Let 'em have a try anyway. They can't be any worse than the last lot." He felt light and free-moving in his blue-grey Harris tweed jacket and grey flannels and suède shoes, no longer the prisoner of scratchy khaki and heavy boots. "But I'm glad old Briller's heart's broken."

"Not so bloody much as you think," Tom said. "He's got some railway stock. His only financial misjudgment. Now he'll make a packet."

"Don't worry about those bastards," Noll said. "They're all the same. They feather their own nests first, last and all the bloody time." Noll was small and broad-shouldered, throwing himself at every situation like a charging centre-half. He had been a bookie's clerk before the war; he was now, energetically and ferociously, looking for a new job.

Jack snapped his fingers. "Same again, miss," he said. He turned to the others. "Thought I was going to do some serious boozing tonight," he said, heavily. "You've talked about nothing but politics. Hell, the war's over and the Reds have brought us home. That's all we put 'em in for, isn't it?"

Dick wanted to argue with him, but the moment had a certain rough charm (thanks initially to three pints of bitter) which he didn't want to dispel.

"I'd do with a woman," he said, and saw that Jack's pale heavy face was settling into a cruel, hunting grin, and Noll's smaller, neater, smoother face with its little toothbrush moustache had a look of dry lubricity.

"We'll have to get organised," Jack said, settling his fifteen stone more comfortably on the little grey upholstered chair. "A small, highly mobile fighting unit, gentlemen. That's what we are."

"Reconnaissance comes first," Noll said. "Let's all go to the Tenessee on Saturday. You know something, animals? A whole new generation of virgins has grown up whilst we've been away."

"Save one for me," Jack said.

"There's Lois Rinchett." Noll's tongue leapt out, small and pink, and moistened his lips. "Her dad's head clerk for the St. Clair Pit. They used to go to the Lupmore Street Chapel, then they moved. She was just a skinny kid, near-albino, and now" – the tongue leapt out again – "she's a dream. You just want to put your head in between them and go ugglewugglewuggle . . ."

"She's only sixteen," Tom said.

"What difference does that make? You waiting until she's twenty-one or something?"

Tom shrugged. "She's nothing to me, boy. Her father knows mine, that's all. Used to know her when I was a kid."

Jack wiped the beer-froth from his mouth with a white silk handkerchief. "There's plenty more," he said. "You don't have to whitter on about one little suicide blonde."

"She's a real blonde," Tom said.

Noll laughed. "You must have known her *very* well when you were a kid," he said.

Dick couldn't have sworn to it, since Africa and Italy and a day's steady drinking had made Tom's face near-scarlet anyway; but he thought that he detected a blush.

"Never even spoken to her," he said. "Used to see her now and again with her dad, that's all."

The damned liar, Dick thought, looking back; even Jack and Noll knew that he was lying, that there'd been many a game of Fathers and Mothers between the little dears until, presumably, Lois's removal interrupted them. And Tom saw her again after the war and discovered that his madcap companion had grown up into a woman . . .

That was today's little lavender-scented story, coming to you through courtesy of Dick Corvey, champion dupe of the North of England if not the world, deceived by his best friend before he'd even met the girl. He couldn't have known then that he'd meet Lois; but when he did meet her he should have remembered that evening at the Frumenty.

But he had been too much the big man, the rollicking good fellow, the hard-drinking man amongst men; he hadn't stored up that piece of knowledge about Tom in case of need, but joined along with Noll and Jack in taking the mickey out of Tom. After all, it wasn't often that one had the chance. It wasn't long, however, before he was hitting back; there was a lull in the conversation and he said to Dick, "Remember Bernice and Rhoda?"

"Can't say that I do."

"We took them in Kellogg's Woods when we were kids. After we'd listened to that revivalist, Delmoose or something, his name was."

"It's a long time ago."

"You remember. Nice little fair-haired piece Bernice was."

"That's right. She was mine. You had the fat swarthy one."

Tom's wide, full-lipped mouth split into a grin under his bristling Western Desert size moustache. "Saw them both in 1941. Rhoda was bursting out all over and busy with a Canadian. So I took Bernice home. She wouldn't play with you at all, would she? Christ, how a girl can change in three years . . ."

"You're a dirty dog," Jack said.

"Not at all. I was behaving like a friend and a brother. Dick couldn't do anything about her in the Far East, so I deputised for him. It wasn't cheap either—she drank four rums and four Worthingtons."

They all laughed; but Dick only went through the motions of smiling. Why had Tom waited until now to tell him the story? Why had he spoiled the picture of Bernice, why had he put a great sweaty fist through the delicate honeycomb of colour and touch and sound and smell that the evening had in the end totalled up to, why had he made something which was like a poem into a Sunday paper paragraph? But, he reflected, the girl who talked about baking to him that summer night, the girl who would do no more than kiss, the rayon and chocolate and orris-root miracle, had no relationship with the girl full of rum and beer, who'd quickly bared what was necessary for the act as if for some emergency operation.

Tom rang the bell for the fourth round of drinks. A new face answered it; over-plump, still a little roughened from a recent battle with acne, but immediately female, soft and yielding and capable of grief and giving.

"What's your order, please?" she asked Tom.

"Two like you, please, miss."

"There's only one like me," she said. "Would you like the same again?" As she leaned over the table to empty the ashtray and collect the glasses a lock of hair fell over her eyes; she put it into place automatically, her eyes on Tom.

"Yes, the same again," Tom said.

He looked at her, smiling; she put the glasses on the tray.

As she turned to go, he said:

"How's your brother these days?"

Her face clouded as if he'd raised his hand to hit her. "Didn't you know? He's dead. He was captured at Singapore."

"Sorry. Hadn't seen him since '40. Haven't been in England since then."

"That's all right," she said, and seemed on the verge of saying more, then glanced at the other three and walked quickly out of the room.

"Hell, of course," Noll said. "Norman Hillberk. Fatguts Hillberk. Don't you remember old Jackson saying he didn't catch the tram home, he just rolled there?"

"A Jap P.O.W.," Jack said. "He'd lose a bit of weight before he died, poor bastard."

"She'd only be a kid then," Dick said.

"Well," Tom said, "she's grown-up now."

"Not half she isn't," Noll said. "Her mum'll have to put a knee into her back to lace up her corsets for her."

"Don't you be so damned skitty," Tom said. "You'll be lucky if you get anything half so good. This isn't like the last war, chum. Not so many killed. There won't be any surplus women. It'll be surplus men."

More people were coming into the room; soon, from all the signs, it would be too full for comfort, but now six of the eight iron-legged tables were filled, it was part of a pub instead of merely a place where the four of them were drinking beer.

The sun was setting now; the faces at the far side of the room glimmered palely, the faces nearest the fire were dramatically lit in red and black, the bitter in the tankard of the old man at the table next to Dick's was changed from straw-yellow to near-amber sown with glittering specks of gold; when the girl, bringing in Tom's round, switched on the light there was an element of annoyance in the glances directed for a split-second towards her; the transition from an atmosphere as cosy as a Victorian ballad had been too abrupt and the room seemed, during that transition, drab and mean. When Tom was paying the girl for the drinks, he said abruptly, "Have a drink with me. Gin-and-orange?"

"Thank you," she said. "Thanks very much. I'll have a grapefruit juice if you don't mind."

Dick looked at Tom in surprise; though Tom wasn't mean and certainly never dodged his round, he'd never bought a drink for a barmaid in his life; he said that they were paid to do the job and the bitches always short-changed you anyway. Then something happened which surprised Dick still more; after the girl had drawn the heavy green velvet curtains on one of the windows Tom leaped forward and drew the curtains of the other two for her.

The girl thanked him and gave him a curiously sacrificial look; she had large hazel eyes and black hair, the same colour as Rhoda's in fact. But why did he think of her as *the girl*, an anonymous figure? That was Lorna, poor Lorna whom Tom used afterwards just as he pleased – used just as Lois had used Dick. She was the reason he hadn't remembered what Tom had said about Lois; he was fool enough to imagine that Tom was, like himself, content with one woman at a time. And perhaps, to be quite honest, she was the reason also that ten minutes later they found themselves in the main bar of the Lord Relton, just off the Tanbury road. Perhaps he'd been a little jealous of Tom's easy success with Lorna, and perhaps that damned submissive attitude of hers, that harem-girl, Master-what-is-thy-will look had put ideas into his head or rather into his loins. Or perhaps the explanation was rather simpler; the Lord Relton was in the half-past ten closing area and the Frumenty was not.

He'd never know, now, nor did it matter. He must, though, have had some good reason to take the car there, because he didn't like the Lord Relton very much. It was a fake-Tudor road-house with a huge car park; even its name was rather phoney, an attempt to identify it with the village of Relton to which, geographically at least, it belonged. But, unlike the Frumenty, unlike even the Ten Dancers or the Blue Lion at Silbridge, the Lord Relton belonged nowhere; it would have been just as much at home in any other place in England. It even smelled like nowhere; it had a smell he'd never encountered anywhere else, undoubtedly clean, and even antiseptic, but also disturbingly sensual, like the flesh of a woman who takes all the deodorants the advertisements recommend.

The smell might have been a good enough excuse for what he did that evening; the smell in the entrance to the pub, and the smell of alcohol and women and cigars in the Long Bar itself with its glittering bottles, one of every liqueur in the world, and the rather incongruous *fête champêtre* mural and the pink wall-lights and the women who, whenever you looked at them, were pulling their skirts down over their knees – the scene was meretricious enough to anyone who'd never left England, but when you compared it with others, when you thought of those happy little games of hide-and-seek with the Japs in Burma, when you thought of the rotten smell of the jungle – sweaty feet and stale cabbage – then it was positively, wonderfully beautiful. That was the crux of the matter: the sudden change from a world in which you existed only to kill or be killed to a world in which giving someone a thick ear would cost you five pounds and killing someone, even with good reason, could lead to you being dragged out screaming and messing your trousers at eight in the morning in Tanbury Gaol; in this world death was a dirty word and they kept you alive, as they kept him alive now at Nedham, whether you wanted to live or not. For four years he'd lived in a totally masculine world, blood and sweat and jungle green, with the strain only lifting for a few days every year; and when it did lift, you knew that whatever crime you committed, from rape to arson, would be forgiven as long as you were an efficient killer. In that world, the world of the killer, the action which even now he wasn't very proud of, the action on account of which Tom, that damned old hypocrite Tom, lectured him like a Dutch uncle, would have seemed both praiseworthy and amusing. Old Dick, they would have said, got on the job whilst the rest of his mates were still talking about it, drank another four double gins, then drove them all home. Not so soft as he looks, isn't old Dick; they wouldn't have got home without old Dick.

She was the first woman he noticed when he went into the Long Bar. His glance, after travelling the room, returned to her and became a stare, which was returned by a smile; a vein in his temple began to throb. Jack had seen her too; he went straight over to her. "How's things, Doris?" he asked. "What you drinking?"

"Gin-and-lime, Jack dear," she said, her eyes were still on Dick and he knew what was going to happen. He went over and sat on the stool opposite the woman.

"How about introducing me?" Now that he was nearer her he caught her smell, closed-in and stuffy and yet exciting, the smell of a woman who lay in bed late each morning, who preferred a scent-spray to soap and water, but who nevertheless devoted a great deal of her life to intensive deeply secret cleansing ceremonies.

"This is Doris," Jack said sulkily. "Doris, Dick Corvey, the reason why it took us so long to finish off the Japs. And this is Eunice."

Eunice was thin and mousy-haired and, though a good ten years younger than Doris, wasn't half as attractive; Jack's nod in her direction indicated that she would do very well for Dick, but the fret of tumescence inside Dick, looking at Doris's plump knees and all too obviously corseted breasts and more than anything else, her slack mouth painted a too-bright and too-young pink, thumbed a nose at this supposition.

She put a hand on his knee. It was soft and as if without strength; she wore a thick gold wedding-ring and above it a narrow platinum engagement-ring. Her face too was as if without bones; it seemed possible that a few more drinks would wash it away to essentials – the hungry blue eyes, that greedy pink mouth. "What lot were you with, dear?" she asked in a husky voice.

"The Chindits."

"My husband was too. Don't know where the bugger is now."

As the word dropped casually from her lips, he had all the evidence he needed; she no longer bothered to keep up appearances, she was a whore, to all intents and purposes now lying moaning underneath him. One part of him was exultant about the fact; another part of him wanted to have nothing to do with her.

Ten minutes later, during which time Doris and Eunice respectively had put away two gin-and-limes apiece, he discovered that his consciousness had made a beautifully smooth gear-change from a heightened, note-taking, fully in control sobriety to the third stage of drunkenness when you were completely, utterly and finally yourself and obeyed without question every order your body and your mind gave you. By that time Tom and Noll had joined them. Noll was, so as to speak, in top gear if not in over-drive; his face was maroon-coloured and his eyes watering and he was talking a little too well, his voice just on the verge of a skid on the slippery tarmac of drunkenness.

He was telling Tom a story with wide sweeping gestures. "Lovely young blonde comes into psycho– psychiatrist's office, see? He's sitting behind his desk – black coat, striped trousers, see? *Good-morning,* he says, *please take all your clothes off. Now lie down on that couch.* She does that, he gets up from his desk, takes his pants off and does – well, what any man would do. Then he gets up, puts his pants on, goes back to his desk and says: *Well, that's solved my problem. Now what's yours?*" Tom altered his scowl to a faint smile; the women screeched their appreciation. "That's clever," Eunice said. "That's what I like. It's clever without being vulgar."

Noll sat down beside her. "I know some vulgar ones, too," he said. He started to whisper into her ear. Tom grunted something in the general direction of Dick and left the room abruptly.

"Your friend's not very pleased with us," Doris said.

"He's not very pleased with anyone today," Dick said.

She stroked his knee; he could feel each finger through the cloth. "You're pleased with me, aren't you, dear?"

"Too pleased for comfort," he said. The smoke was very thick; he took out a white handkerchief from his breast-pocket to wipe his eyes. When he finished she took it from him and deftly refolded it. "I like to see a man look neat," she said. Her eyes were rather protuberant, pale blue and slightly bloodshot; he felt as if he were exposed naked in a dream. The tumescence changed from a fret to something near pain; he squeezed her hand and saw her eyes widen.

Out of the corner of his eye he saw that Jack was pushing his way through to the bar. He'd be at least five minutes; and Tom hadn't come back yet.

"I'm going out now," he whispered. "See you at the front in two minutes."

He met her outside in a minute less than that; she took his hand as she climbed into the Ford.

"You'll take Eunice back, won't you, dear?" she asked as he drove down the narrow lane, just off the main road. He nodded.

"It's a long way to Luckthorpe. Turn left here, dear. Then sharp right." He saw that they were approaching a fir plantation; the car pitched and rolled on the unmetalled surface and he found it difficult to hold a straight course; his hands were shaking and sweaty as if there were no strength in them, as if all the strength that normally resided in the various parts of his body had been gathered up into its centre.

"Wipe the lipstick off, dear," she said as they stopped outside the pub.

She leaned over him, billowing and oddly maternal in her blue satin blouse and black skirt. "Put out your tongue. There." She wiped his lips with the moist handkerchief; when she'd finished he felt as he had always done when his face had been cleaned in that way as a child, not cleaner but dirtier.

"We've been away a long time," she said. "We'd better not go in together." She looked at him anxiously. "You will give us both a lift back, won't you, dear? It's not far out of your way."

"Of course I will," he said; but as he entered the pub he knew that he neither wanted to see her home nor take back Tom and Noll and Jack; he only wanted to drive away by himself as fast as the car would go until he reached the stage, at sixty-five miles an hour, of not thinking about anything except the necessity to hold the car on the road.

When he came into the Long Bar Noll burst out laughing. "Sly devil," he said. "Bet you daren't say where you've been."

"Went to wash my hands."

"Fifteen minutes it took you. Feel better?"

Eunice pursed her lips as if in censure and then began to giggle when Doris appeared.

"You look lovely, darling," she said. "Really freshened up. Dick looks a bit pale though. Dick!" The giggle turned into a screeching laugh, in which Doris joined.

"I'll get some drinks," he said and went over to the bar. He couldn't bear to look at Doris any longer; she'd suddenly diminished from a white-thighed dispenser of apocalypse to a plump middle-aged woman with the seam of her left stocking awry.

Tom was standing by the bar with Jack. When he saw Dick he raised his hand to Dick as if to hit him. "You bloody fool!"

"You're not my keeper," Dick said.

"You need a keeper," Tom said. "Look at them now." Noll had suddenly embarked upon another of his stories; Doris and Eunice were screaming with laughter again and, whenever he leaned forward, pushing him away with the ineffectual gesture of the loose woman.

"Jesus, what a horrible laugh they both have," Tom said. "Goes right through your head. Remember once when I was in Kent, a Jerry pilot bailed out and some hop-pickers caught him. We couldn't do a thing about it, of course; wouldn't have faced those bloody women for a fortune. Saw some of 'em in the pub that same evening. They were laughing just like those two bitches there." He pulled a face and drained his pint.

"You can't blame them," Jack said.

"Doesn't matter a toss," Tom said. "The war's over anyway, until the next time." He looked at Dick. "I hate to remind you, lover-boy," he said, "but it's your round. Have you enough strength to get some money out of your pocket and raise that seductive caressing voice of yours?"

Clever, sensible Tom, Dick thought, remembering the air of absolute superiority that he had worn that evening and the way they'd all of them talked to him that night after he'd dropped the women at Luckthorpe; they'd grumbled so much about going out of the way that you'd have thought it was their car and their petrol. Jack, puffing a pipe and trying to look like one of those wise old characters in the tobacco advertisements, had pointed out that there were no propho stations in Civvy Street; Noll had said, with an air of great virtue, that he didn't mind a mucky story now and again but, by God, the ones those old bags told *him* made his hair stand on end, and Tom, pillar-of-society know-where-to-draw-the-line Tom, had pointed out, to round off the joint admonition, that Dick had come back into the pub with lipstick on his cheeks and his fly wide open. "It's still on," he said, viciously. "She didn't clean your face very well."

Yes, it was all in fun and all in friendship; but, as always, he was the one in the wrong, he was the one who made a fool of himself. But he hadn't let them absolutely terrorize him; when Noll and

Jack had got out, he'd said rebelliously to Tom, "Just the same, she was nice."

"I don't deny it," Tom said. "But they're all the same. I mean, the act's always the same. Why not do it with a nice-looking young girl? You've no common sense."

"I never had," Dick said.

"N'importe," Tom said. He passed his hand over his forehead. "I'd do with a cup of tea and then a hundred years in bed."

"Nil basterundum carborundum," Dick said automatically. The road surface changed from tarmac to cobblestones and the lights from fluorescent to gas. Silbridge was deserted but not empty; after Burma it still had at odd moments the power to make him happy. The light in the living-room at his home was the main factor at that moment; they found his father checking sweet coupons when they entered.

"Hello, you dirty-stay-out-lates," he said. "Smashed t'car up, I shouldn't wonder." In his shirt-sleeves, smoking a small cheroot, he was happy and expansive. "Your mother's gone to bed. So's your brother. In fact, all decent folk are in bed long sin'. Fancy a cup of tea and summat to eat?"

He went into the kitchen and they heard the running of water and the plop of a gas flame. He came out with a plate of sandwiches. "Goose," he said. "That'll put some hair on your chest. Well, Tom, how are you, lad?"

"Just looking round for a job, Mr. Corvey."

"Aren't you going back to Hancott's?"

"Might for a while. There's not much future in it, though."

"He's got two sons. They'll spend his brass for him, like Dick does mine." He pushed the coupons and some buff forms aside. "This damned rationing," he said. "Enough to turn your hair grey. I'm working for t'Government, unpaid."

"Never mind," Dick said. "You sell all the stuff."

"I don't deny that," his father said. "But they could stop rationing tomorrow if they wanted. What the hell's the point in winning the war if they can't?"

The man who'd said that, sitting in the old velvet upholstered high-backed chair, a wedding-present from his grandfather, was a man he'd never see again. His hair was short and well-brushed, his shoes shining, his trousers sharply creased; he still had his collar and tie on and his tie was a good one, all silk fastened with a diamond stick-pin. He used to shave every day then; his cheeks were always pink and smooth and he laughed easily. That was the trouble: he was too happy, too healthy, not very far off being handsome with his straight nose and good mouth and pink cheeks. So he'd been seen to, altered, cut down to size. And Tom had shot up very quickly to his proper size; he had, you might say, been groomed for stardom.

Maybe it was his father's own fault; something that he'd said, said in a tone which indicated that it didn't really matter that he himself was perfectly safe, entitled to continue in a state of contentment, came back to Dick.

"I was talking to Marples' brother-in-law last night at the Liberal Club," he said. "According to him the Council's dead eager to do some rebuilding. They shelved the plans when the war came. Well, they won't rebuild here; this is no slum area. They're damned well-built houses, good for a hundred years. It'll be the top end. Merret Street way; they've some real slums there." And he'd taken another swig of tea and a bite of goose sandwich, sublimely sure of himself.

But Tom had hardly listened to him. "There's no future at Hancott's," he repeated, half to himself. "Wish I could buy a shop. That's the only way; you've got to work for yourself. I'll find something, though . . ."

Dick looked at his face. The hardness of his expression surprised him; his body in the skimpy blue demob suit was tensed as if to spring at some enemy.

8

Tom left Hancott's, of course; Tom always knew where he was going and didn't have a shooting-brake or eight pounds a week pocket-money to distract him. Some two years after he was demobbed he'd taken an Emergency Training Course and was teaching at

Silbridge Elementary School. He was still studying hard – the two-year course types, he said, hated your guts, so you had to get ahead of them somehow – and had lost his suntan and something like a stone in weight and tended to be short-tempered and twitchy. But Dick was in splendid shape, sampling every delight Civvy Street had to offer. He went to dances, he went to pubs, he went to concert halls, he went to race-tracks, he joined the South Silbridge Tennis Club, he joined the Tanbury Film Society, he visited the theatre in Manchester and Leeds; and he even bought himself an evening suit. He grimaced at the recollection; what particular misconception of himself had led him to that absurdity? Dick Corvey, man-about-town? Dick Corvey, playboy? Dick Corvey, future big businessman? Not that there was anything wrong in itself about buying one; but there had been more important matters to think about.

Tom, he was quite sure, possessed now both a dinner-jacket and tails, but he didn't then; his response was lukewarm when Dick one winter evening in the Grey Lion told him of his purchase.

"Suppose it'll save you money," he said, "but the bloody shopkeepers always tell you that when they're trying to sell you something."

"Don't be such a damned old wet blanket," Dick said. "Think big, man, think big."

"I do," Tom said. "And I don't see how a soup-and-fish is going to help you, unless you want to be a waiter or something."

"Waiters wear tails," Dick said.

"All right, then, you can be a cinema-manager." He looked around. "No-one here tonight."

"Noll and Jack generally come in for the last half-hour."

"That makes me deliriously happy," Tom said. He huddled into his black duffle-coat as a blast of cold air came into the room. "That's someone coming in by the front door," he said peevishly. "There's six rooms in this place, they've all got draught-screens, and yet you're frozen to death every time anyone comes in."

"They train their draughts," Dick said. "They train them to attack niggling cantankerous old bastards like you." He lit a cigarette; after the second puff the cough began. Though it wasn't he knew now, any ordinary cough: it was Rita.

Mick Rorler after reading an account of some American hurricanes, had named every cough in Ward M2. And his had been Rita, gay, irresponsible Rita, dancing gaily from his chest to his throat and then down to his stomach so that he nearly brought up his beer. When he recovered his breath, his eyes were watering and the room for a second was hazy; he couldn't read the words on the little cards over the mantelpiece (*The Banks have entered into an agreement with us . . . If drinking interferes with your work . . . Hear all, see all, say nowt . . .*) or discern as more than a pink and black blur the girl on the soft drink advertisement just under the cards. Yes, that was Rita, Rita at Force One, Rita when very much younger, Rita at the stage when she could have been thrown out of his body with very little difficulty.

Tom lit his pipe, something he'd taken to at the training college. "You want to lay off cigarettes, man," he said.

"The smoke went down the wrong way," Dick said hoarsely. He finished his beer.

Tom pressed the bell by his side. "That's your story and you're sticking to it," he said. "For a moment, I thought you'd had it. Fine bloody place to die in."

Dick had laughed it off then. "Thought so myself," he said. "It'd be damned funny to die just after seeing *Orphée.*"

"You were purple in the face," Tom said. "I half expected to see those outriders come for you. Black and grim and gauntletted."

"Wouldn't mind meeting Death, though," Dick said. "God, wasn't she a smasher?"

Tom paid the waiter for the drinks, carefully counting out the exact change. "You've got something there," he said. "Cold and hot all at once, like dry ice."

He'd seemed on the point of cheering up then; but before they left the Blue Lion he was as morose as when he'd entered it. So much so, Dick reflected sardonically, that he'd actually been worried, had asked him if he were in some sort of trouble. There wasn't any need for him to worry about Tom though – like the hero of one of those serials they used to see at the old Electric Palace, he always escaped the avalanche, the dinosaur, the flooded tunnel, his aeroplane would never crash.

And when they went into Tom's house that night help had come for our hero, the jammed control stick had been freed and he was climbing upwards. Help was waiting for him in the form of Barney Rowmarsh, a stooping, middle-aged man with an incongruously thick and curly mop of fair hair standing by the drawing-room fire with a cheroot in his mouth. The big old roll-top desk was open and crammed with typescript and legal documents and coloured drawings; there was an open tin of Romany Cocktail Biscuits and six pint bottles of Tetley's Bitter on the mahogany table.

"Come up on the horses?" Tom asked his father, who was seated by the table, a glass in his hand.

"No, you cheeky young devil. And leave that ale alone. Where's your manners? Ask Dick if he wants some first." He seemed in high good humour, spruce in a green check worsted suit and green suède shoes. "How are you, Dick lad? Bit since we've seen you. And how's your mother and father?"

"Mother's not so well," Dick said. He hoped that Tom's father wouldn't ask what her illness was, though his stock reply was that she had stomach trouble, he was tired of giving it and of hearing the stock answer – *They can work wonders these days, she'll soon be better, never fear* – or worse still, the stock answer one received from a certain type of woman – *She's been poorly for a long time hasn't she? You want to get something done, you know. See a specialist* . . . But Tom's father wasn't really very interested; he pursed his lips and looked sad for a second, then poured Dick a glass of beer, and gave him a Cope's Court and introduced him to Barney Rowmarsh.

Tom in the meantime had helped himself to beer and was sprawled in an armchair, looking at his father and Rowmarsh with an expression of weary tolerance. Dick looked at father and son. At that moment they looked more alike than ever he'd noticed before; they might almost have been brothers, and Tom, in his shiny navy-blue serge suit and heavy black shoes, the lines on his face like knife scars compared with his father's, might almost have been the elder.

"So you've finally done it?" Tom said in a flat voice.

"Of course I have! Best thing I've ever done!" He turned to Dick. "You're the first to know, Dick. Barney and I are going into partnership. Meet Rowmarsh and Coverack Limited, manufacturers." He opened another bottle of beer and filled his glass with his usual competence; none frothed over and there was exactly the right amount of head on it to make it immediately drinkable. Tom had once commented to Dick with some bitterness on this trait of his father's. "My Old Man," he said, "can do any little thing you can mention, from mending a switch to pouring a glass of beer, like a professional. It's the big things, the important things, he messes up." Just then, however, to any outsider Tom's father looked every inch the successful *entrepreneur*, there was even a hint of patronage in his manner towards Rowmarsh who, he said, wasn't very practical.

"Used to work for Toverleys, Barney did. Best toy designer in the business. Worked his guts out for them in the war and then they promoted the boss's brother-in-law over his head. Promised him the moon if he'd work twenty-four hours a day."

"Eighteen," Rowmarsh said in a weak husky voice. "They let me sleep sometimes."

"Toys are going to be big business," Tom's father said. "There'll be more money about than ever before for people to spend on their kids. I can smell it, I tell you."

"I hope you can, father," Tom said.

"Of course I can!" Tom's father flushed angrily. "I'll tell you something else, too; there's more money in it than teaching. Teaching! Phooey! It's a job for old maids! Did you ever see a teacher who was rich?"

"I never saw one who was poor, either," Tom said. "I never saw one in debt. I never saw one on the dole."

His father drained his glass of beer at one gulp. "Well," he said. "You never saw an independent businessman on the dole either. Because there isn't any dole for him. It's bankruptcy first and then National Assistance."

"We won't go bankrupt," Rowmarsh said in an assured tone.

"That's right, Barney," Tom's father said. "We won't, because your stuff's too damned good."

"I know it is," Rowmarsh said, his eyes glittering. "Better than ever they let me make it."

"There'll be a division of labour, you see. Barney'll make the stuff, I'll sell it. I *can* sell, God knows. I've sold enough stuff in my time."

"Ah, to hell," Tom said. "Tell me, what does Mother think about it?"

"She agrees with me."

"Funny thing she's out of the way tonight," Tom said.

"She knows all about it," his father said. "Ask her when she comes in if you like." His voice was unexpectedly conciliatory; though kind and easy-going his temper would normally have flared up long since. He came over to Tom and put his hand on his shoulder. His voice was wheedling. "Now you're being unfair, son. You're really being unfair. I've made my mistakes and I admit it, but I'd never do anything behind your mother's back . . ."

Dick saw that he wasn't really wanted; he put his empty glass on the table and rose to go. Tom's good-night was no more than a grunt, his father's and Rowmarsh's the bare two words. As he went out of the room he saw that Rowmarsh's face was perfectly calm; he was obviously relying on Tom's father to get whatever it was that they both wanted from Tom.

He walked very slowly to the Ford; when he got into the driving seat, he sat immobile for a minute before he turned the ignition-key, wondering if he shouldn't find some excuse to go back.

The keystone of the Coveracks' doorway was, in contrast to the red brick of the house, in a pale-coloured stone. It had carved upon it in bas-relief the lifesize head of an old man with a long beard; Dick had seen it often before, but had never realised until now how much he disliked that frowning, blank-eyed face. He pulled the starter and rammed the gear lever into first, aware, as the car moved away, of having somehow let Tom down.

9

His job at Larton's had been welcome enough before the war; but it was idiotic to return to it. He'd known the very first day there, that he wasn't going to enjoy himself; and if he'd followed his instincts he'd have given in his notice immediately. And if the shop hadn't subsidised him, if he'd been solely dependent on the job at Larton's, there would have been no question of his staying either.

Seeing Isaac Larton, the Managing Director, had been a deceptively promising start to the day. Larton's private office hadn't changed in the five years since he last saw it; it was still kept stiflingly warm, the long black mahogany desk was still unscratched and shining, the thick black and white fitted carpet showed no signs of wear, there were the same books in the white-painted steel bookcase, there was the same plain grey vase, shaped like a bomb, on top of the cocktail cabinet, and there was the same radiogram, long and low-set with a plain loudspeaker grille, its only decoration the manufacturer's name on the handle of the record compartment. The radiogram, the Larton Five-Six, a hundred pounds in 1931, had made the firm's reputation and enabled it to ride out the Depression. It was Isaac Larton's chief achievement; but it was now in better shape than he was, for within five years he'd become an old man. He still held his head erect in a high-winged starched collar, his black broad-cloth suit was brushed and pressed, there was still the same gold pen and pencil in his waistcoat pocket. But his eyes had lost their cold sharpness, had become vague and puzzled, and his voice had begun to quaver a little. Before him were two thick bound folders, one in red and one in blue; as he spoke to Dick, he riffled them casually.

"It's very gratifying to see you, Corvey, very gratifying indeed. Yes, indeed. It's good to see the warriors return, and more warriors, thank God, than last time. Don't stand to attention, my dear chap; sit down and be civilian. Have a cigarette" – he pushed forward a silver box of Chesterfields – "they're American, everything's going to be American."

He took one out for himself and put it into a long black cigarette-holder. Exhaling the smoke slowly, he looked at Dick. His smile vanished. "You must use a holder, my boy," he said, sternly. "I've smoked thirty a day since I was twenty-one and never had a cigarette cough. Never one in fifty-three years. It filters the smoke, you see. Yes." He thumped the desk with his fist. "*Filters* it."

"It's nice to see you looking so well, sir," Dick said. "You don't seem to have changed at all."

"I've not changed," Larton said dreamily. "The factory has, though. It's bigger now, much bigger; all that war work . . . Do you know we're still on war contracts? I asked the gentleman at Whitehall who's in charge of the order what we should do about it. They would have been within their rights to cancel the contract, of course. He was quite indignant that I should bother him. I've received no orders, he said . . ." He chuckled. "Yes, Corvey, there are going to be changes, far-reaching changes. You're a very fortunate young man . . . on the threshold of a new era . . ."

"Fortunate to be alive, sir," Dick said, smiling.

"Yes, indeed. Alive and unscathed. And older, too, much older . . . but your job's waiting, it's not like the last time. Your confrère Liphook is now senior clerk."

"He deserves it," Dick said.

"Yes, yes, absolutely. Had a very rough time, poor chap, when he lost his leg. But work's the best medicine . . ."

His voice rambled on for another ten minutes, brought to a stop only by the arrival of his son Henry with a sheaf of papers. Henry was a tall and muscular man in what only could be termed the prime of life; soon whisky and steaks would bring the broken veins to his cheeks, the heavy jowls would become a double chin, and he'd start worrying about his heart. But just now he was full of bounce; his father seemed a ghost beside him. "Look, Father, these all need signing," he said. "Don't sit on them like a bloody hen—" then broke off when he saw Dick. He put out his hand and pumped Dick's vigorously. "Well, look who's here!" he said. "Dick Corvey! You were a skinny little lad when you went away, and now you're a grown man." He emitted an abrupt guffaw and slapped Dick on the back. "Just shows you, Father. Killing Japs is good for you. I'm sorry I missed you when I was away, Dick, but I had to go to London to drive some sense into a Civil Servant's silly head . . ." He glanced at his watch. "Well, I've got to work like the clappers this morning," he said. "I'll be seeing you, Dick." It was plainly a dismissal; Dick stood up.

So far it hadn't been bad; the old man was kind enough, and

obviously Henry had more to do than to form a one-man deputation of welcome for him. But Ron Liphook's greeting when he went into the Despatch Office, was more in the nature of a threat.

"I shouldn't spend too much time there if I were you," he said in his low harsh voice.

"He asked me to go," Dick said.

"I'm fully aware of that. Just a word to the wise, old man."

"It's jolly good of you to take the trouble," Dick said.

"H.L.'s the man to go to if you want anything."

"I grasped that."

Liphook sucked in his lips as if he weren't very pleased that Dick had already grasped it. "You'll find the whole setup very different now," he said. "The place has expanded enormously since the war. And now we're going to inaugurate—" he paused and gave Dick a tiny smile. "Er – to *set up*, a new department. Television. We've got the floor space because we extended to meet our war contracts."

"You're still busy with them, aren't you?"

Liphook frowned. "Keep that quiet," he said.

Dick laughed. "O.K. Ron, don't be frightened."

Liphook's frown didn't lift. "A sound idea, a really sound idea, old man, would be for you to have a look at our organisation chart. And this is a report I did for H.L.; we knew early last year that the war wouldn't last much longer, so we clarified our thoughts."

Dick was on the verge of making some quip about Liphook's rising in the world very quickly, then thought better of it. He looked at Liphook thoughtfully: without any doubt his former confrère had become every inch the smart young executive; he still used hair-oil but didn't have dandruff, and his finger-nails, which used to be bitten, now were, unless he was very much mistaken, manicured. And that bird's-eye worsted suit he was wearing couldn't have cost him less than twenty guineas. Ruby was moving up all right; the war had given him the chance to make himself indispensable and now he was ten years ahead of the field; he, Dick Corvey, representing the field. He glanced through the report; it ran to a hundred quarto pages. "I'm sure this'll put me in the picture," he said.

"You mustn't regard it as Holy Writ," Liphook said. "We're

still in a transitional, an" – the tiny smile returned to his face – "*in-between* stage. Still, as you say, it'll put you in the picture. Things are bound to be a bit confusing at first. I know what it's like myself. Though *I*" – the smile broadened – "had to pick up the threads *very* quickly." He picked up a sheaf of papers. "Must push off to see H.L. now, old man. Senior Conference, mustn't be late."

"That's a new thing."

"There's a lot of new things here now," Liphook said. He walked, or rather limped quickly, out of the dark little office; it was a pretty good limp, Dick thought, not so pronounced as to be distressing to watch, but just sufficient to be romantic, to make it clear that Liphook had served his King and country.

He read the report very slowly; there was no hurry, because he could tell that R. A. Liphook, Senior Administrative Assistant, Despatch Dept. halfway up the chart to the left, hadn't any real work for him for at least a week.

The report was written in a style from which all traces of personality had deliberately been removed. The last publication of its kind he'd seen had been a progress report from old Isaac in 1939: it was quite horrible, full of references to this great industry of ours and golden futures for us all, for we are all one happy family, but at least it was recognisably the work of a human being, even if he were a greedy Pecksniffian old get who used to sneak around the factory in carpet slippers so that they wouldn't hear him coming. Larton's wasn't any paradise before the war; but at least it wasn't so damned efficient, so progressive, so dynamic as it promised to be now. Old Isaac did have the decency to offer a golden dawn, he did hold out a large juicy carrot; but this grey slab of typescript seemed only to say that whilst hard work – or, in its own language, unremitting effort – was absolutely essential on everyone's part, it wasn't going to be much fun and, what was more, they needn't expect any vastly inflated wages, because that wouldn't only be bad for Larton's, but for the country, and in the end they'd be cutting their own throats.

At the same moment that he was sitting in that shabby little office – if so it could be termed, since they'd done no more than partition a corner of the General Office with matchboarding

– Tom would be sitting in an equally shabby little office on the same kind of office chair behind the same dark-stained office desk, producing prose poems extolling the beauty and solidity and the laughable cheapness of Semi-Detached and Terrace and Bungalow and Old Property Repaying Attention and Large Detached Suitable Conversion. Tom enjoyed his job no more than Dick did. (Though at least he had a desk of his own. When Liphook returned from the senior Conference and saw where Dick was sitting, he went out without saying a word, and ten minutes later two workmen delivered a small deal table and a plain wooden chair.) Tom would have in his pocket though, the Ministry of Education form which was to be his ticket out of the estate agency business; and that was the difference. Dick had, somehow or other, lived through the day, had endured until half-past five and the twenty-five to six bus and liver and onions and floury potatoes with butter and broad beans and blackberry and apple pie with fresh cream. And he'd listened to the radio and then at nine o'clock had taken Sam and his father and mother to the Grey Lion, since it was his first day back at work.

The menu wasn't always the same, naturally; and it was very rare for him to go out with Sam and his parents, not because he wasn't fond of them but because Sam preferred the Seven Dancers and his own age group, his father the Liberal Club (one pint of mixed, one large Lamb's Navy rum, every evening at nine-twenty precisely, except Wednesday and Sunday) and his mother rarely touched alcohol at all, much less visited a pub. That visit to the Grey Lion had been to please him and Sam and his father, a departure – to judge from her blushes and giggles over two Advocaats – from the habits of a lifetime. Dick smiled as he remembered her in a lace blouse and black satin skirt, lipsticked very discreetly and smelling of eau-de-Cologne, her Wednesday and Sunday 4711 from the big bottle his father had given her for her birthday.

But essentially each working day for the next two years *had* been the same; there were four increases of salary, he learned whom one must sir, mister or Christian name, he was drawn into the routine again. But Tom had escaped the trap; even as an elementary school teacher, he was more free than Dick; Dick was tied down to one place, whilst Tom would go almost anywhere in the United Kingdom. And Tom's future was, even if he never rose higher than an assistant teacher, secure; Dick's future was bound up with Larton's, and the radio industry, and his father's shop.

It took him two years and that meeting with Barney Rowmarsh to realise it, to realise that he'd been wasting his time and not even deriving any great pleasure from it. If Tom hadn't after all gone into business with Rowmarsh and his father, if Tom hadn't resigned from his nice safe job, it would have been different. And perhaps it would have been different again if he hadn't gone to Hubert Tarken's party soon after that talk with his father.

No, not *that* talk; that *Friday* talk. Friday was the night when, on his father's return from the Liberal Club on Charlton Street (10.5 on the dot) they made up the accounts for the week and, what was at that time even more important, checked the coupons and Ministry of Food forms.

When they'd done that they always had a couple of bottles of beer apiece and split a packet of Mannikins; on no other day in the week in fact, could you smell cheroots or liquor in the house.

Dick's father had taken a drink of Family Ale and was exhaling a mouthful of Havana, happy and well-adjusted and a little overweight, as well he might be with a week's takings of over ninety pounds when Dick said casually: "Tom's left Silbridge Road School."

"A better job already?"

"He's left teaching." Dick's mother had been baking tea-cakes that day; the smell of new bread still pervaded the house, along with the smell of the Mannikins and the beer.

"Is he in trouble?"

"No. He's going into business with his father and Barney Rowmarsh. Barney used to work for Taverleys. You know, the toy people."

"Of course I know, Dick. I've lived in Silbridge a damned sight longer than you."

He reached out and took a handful of potato crisps.

"Funny devil that Rowmarsh. Forty-two and not married. Comes from God knows where and He won't talk."

"He's good at his job."

"He may be. I wouldn't trust him as far as I could throw him. Tom wants his bloody head examining. By God, they're a right pair, Barney Rowmarsh and Harold Coverack. Harold's lived hand to mouth all his life – big ideas and nowt to back 'em up with, that's Harold. And Barney – he's the original mystery man, is Barney. Your pal Tom's gone stark staring mad." He unloosened his collar and tie. "Still, he's young enough to take a risk."

"You want to take a risk yourself, Dad," Dick said. "You should branch out a bit now whilst you can. Remember the soda-fountain before the war? Well, there's only one café in the whole of Silbridge. Why not cash in whilst the going is good?"

His father laughed. "I'm too old, Dick. And times have changed. You need a licence for this, a licence for that, you've got to prove you're solvent, you've got to see one little tinpot clerk after the other – it's not worth the effort, lad."

"O.K. O.K. But someone else'll do it if you don't."

"Let 'em. This shop's in a good position and I've lived in this town all my life. I've earned a decent living for thirty years and I reckon I'll keep on doing it. Let others run t'milk bars and cafés. If folk want summat to eat they can eat at home and if they want summat to drink they can go to t'boozer. Even that soda-fountain you talk about was more worry than it was worth. My shop was turning into a hangout for all t'roughs and little fourteen-year-old tarts in town."

"That's quite different," Dick said, with some irritation. "I mean a proper café, nicely furnished. There's a shop vacant on the High Street."

"Aye," his father said. "I know it. There's been a dozen shops there and every bloody one has gone banked. And it's a good mile from here, on t'wrong end of t'High Street."

"They may build there," Dick said.

"They may make me Prime Minister, but I'm damned sure they won't."

"Father, just let me point this out; there's only one café in Silbridge and that's no more than a lorry-driver's pull-up. Of course there's a bit of risk attached to any new business, but you can't make any money without taking a few risks."

His father smiled. It wasn't a sneer; his father wouldn't know how to sneer. But it was patronising, superior, cocksure at Dick's expense; he didn't like it at all.

"Listen, Dick, people who take risks don't end up making money. They end up losing all they've got." He pointed with his cheroot to the figure of £92 1*s.* 11½*d.* on the sheet of paper on the table. "That's solid, lad, that's assured. When I retire I want to hand over the business to you in going order." He smiled again; this time it was a good smile, tender and warm. "That is, if that's what you still fancy, lad. You've always been my right-hand man since you were a bairn. But I don't want you to work full time in the shop now, I want you to enjoy yourself. You've not had much youth, same as me. Time enough to start worrying when you're wed."

Dick very slowly and laboriously changed his position so that he was lying on his right side, knowing drearily as he did so that within ten minutes his back would ache just as fiercely again.

Time enough to start worrying when you're wed; but there hadn't been time enough. He had known this, had known that the change had to be made; his father, cheerfully puffing out clouds of Havana smoke, had travelled past the right station. And Dick, instead of yanking his father out with him, had let himself be argued down, let himself be argued down far too easily, because it was so warm and comfortable in the compartment and he was enjoying his cheroot.

And now there'd never be any more of those cosy Friday nights, he'd never again see the fire burning bright in the Dentdale, he would never again taste tobacco, much less cheroots, never again have his tongue prickled and stomach warmed by beer, never again see his father look at him otherwise than sadly. The heater was off, the lights were off, and the train was going faster and faster into the night, into a country he didn't know, black, stony, barren and cold.

10

BUT the landscape in fact didn't become suddenly grim; it became more and more bright and beautiful, for after Hubert Tarken's birthday party it included Lois. Tom and he were mildly puzzled by Hubert's invitation; though they'd gone to Tanbury High School together, their acquaintance since VJ Day had been limited to about four drinking sessions, all accidental rather than planned. They'd been quite enjoyable: Hubert, small and skinny and waxy-faced like his father, had an astounding capacity for hard liquor and the ability to play by ear any tune you cared to mention. Like Dick, he was being allowed to have his fill of wild oats before he finally settled down; but the Tarkens' family business, a newsagents' and stationers' and confectioners' in the centre of Silbridge with two branches in the outskirts, was a far more solid and prosperous concern than the Corvey family business. In short, it *was* a business, registered as a limited company (something which his ass of a father, because of his hatred of lawyers and accountants, never bothered to do until it was too late) and carried Hubert as a passenger with no signs of strain; Tarken Senior said that he'd rather give his own son ten pounds a week in wages than those Socialist bastards six in tax. The Tarkens were far from being millionaires and certainly would never get their pictures in the *Tatler* or the *Queen* or even very often in the *Tanbury Gazette*; but they were as much out of his class financially as he was out of Tom's. Tom had resigned from his job at the Silbridge Elementary School and was now using his status as an ex-Serviceman to obtain licences for plastics and lead and export-only paint of the kind which Rowmarsh said he couldn't begin to work without. And after he'd obtained these and about a hundred other licences he had to use his intelligence and common sense and willingness to lick anyone's boots, no matter how dirty, to get the money for the first inescapable hundred down-payments and also had to prevent, sometimes almost by physical violence, his father and Barney running the business into the red before they'd even had a sniff of the black. So Tom, that evening, wasn't really enjoying the party; he'd put on his best suit, which fitted where it touched, and his stiff white collar was spotted with blood; his mind hadn't been on the job of shaving but had been instead scrutinising Government forms and bank statements. But Dick Corvey, the Triumphant, Clerk Extraordinary of Isaac Larton Limited, Heir Apparent of Simon Corvey (Est. 1919), was wearing a clerical grey worsted suit with hand-stitched lapels and an American nylon shirt which he'd obtained through one of his father's customers, who was a chain-smoker. There weren't many nylon shirts on the English market at that period; when you did get hold of one it was generally very skimpy, totally transparent and made from parachute fabric. His was a real shirt made from shirting material, though the cut was rather odd. Hubert noticed it immediately he was inside the house and because he noticed it, so did everyone else.

"Hey, Dick," he said, "what the devil are you wearing? One of your mother's blouses?"

"Nylon," he said. "Everyone'll wear it soon. Wash in a hand-basin and hang it up to dry."

"Where'd you get it?"

"You can only get one like this for dollars." He winked. "Don't ask questions."

And that, he thought with derision, was his big moment, the crest of the wave. There he was, standing by the Larton Ninety-Four, having helped himself to a State Express 555 from one of the boxes which were lying around the lounge, sizing the women up and, finally, deciding that he wanted the tall blonde in flame taffeta; there he was in his mind's eye now, so clearly that it hurt, strutting straight towards the banana skin to end all banana skins. For then, seeing Lois in that taffeta dress which was a shade too tight round her hips, he had begun to think of marriage, he had, his fingers trembling in his haste, begun to unbuckle the armour of common sense which had previously saved him from being hurt by any other human being.

He remembered something else too; she was sitting beside Tom on the three-seater sofa though they weren't speaking. They wouldn't need to speak; those two were past the need for words whilst they were still at Elementary School.

But he had been too stupid to put two and two together, gazing open-mouthed at her whilst Hubert briefed his guests in his best Chief Salesman's manner, hearty and matey but with a hint of menace.

"Now, ladies and gentlemen, before I push the boat out, all I've got to say is this: the house is ours, providing no-one's sick on the carpet, providing no-one goes in the shop, providing we keep the radiogram sweet and low after midnight. And providing no-one puts their glasses on that same radiogram as I was going to do before Tom scowled at me . . ."

His little harangue had been of course quite superfluous; he must have known that no-one there would seriously misbehave – that was the reason they'd all been invited. The hard drinkers and yobbos were excluded; Hubert liked their company outside his home but not in it. It had been a satisfactory enough party with more than enough to drink; that was the first time he'd ever had more than a glassful of wine, and he remembered how delighted he was to find an alcoholic drink which neither made you run to the bathroom every ten minutes nor made you nasty drunk in fifty.

Their relationship had ripened too quickly, everything had gone too smoothly; from the beginning it had been a Bordeaux and State Express 555 relationship. Scraps of their conversation came back to him, mushrooming like dumdum bullets.

"I'd like a room like this one day," he'd said, looking around the lounge.

"It's lovely, isn't it?" she said. "That parquet floor's super." She leaned towards him. "They say Mr. Tarken's spent *two thousand pounds* on this house." She took a sip of white wine. "It's deliciously cold," she said. "Let's try yours." She sipped it and made a wry face. "It's bitter," she said.

"It'll taste sweet now you've put your lips to it," Dick said.

"You're flirting with me," she said delightedly.

"I'm a very sincere young man," he said. He took her hand and kissed the palm, then closed her finger gently. "That's a present to prove it."

And so, later on when all the lights but one pink table-lamp had been turned off, he found himself kissing her, very gently, and stroking her long yellow hair as Hubert at the white baby grand played *Mood Indigo.* It was incredible to believe now that he could have been taken in so easily by that pinchbeck set of circumstances – wine, a pretty girl, soft lights, and some rather flashily played jazz.

But he had been taken in; instead of enjoying the experience for what it was worth, enjoying it with his tongue in his cheek, he had taken it seriously, he had reflected that, after all, it was time that he settled down. And very soon, perhaps partly because of the new Morris, perhaps because of the new suit, perhaps because he always had plenty of money in his pocket, they were going out together regularly, at first once a week, then twice. And Tom, his clever friend Tom, wasn't worrying with women at all. His only relaxation at that time seemed to be a Sunday evening drink with Dick at the Blue Lion. There was Lorna Hillberk, of course; since that night at the Frumenty Dick kept seeing Tom around with her. She'd lost her spots and some of her plumpness but she still had that sacrificial swimming-eyed look, a look dedicated to Tom and no-one else.

Casually, that evening in high summer, he'd said to Tom: "It's time you put her out of her misery."

"Who?"

"Lorna. Who else?"

Tom took a bottle of B.P. aspirin from his pocket, swallowed two with a grimace, and washed them down with a swig of bitter. "She's becoming a bore," he said.

"Her bosom doesn't seem boring to me."

And as he uttered the flat banal words, he remembered her on the night of Hubert Tarken's party: because of Lois, because of his own immediate obsession, his own straight-to-the-bull's-eye obsession, he hadn't really seen anything that night but a halter-necked taffeta dress and long yellow hair and that open, terribly young, like a polished bayonet striking home, face; but there was, out of the corner of his eye, a picture of a square-cut black dress in a material which seemed to have been woven with the dust of the warehouse still in it; and, living, blindingly white contradictions of that blackness, Lorna's big ebullient breasts and that vulnerable, female face, looking at Tom, her soul in her eyes. Yes, her soul in her eyes. That was her bad luck, her trouble and her glory. And when he talked about her bosom, when he uttered the phrase – God knows a reasonably innocuous one – he was prickled by an enormous unspecified lust and, to a lesser degree, an aching guilt.

"They're lovely," he said in an attempt to exorcise the guilt. "You're a fortunate man."

"Listen, you can't be feeling her tits all the time." Tom's tone was casual, but his eyes evaded Dick's.

"Well, I don't see anything wrong with her."

Tom hit the glass-topped table so hard with his fist that Dick half-expected to see it splinter. "Jesus Christ, I've got enough to bear with my bloody mother going on at me!" he shouted. He took his pipe out, filled it with his hands trembling, then dropped it on the floor; the stem broke and he kicked it across the room. "Give me a cigarette, damn you!" he said to Dick.

Dick raised his eyebrows but threw a packet of Player's across to him. "Baby all done with tantrums?" he asked after Tom had lit the cigarette.

"Don't be so bloody patronising," Tom said. "And don't go on about marriage, for God's sake. I can't afford to keep myself, let alone a woman."

"Everyone we went to school with's married now," Dick said. "Did you see Piggy Runkett's picture in the *Gazette* last week?"

Tom smiled, though bleakly. "Piggy. Yes I saw it. Top hats and morning-suits and the whole bloody boiling canned, right down to his half-wit brother Vernon." He looked round the Bar Parlour, empty except for the hard core of regulars, retired men of substance who sat there regularly from eight to ten every night, speaking very little, ordering their drinks with a nod or a grunt, happy in an emotional limbo which could only be disturbed by the entrance of a woman or, almost as bad, someone from the taproom. They had booked first-class corner seats to death, all of them – the ex-printer, the ex-schoolmaster, the ex-solicitor, the ex-builder – and they would reach their destination before Tom and Dick. So they took no notice of Tom's outburst and this only served to annoy him further. "That bloody Piggy Runkett," he said, in a deliberately loud voice, aware that each of the regulars had had business dealings with the Runkett family. "Christ, you remember Piggy at school? They paid his fees because he couldn't pass his scholarship, then they paid for about a hundred tutors so he could just scrape through his School Cert. The degenerate heap of uselessness!" He was really yelling now. But the Bar Parlour, tucked away in the west wing of the Blue Lion, at the end of a maze of passages and draught-screens, might have been designed especially with the purpose of letting people like Tom explode slanderously with no harm done. The ex-printer's square sagging face twitched, the ex-schoolmaster looked as if he were thinking of bad reports, the ex-solicitor's appropriately thin lips smacked together dryly and the ex-builder momentarily looked puzzled. Tom, with an abrupt gesture, loosened his collar.

"Piggy Runkett," he said in a lower voice. "Our chum. Remember when his father gave him a Brough Superior?"

Dick giggled. "I remember him running it into that dry-stone wall on Boggart Moor."

"My God, yes. He bled like a pig. Blubbered too. But Daddy bought him a new bike, and now Daddy's bought him a new house with a double garage and G-Plan furniture." Tom puckered his mouth as if to spit and finished off his beer. "This stinking hogwash . . ." He put both hands to his head. "Once over the next hump, kid, and I'll never drink it again . . ."

"Doing well?"

"We've plenty of orders. That little runt Rowmarsh's the worst in the world to work with, but he knows his job. Trouble is, we're working on a shoestring."

"Don't worry," Dick said. "The market's wide open. You *won't* fail."

Tom put his hand to his stomach and sketched the action of vomiting. "Please don't, please don't. We damned well can. And when we do, it's going to be the biggest balls-up in the history of the human race. I've spat in the face of the Ministry of Education; the Government as a whole hasn't realised it yet but when they do, when some evil little clerk looks up C-O-V-, the bloody roof'll fall in on me. My Old Man's given up a good job at Ridgton's to be a Captain of Commerce; and if it all nose-dives, he'll be lucky if he even gets National Assistance. Might be able to help him, though. I can always join the Army again, if they'll have me." He squinted at his empty pint-pot. "Look, Dicky-boy, d'you mind if I have a gin, a large gin? Tell them to bring a bottle of orange, too."

That typical Tom Coverack touch about the bottle of orange nearly made Dick cry. Tom, he was well aware, was beaten down to his knees, but even then he didn't want to run the risk of being swindled or even being vicariously swindled.

"You have a whole bottle of gin if you like," he said. "Anything to make you happy, you worn-out Persian pillock."

He had felt enormously sorry for Tom, yet at the same time exultant. It was like watching a trapeze artist at the circus: you didn't, as a sane and decent member of society, want them to be hurt, but somewhere in the back of your mind, or rather in the cellar, the disused smelly cellar of your mind, you did want them to be hurt, you waited, urgently, quiveringly, for the missed hand-hold, the split-second incredulity, and the long scream.

"Thank you for nothing," Tom said. "You're making up for the rounds you've dodged, you mean bastard." But there was moisture in his eyes; and Dick felt the need of a gesture to match that moisture. "I'll lend you a hundred," he said.

Tom was looking intently at his gin. "Only just enough," he said. "If you'd asked for gin-and-orange you'd have got about one per bloody cent—"

"I'll lend you a hundred," Dick repeated.

Tom coloured his gin with orange-juice. "I wasn't asking you for money," he said. "Forget it."

"You need it, don't you?"

"I don't need anything. I'm big enough and ugly enough to look after myself."

"You bony old baboon," Dick said. "I told you: I'll help you out. Give me something in writing if you like."

"I could give you some shares," Tom said.

Dick blankly organised his face into a smile. "Right, Tom. Give me some shares."

Tom looked at him sadly. There seemed to be no question now of his ever having been in charge of their relationship; he had shrunken into a bag of bones, galvanised into a semblance of life by alcohol and tobacco. "When I'm a millionaire I'll remember your faith in me," he said. "Get some more gin."

"Don't be so bloody silly," Dick said, ringing the bell. "I'll take your shares. Make my fortune."

"You know damned well that's not what you're thinking. Be honest."

Dick swore at him. "Look, Tom, you're a boozer and a lecher and a rotten old twister. But I know one thing: you'll pay me back."

"Don't be so damn sure, mate," Tom said. "I mightn't be able to."

"Doesn't matter."

"Very well." Tom's voice was clear and decisive now. "I'll tell you what I'll do. I'll see you here next Thursday night and if you still want to lose a hundred pounds, I'll borrow it. Six per cent. The solicitor'll draw up the agreement. But it's entirely up to you. If you still want to lend me it, say so straightaway. But if you don't, or you haven't got the money, don't say anything. And then we'll forget the whole thing. Right?"

"Right."

"Let's get stinking," Tom said. "Let's get really stinking."

But they hadn't; for, a good half-hour before closing time, Tom had been violently sick. He only just managed to reach the Gents before it happened. Dick stood beside him as he bent his head in the direction of the w.c., his shoulders were shaking and he looked old and shabby. The sunlight pouring in through the frosted glass windows made the event even more unbearable and sordid; the window over the w.c. was open a little and there was a smell of grass and trees, like women's perfume at an execution.

Tom pulled himself upright and wiped his mouth with his handkerchief. "Sorry, Dick," he said. "I'm not very good company this evening." He rubbed his eyes; they were red-rimmed and on the lid of the left a stye was beginning. "I've been out of sorts all day," he said as they walked out of the Blue Lion. "I was up till two this morning with the books and at the factory at seven. I don't know whether I'm alive or dead."

"You want to go home?"

"We'll have some coffee first." He slumped into the seat of the Morris. "Keep the windows open, I can hardly breathe."

"Are you sure you don't want to go home? You look bloody awful."

"My father's getting cold feet," Tom said. "He'll be at home tonight, moaning half the time and the other half putting out ideas which'll be so downright idiotic that they'll make me feel sicker than I already am. And Mother won't say anything but she'll look at me as if it were all my fault. Like that damned Lorna—" He went on complaining, his voice a monotone, as they passed the Kasbah and the entrance to Kellogg's Woods.

"It's always my fault, everything's my fault. I always carry the bloody can back . . ."

And before Dick took him home, he said in a whining, wheedling voice, without a trace of his usual self-assurance, "Sure you don't want those shares, Dick? Quite sure?" And when he'd seen the answer, apparent from the expression on Dick's face, he'd cringed away from him as if he'd been hit.

And Dick, without knowing it, had made another mistake, for those shares were slowly but steadily rising now. It didn't really make much difference; money at present was of no more use to him than clothes were. He hadn't thought of money for six months, any more than he'd thought of the tweed jacket and pair of flannels and the five shirts and two pairs of shoes in his wardrobe; he'd once asked his father to take them home for him, but he wouldn't entertain the idea. "You'll be making your will next, you silly young idiot," he'd shouted. "You'll wear those clothes again soon."

"In my coffin," Dick said.

"You'll walk out in them. Now stop talking so daft, sonny, please."

Still, there would have been an enormous satisfaction in cutting the last ties, in looking the truth squarely in the face. He stretched his hand to the towel-rail on his bedside locker and took down his sponge-bag. He lay panting for a minute, recovering his breath, then he pulled open the drawstring. He was looking at the razor in its neat blue-and-silver plastic box, though not touching it, when Nurse Mallaton came in with a cup of hot milk. She put the milk down on the top of the bedside locker, then leaned over him to close the sponge-bag and hang it up again. "You're shaved already," she said.

"I was checking my toothpaste."

"It's a new tube." She looked at him gravely. It was the same kind of look his mother gave him when she discovered him in the pantry, his hand near the bowl of fruit-cake mixture. "The milk won't be nice if you don't drink it soon," she said. She helped him up into a sitting position again; he smelled on her breath apples and new bread and coffee and, even better than that, the odour of female sleep.

"O.K.," he said. "Maybe it'll finally rid me of the taste of those fishcakes."

"Don't be so faddy," she said, "they were perfectly good fishcakes."

"You didn't eat any," he said.

"How did you know?" She turned her head away from him for a moment; he saw with a stab of delight that she was blushing. The delight was wholesome and immediate and with it came knowledge, only lasting for a split second, but, whilst it lasted, blindingly undeniable: if things had been different, if he'd met her under any other circumstances, they would have liked each other as human beings. A line of poetry read somewhere during the War came back to him, looking at her half-averted profile:

Overcome, O bitter sweetness,
Inhabitant of the soft cheek of a girl . . .

He repeated the words aloud to her; she turned her face to him, smiling now. "Don't you know the rest?" she asked.

"That's all I can remember. I wouldn't have remembered it at all but for you."

"Oh, you shouldn't—" she began, then put out her hand and

stroked his gently. "You really are nice, Dick," she said and took the tray and walked quickly out of the cubicle.

He raised his cup to his lips and set it down again hastily – his hand was trembling so violently that he couldn't hold it straight. With a growing amazement he recognised the sensation, the sensation he hadn't experienced, except in his mind, since the Bug had moved over to the right lung – my God, he thought, it's real, I could at this very moment . . . His hand steadied after a moment; as he drank the milk he tried to forget what he'd just seen and to remember the rest of the poem.

"*Overcome the empyrean*," he said under his breath. "*Overcome the empyrean.*" The smile on his face broadened.

II

THE circle began by the administration block, three wooden ex-Army huts connected by a covered passage, made a wide detour by the Operating Theatre, a square red-brick building with tall frosted-glass windows, bypassed the Nurses' Home and then gradually climbed to Block M2. The path was bordered by pines, but nowhere were they thick enough to afford any cover. Rock and Basil began to walk up the hill briskly, swinging their sticks, but halfway up, Rock slowed down, his hand to his chest.

"They made this bloody walk for mountain goats," he said, panting.

"It's your P.P.," Basil said. "You want a lobe like me, man." He was wearing a green tweed suit and highly polished tan shoes; his plump face healthily reddened by the wind, he had the air of a country squire surveying his domains.

"I don't want anything but to get out of here in one piece," Rock said.

"They say they're trying to fatten Dick Corvey up for a thora," Basil said.

"You always know everything, don't you?"

Over the brow of the hill two girls approached. Basil smiled; his face suddenly turning older, his eyes greedy. As they passed he threw each of them a toffee from the bag he always carried. He watched them go out of sight over the hill, his face doting.

"You get dafter," Rock said.

"What harm is there in it?"

"You can't do anything about it here."

"I shan't always be here," Basil said. They went past the Women's Block and the Matron's Quarters, both sheltered from the eyes of male patients by a stand of firs and their position in a dip beyond the crest of the hill. Janice Marton and another girl, plump and bespectacled, came towards them! Basil took a thick envelope from his pocket.

When they had reached the South pines Rock said crossly, "I don't think much of your choice."

"Janice is Peter's woman," Basil said. "Anyway, I like Millie best." He stopped for a moment looking out over the valley below, and took a deep breath. "Just look at that view, Rock," he said. "Makes you feel glad to be alive. Look at those fields and those woods and that nice little river. And there's some lambs in that field over to the right." He feinted at Rock's belly, dancing around him. "Spring is here, Rock."

"It's here too soon," Rock said, shading his eyes against the sun. "Those lambs were in too much of a hurry to be born. They'll be sorry."

"Can't you enjoy anything, you grizzling devil?" Basil said, looking again at the rich green patchwork of the valley, silk with the silver lamé thread of the river running through it.

Rock did not seem to hear him. "I wonder what the hell they cure us for," he said. "What's the point, for Christ's sake?" His G.I. jacket flopped loosely over his thin chest; the bright colours of his open-necked shirt seemed almost obscene in contrast with his thin, savage face.

Basil's expression was almost paternal, his round face wrinkled with concern. "Have you heard from her again?"

"She wants a divorce."

They walked on a little farther towards the seat overlooking Ward M2. They sat for a moment in silence, then Rock handed Basil a typewritten envelope. Basil glanced at it and handed it back to Rock.

"Give her it."

Janice Marton and Millie came round the Circle again; Basil, out of the corner of his eye, saw them and gave them a perfunctory smile. Rock's expression remained unchanged but, glancing in the direction of Janice's white unstockinged legs, he said under his breath: "The whore. The dirty little *whore*."

"Give her the divorce," Basil said. "Get rid of her. Forget her. Start again."

Rock grinned. "No, Basil. I won't give her a divorce. That's what she wants, the bitch. But I'll get my discharge, one of these days. Then I'll give her something she won't forget."

"I wouldn't if I were you."

"But *I* would." His voice was soft and dreamy. "She has lovely white teeth. Hell, when people meet her for the first time they don't believe they're real." He giggled. "When I've finished with the nasty lying little trollop, she'll have to get some false ones. And I'll spoil that nice little straight nose of hers. And her boy friend, my pal who saw to it that my wife wasn't lonely – I'll use my feet on him too. And I know where I'll use my feet first. I'll make sure they don't have any more fun. And I'll take my son back, and I'll tell him his mother's a whore, a dirty rotten little whore, who couldn't wait six months for her husband, not six lousy months before she went off with another man."

"My God, Rock, he's only four."

"He's not staying with that pair."

"If you do that to them, he will. You can't look after him in jail."

"I'll see he's all right."

"He's your son."

"Is he?" Rock stood up suddenly and kicked the leg of the seat so hard that it shook. "No. He *is* my son. I'm sure of that. Lucy was all right until she met that chap. Christ, if only I'd not been married to her . . . Chaps like Dick Corvey don't know how lucky they are."

"You're not so different from him," Basil said.

Rock snorted. "I'm not as bloody soft as him. I can remember the day she broke off the engagement. He'd just been given a cubicle, remember? She ran out down the drive, blubbing. And then he didn't speak to anyone for days. Doesn't speak much now for that matter."

"It takes different people different ways," Basil said. "But you're still no better than him. He let it make him ill, and you let it make you vicious, that's all."

They had nearly completed the Circle by now and were passing the south end of Block M2, a two-storeyed flat-roofed building in ferro-concrete with bay windows at each end.

Rock looked at it glumly. "It looks like a tram," he said. "A big concrete tram that's going nowhere."

"Let's go and see Dick," Basil said.

"If he's as mangy as he was the other day I'm damned if I want to."

"You were here yourself once," Basil said. "And we've not made the rounds for shopping yet."

Rock shrugged his shoulders. "O.K., if you want your head bitten off."

When they went into the cubicle Dick smiled at them. "I thought you'd forgotten me, you bastards."

"We'd never do that, Dickie boy," Rock said. "Want anything from the village?"

"A pad and envelopes and a *Lilliput*. And a jar of Silvikrin."

Basil raised his eyebrows. "Are you courting, Dick?"

"Don't be so bloody nosey," Dick said. "I've got dandruff, that's all. And don't bring me last month's *Lilliput* or I'll beat your brains out with it."

The sun had gone under a cloud now and it looked as if it were going to stay under it; but he still felt happy, calmly, steadily happy. It was idiotic of him to allow himself to be in this state; for two whole days now he'd enjoyed it, in fact, ever since Nurse Mallaton had touched his hand, had looked at him as a human being. No matter how he tried to reason that moment away, he still had the tenure of happiness.

She passed by at that moment; he waved at her. She didn't wave back, but smiled at him. He felt his face flushing and leaned back on his pillows, feeling that somehow his well-being was confirmed. "She's better than your stinking old strep and P.A.S.," he said.

"You're on the mend, boy," Basil said. "She's a bobby-dazzler." He put his head out of the cubicle entrance. "Walks as if she were on springs."

"She looks like a horse," Rock said. "A clean healthy young horse, but a horse just the same."

"They all look like horses to you," Basil said.

"Hacks," Rock said. "Hacks with a different rider each day. This one's rider has a Ford V8. I saw him collect her from the Nunnery last night."

Dick's face darkened. "It's nothing to do with me," he said.

"They're nothing to any of us," Rock said.

Dick opened *Picture Post* after they had gone, but closed it when he came to the photograph of a society wedding. The bridegroom reminded him too much of Tom, everyone in the group looked too healthy, too successful. Good old Rock, he thought, he's straightened me out. Clear-thinking, clear-sighted Rock, my friend of twelve months' standing; I was dreaming and he woke me up, I was happy and I had no right to be happy – Evelyn isn't for me. On the line I'm travelling on you mustn't expect, when you press the bell-push marked *Attendant*, that anything will happen. There won't even be someone coming round with a tray of chocolate and cigarettes, there won't be any trolleys of tea on the platform at the little gas-lit wayside stations, only a high angry voice shouting a name no one can catch. You put up your feet on the dusty red upholstery with the stuffing leaking out of it, you throw aside the newspaper you've read twice from cover to cover, and you make yourself as comfortable as possible until you reach your destination, which will be soon enough, quite soon enough. But why shouldn't he dream? Why shouldn't he press the bell-push? He'd had it, utterly and finally, there was no hope, but if he wanted to gloat over – no, not to gloat over, to treasure – that liveable from egg to apple moment that she'd given him two days ago, he'd do so and to hell with Rock and the lover with the V8.

He picked up the *Picture Post* again and searched for the wedding photograph. He had been mistaken; the bridegroom didn't look in the least like Tom. But he knew whom he could, if he used his imagination, make him turn into; and, what was equally important, he knew who the bride would be.

The sky turned hodden grey and the rain began, at first no more than droplets splattering the tarmac path outside like buckshot, then becoming a downpour, driving into the cubicle and splattering his face. There was the sound of doors and windows closing all over the ward. When Probationer Laggons came in to close the two doors of his cubicle, rattling and creaking on their hinges with the force of the storm, he didn't bother to look up but kept his half-closed eyes fixed on the magazine.

12

HE didn't see Nurse Mallaton at lunch-time, but wasn't disappointed; he wanted to compose fantasies with her for theme, pastel-coloured fantasies of drives in the Morris, of the Last Waltz and walks in the country, and her actual presence would have turned those fantasies into simpering, unreal little B features or, worse still, would have given them a sharp edge of longing, would have made them instruments of self-torture. But by a quarter-to-six he was willing to take either risk; he had a sharp, compelling need to see her, just as he once had a sharp compelling need for a drink, or a cigarette or Lois. The difference is, he thought, hearing the rattle of cutlery and meal-trolleys along the passage outside, that he needed to see Nurse Mallaton more than ever he needed to see Lois; when he was going about with Lois she was his selection out of almost the whole unmarried female population of the Silbridge district, whilst Nurse Mallaton was Hobson's choice . . .

Then, as she came into the cubicle with his supper he knew that wherever he had met her, she would have been exactly the sort of woman he always wanted. *She'll make you a good wife*, his mother would have said – something which she'd never said about Lois, though of course she never criticised Lois in his hearing. That was his mother's accolade: it was what she'd said about Lorna Hillberk – *She'd make Tom a good wife, but he hasn't the sense to see it* . . . And there it was; the right woman, the good wife, had been discovered,

discovered too late; it was like those films he used to see at the old Electric Palace in which some grizzled old desert rat, generally played by Walter Huston or someone who looked like him, would expire in the hero's arms, gasping *The treasure's in the . . .* leaving the hero to complete the sentence, leaving the handsome healthy hard-riding hero to find the treasure. Well, there was one consolation; he knew where the treasure was. He'd never spend it; but at least he could look at it.

"I missed you at dinner time," he said to her.

She helped him into a sitting position and pulled forward the green Formica-topped table to straddle his bed.

"I had to go to the Women's Ward."

"It's a waste," he said. "A sad, wicked waste."

"It's very good of you to say so, Mr. Corvey," she said, and made as if to curtsey. She didn't actually do so; but she did touch the hem of her skirt, revealing a millimetre of black petticoat.

"It'd be very good of you to bring me some chicken instead of this muck," he said, pointing towards the shepherd's pie.

"That was an exception," she said. "A very great favour. But it's not too bad. Put some butter on and eat it all up."

"I will for you," he said. "If you'll hand me my butter ration. Left-hand side of the locker." He looked at her bent head; her hair wasn't yellow like Lois's, nor was it dyed; it was a shade darker than ash-blonde, glossy and, so near to him, clean-smelling. He could identify the smell; his sister had used that shampoo back in the days when the whole world was secure, back in the days before Nelly had begun to roll up her sleeves and get to work on him.

"Here you are," she said, straightening up. "You don't use much, do you?"

"I have to watch my figure," he said. "It'd be awful to die of thrombosis."

"Don't worry about that," she said. She took hold of the trolley again; as she was going out of the cubicle, he said desperately: "You don't come from these parts."

She stopped at the doorway. "But I do, Mr. Corvey. Tanbury."

"That's practically next door. Which part?"

"Rincort Street. Near the High School."

"Have you ever been to the Raynton Hotel?"

"Only once. It's awfully expensive."

"All right, Eve," he said, without noticing that he had used her Christian name. "I'll take you to dinner there. We'll have cocktails, wine, liqueurs – the lot. Will you?"

"That's very sweet of you," she said. Her voice was shaking. "Look, Mr. Corvey, I must go now. I'll bring you your pudding." He heard her feet running down the passage and the tortured squeak of the trolley wheels; he cut into the packet of butter viciously.

"You've eaten it all up again," she said when she returned with a plate of jam roly-poly and a jug of custard.

"I told you; I always eat everything up for you."

She touched his hand for a second; his hand knew that it had happened, just as his back knew that she had helped him to sit up, but he could not tell whether the gesture was a very light admonitory slap or a deliberate caress.

"If you always eat up all your meals, you'll soon be better," she said.

"Will you have dinner with me at the Raynton?"

"No, don't—" She stopped. "Yes. Yes, I will, Mr. Corvey. On one condition: that you gain three stones. O.K.?"

"O.K.," he said. "Is that a promise?"

"It's a promise."

"Cross your heart and swear to die?"

"I never cross my heart. You'll just have to take my word."

"That's good enough," he said, and started to spoon up the pudding.

She poured out his tea; a lock of hair fell over her eye and she pushed it back with a tired, end-of-the-day gesture, poignantly domestic, which nearly brought the tears to his eyes.

"It's been a long day for you, love," he said.

"I'm all right," she said, brusquely. "Is there anything else you need?"

"You could give me *The Lady in the Lake.* Second shelf of the wardrobe, right-hand side."

As she put it on the table, Lois's photo fell out of its pages. "She's very pretty," she said.

"You're much prettier. What'll you wear when we go to the Raynton?"

"I'll tell you when you've put on three stones."

He took a mouthful of roly-poly. "I'm going to do just that," he said. "Make no mistake about it."

"Of course you are," she said, soothingly. "Of course you are, Mr. Corvey. Goodnight."

"Goodnight," he said to her retreating back and savagely gobbled the pudding. He hadn't missed the note of pity in her voice; and why had she been in such a hurry? A date with the Ford V8 boy-friend presumably; and who could blame her?

The pudding had rather more crust than jam; but he ate it all and spooned up the custard. To finish it all was somehow mixed up with defeating Nurse Mallaton's rich healthy boy-friends; the tarnished chromium dessert-spoon he was holding wasn't much of a weapon, he knew, but it was the only one he had.

When the plate was emptied, he lay back, his hand near the packet of Rennies he always kept on the top of the locker, waiting for the usual bout of dyspepsia. To his surprise the pain didn't begin; though the circumstances – the steady drumming of the rain on the windows, the grey sky now darkening into night, his irritation with Rock, the twice-cooked taste of the shepherd's pie and the hard crust of the pudding and, more than anything else, Nurse Mallaton's obvious pity, the promise which she made so easily because she knew she'd never have to keep it – all these normally would have guaranteed not just indigestion but actual vomiting. But he felt fine; his stomach wasn't exactly overjoyed about his supper but it would stay down. And he himself, though he wasn't exactly happy now, at least felt alive, healthily angry, angry with himself for being a consumptive, angry with Nurse Mallaton both for being so attractive and for her pity, her damned female pity.

Lois, he remembered, had always liked the Raynton; and though it was hardly Yorkshire's answer to the Savoy, Raymond Postgate had once lunched there, and the service was good and the carpets thick. And it was expensive; that appealed to Lois. Not that she was a gold-digger; but once he started going around with her there were more withdrawals than deposits in his Post Office savings book. But the day that they were engaged was the last time he took her to the Raynton for dinner; even she, when she saw that the meal left little change from three pounds, saw the red light.

"That was gorgeous, darling," she said, when they were out in the street looking at the Wedgwood tea-set in the window of Runcelby's, the more superior of Tanbury's two department stores. "But it was just a very special occasion. We'll have to be very economical and save like mad."

"Don't worry," he said. She was wearing a maroon button-through dress with a low neck; the wine and the food and the brandy were all combining to stimulate his desire again, to make him forget his fatigue after a drive of seventy miles and an afternoon under a blazing sun on Haworth Moors exploring the texture of the fine wool of the dress and the skin underneath it. There was still enough sunlight in the air, the dregs of the golden light which had poured down upon them all day to rid the fluorescent street-lamps, now just lighting up, of their interstellar bleakness; and the black stone buildings seemed not to be blackened by soot, but as if they had always been that colour, as if that colour had been chosen to give pleasure, like the shade of a woman's dress.

There had never been in all his life such a concentration of contentment. He didn't want to go home, he didn't even want to move from the spot.

"Will you buy me that tea-set when we're married?" she asked.

"Now, darling, if you like."

"Not all at once, silly, bit by bit." She squeezed his arm. "Wasn't it lovely at Haworth? Like heaven. Absolutely like heaven."

Her face had caught the sun a little; he touched her cheek gently and felt a slight roughness. She smiled at him, her eyes crinkling.

"I love you mucher."

"Plenty mucher? Me tooer."

What had happened in that hollow on the way to the waterfall had been the culmination of a dozen trips to theatre and cinema and dance hall each ending in embraces which had become progressively more intimate; and there had been the walks which weren't really walks but simply attempts to find a secluded spot, which wasn't easy either in Silbridge or Tanbury. And this time, because he'd been able to get hold of three gallons of petrol at ten shillings a gallon, they had found themselves quite alone but for a sheep and a flight of curlews and then the urgent whisperings between them and then finally no light, no sky, no earth, only a terrifying swoop into the dark caves of pleasure with two voices (his own, he recognised with surprise, was one of them) crying out like lost children.

Dick reached out angrily and threw the photograph on the floor. He was no better, he thought with disgust, than those squalid adolescents whom you kept reading about in the papers, discovered self-trussed and hanging by the neck in their bedroom, their only epitaph some lying banality to say that he was a happy healthy lad with a great interest in Westerns or that he was well-liked and a promising scholar, but sensitive and withdrawn. He was hurting himself, mixing it all up with sex and failure; and, he knew, instinctively, that wasn't the reason for his wanting to remember that evening. He wanted to remember it because at some time that evening there had been a clue, a clue to the situation in which he now found himself, his only positively pleasure as a man and as a human being a flirtation with a nurse, the condemned man gulping down the spiced wine at the last stop before Tyburn. There was a clue, there was an answer. Perhaps it couldn't help him now; but he still wanted to know, to know if only to spit in the hangman's eye. He had to know – and then without knowing it, he fell asleep, to awake at a quarter to nine, alone, totally alone, completely aware of every physical circumstance from the warm softness of the day blanket which someone had pulled up to his chin to the orange glow of the lamps of London Road crossing the southern half of the valley.

The London Road was a two-lane carriageway; he'd touched seventy on it coming back from Haworth the day of his engagement, the day they'd first gone to heaven. That was what they always called it afterwards, even when they were alone together; and of course it was a great joke to use the phrase apparently in all innocence when in public. Scraps of conversation floated into his mind. *When we're married we'll go to heaven every day . . . Anything might happen, Hubert; just for argument's sake, suppose Lois and I went to heaven tonight . . .*

He took a sip of the now cold milk on the locker; that wasn't the clue. The clue had been there plain to see at Haworth and you couldn't say fairer than that. Nelly had played absolutely fair with him that day: the place and time of the warning were calculated so that it should have its maximum effect. He and Lois were sitting in the bar parlour of the Black Bull drinking beer and eating sandwiches made from Nisbauer's sausages, when Lois coughed. He'd been a little annoyed at being interrupted in his enjoyment of the sausages; Nisbauer, a fat, ill-tempered German, had been making them for some thirty years now, scorning to recognise the existence of the Ministry of Food; Nisbauer's sausages and black puddings and pies were, during both wars, his father said, the only eatable foodstuffs to be bought in Silbridge and when some yobbos in 1916 broke Nisbauer's shop window the police gave them such a clobbering that he never had any trouble again. Nisbauer's sausages, rich and highly spiced, eaten between slices of home-made bread, washed down with beer – that was another never, another never again.

Lois went on coughing; he hit her gently on the back.

"I've caught cold," she said. "Or maybe it's T.B."

"I'd still love you," he said.

"I wouldn't be much use to you then," she said. "I had a cousin – I never met him – who died of T.B. at twenty."

He laughed. "If you never met him, then what of it?"

"Mummy's always a bit scared of it," she said. "She makes me drink two pints of milk a day."

"That's what gives you those lovely white teeth," he said.

"Those poor Brontë girls," she said. "All dead. What did it say in that letter? *I vomit blood . . .*"

"Don't think about it. You can't help them now."

The tone of her voice when she'd talked about T.B. and the way in which there had been invoked the gigantic spectre of her mother, her bustling good-hearted mother who loved her little daughter – it was a plain enough warning, not far from the Rectory with its view of graves, in the very room where Branwell, showing unusual good sense, had decided it was better to die quickly of drink than be eaten up piecemeal by the Bug. And because of the miracles of modern science, because of the doctors being so damnably clever, he himself hadn't had that choice. They kept him alive, as they kept his mother alive for six months, to keep themselves in jobs, to obtain the subject-matter for clever little articles in the *Lancet*.

And that had been the end of a perfect day; he'd rushed in, the triumphant young lover, the selfish big-headed, hard-hearted young lover, shouting like a fool: "I'm engaged!"

Joyce was staying with them; when he came into the living-room she was talking in low tones to her father. They were sitting together at the table, which still had a litter of tea-things on it. She was wearing a cream silk housecoat, and she'd taken the pins out of her long black hair; she had her arm around her father's shoulders.

"Where's Mother?" he said, impatiently. They looked up at him but didn't speak. Even at that moment of anxiety he noticed with pleasure how Joyce's hair shone, how pleasantly it smelled of Amami; having her in the house again took him back to the days before the war, the days when Sam was living there too, the days when the whole world was secure.

He took a seat by the fireplace. "What's the matter?"

Joyce left her father and came over to him. "The results of the X-ray have come through." She put her face against his and started to cry. "It's what we were frightened of. In the stomach."

He turned to his father and said fiercely, "Why didn't you tell me?"

"We didn't know till today. It wouldn't have helped, Dick. It's what we suspected but it wouldn't have helped to tell you."

"Have you told her?"

"No. No. That's a bridge to be crossed. She's sleeping now; the doctor gave us some tablets."

"If only I'd known earlier," Dick said. "If only I'd known earlier . . ."

Joyce suddenly, briskly and unseeingly, took the tray from the Welsh dresser and put the tea-things on it.

"I heard you say something about being engaged," she said.

"Lois Rinchett."

"I remember her. Mother will be pleased. Now, you mustn't worry, Dick. There's an operation that'll put her right, if it isn't too late—"

But his father didn't speak again that night; he sat staring at the table, Joyce beside him stroking his hair. About five minutes later Dick muttered something about being tired and went up to bed, leaving them huddled together like the survivors of some great storm.

13

THE next morning both his father and Joyce looked more cheerful; the day was so bright as to make even the spotless yellow cretonne curtain, the crisply laundered red-and-green-checked tablecloth, and the gleaming plates in the Welsh dresser appear for a second a little dingy. There was a smell of bacon and mushrooms frying; this was Sunday morning, the day of the big late breakfast and the pealing bells; and, he realised, as Joyce bustled about the kitchen, the first Sunday, the first Sunday ever, that his mother hadn't cooked the breakfast.

"Take your mother up a cup of tea, Dick," his father said. "It's about time she saw your face, you devil. And tell her your news."

"Are you sure?" He stopped because he didn't know how to put it.

"It'll do her good to hear it," his father said. "It's high time you settled down."

"If only I'd known, I wouldn't have—" He stopped again. He hadn't cried at all during the night, but had gone to sleep immediately, despite himself; he'd been so tired that he hadn't even bothered to put on his pyjamas. Now his lip was quivering.

"Don't be so soft," his father said, roughly. "People have got to keep on living. If you go up blubbing like a great bairn, that won't help her, will it?" He went to the dresser, took out a bottle from inside it and poured rum into Dick's cup of tea. "Pull yourself together," he said, his voice unexpectedly military.

Joyce came in from the kitchen. "Just look after the bacon, Daddy," she said. "Keep the gas low, that's all you've got to remember." She pressed Dick's hand. "Wait until I've been upstairs for the tray, will you, Dick?"

When she returned and was putting out the small teapot and a plate of thin bread-and-butter, she said in a fierce whisper: "Don't mind Daddy. Be cheerful, that's all. Tell her all about the engagement."

But the few steps it took to ascend that narrow staircase were the most difficult he'd ever taken. He couldn't face what was beyond that shining cream flush-fronted door, that door which was a manifestation of his mother's personality; a year ago she'd decided that the house was to be light and gay and, to use her own adjective, modern. He didn't himself quite approve; he had an intuition that the modernising process would eventually sweep away the Dentdale and the old gas stove and even the Welsh dresser. And then as he put his hand to the strip of chromium where the door-knob used to be, he had to choke hard so that he wouldn't do the very thing his father had told him not to do; for guilt, the guilt he'd disregarded yesterday, had now a tight hold of him.

But when he entered the room, his mother in a pink quilted satin bedjacket was looking better than ever he'd seen her, her cheeks rosy with sleep, her black hair, exactly the same colour as Joyce's, glistening and neatly braided. The room smelled of lavender water and 4711 and there was a bowl of carnations on the new walnut tallboy.

What she said when he told her of his engagement was significant.

"She's a lovely girl," she'd said. "A really lovely girl." And she'd laughed. "There's one thing sure, you'll have nice-looking children."

But she didn't say that Lois was a good girl. She was a lovely girl, his mother knew that; and his mother knew nothing against her. And she was pleased at the engagement, as she would have been pleased at his being given promotion or a Royal Humane Society medal.

"Are you feeling better now?" he'd asked.

"It's only my stomach, Dick. And I'm a bit run down, the doctor says. But I feel on top of the world. It's a fine sunny day and my son's going to be married."

"You'll be up and about soon," he said. "I'll take you and Dad to Morecambe and bring Lois along too."

"Of course we will," she said. "And we'll go to see your Uncle Henry at Morecambe; he's always asking us to come over. The air'll do us all good. You and your Dad are looking a bit peaked lately."

"We'll fix it for Sunday then."

"Yes," she said. "I'll drop him a line."

Her eyes were perfectly expressionless, but suddenly her hand tightened on the handle of her tea-cup; her knuckles whitened with the pressure and the handle broke off.

"I'll fetch you another," Dick said. Then Rita came, at something like Force Four; he had to wipe his eyes when he'd finished.

"I won't be a minute," he said, going to the door.

"No," his mother said sharply. "Dick, love, listen to me. I don't like that cough. I've heard it too often lately."

"I'm smoking too much, Mother. I'll cut it down."

"I don't think it is that," she said. "I'm not saying it's nothing that won't be cleared up, but you must see the doctor. You don't realise it, son, but you've been under a great strain the last few years, living under terrible conditions and eating all the wrong food" – she spoke of his service in the Far East as if it had been a stay at some unsatisfactory boarding-house, Dick thought with an amused tenderness – "and it takes time to recover. Promise me to see the doctor, Dick, please." She took a drink of tea, holding the cup in two hands. She drank it quickly, as if it were alcoholic, and her face reddened slightly. "Pour me another cup, please," she said. "Don't mind me fussing, Dick. It'll be someone else's job soon. You mustn't deprive me of the pleasure."

And he'd promised to see the doctor and to go to bed earlier and always, above all, to eat a good breakfast and not to smoke too much. But he hadn't seen the doctor about Rita; he kept meaning to do so, and kept putting it off and then, as a result of a scream one morning a month later – the scream was his father's, which made it all the worse to bear – his mother was taken to hospital. And there her face was gradually sponged of its identity by morphine, and the 4711 she now used every day couldn't quite disguise the smell of death about her, the smell which had come from his parents' room so strongly that morning, that light and gay and modern room, the room which his father wouldn't let him enter but pushed him away from – *Don't stand there, you bloody fool – fetch the doctor, for Christ's sake fetch the doctor.*

It had been easy to tell lies to that shrunken, waxy face, because it wasn't with him or his father or any human being any longer, except that now and again the eyes would recognise the loneliness in his father's face and give him a puzzled, almost resentful look.

He didn't know whether she was fully herself again before the end; she died four months after entering hospital whilst they were debating the pros and cons of some operation which would take her even more irrecoverably out of the ordinary human world than she was already. And then the heart condition which was one of the cons as far as operations were concerned became the crowning mercy; or at least, that's what the doctor said.

After that, he still didn't see the doctor about Rita; or about his indigestion, or about his fatigue not just at the end of the day but the middle of the day, or about his night-sweats. He drank and smoked more, he started carrying digestive tablets and glucose tablets, and when he woke in the night with his pyjamas soaked in sweat, he took them off, rubbed himself down with his towel and slept in his shirt. But sleep was the wrong word; he'd lie half-awake listening to the hours strike on the Town Hall clock, to awake, more tired than when he'd gone to bed, at half past seven, to breakfast on bread-and-butter and tea and a cigarette.

Not that he'd been unhappy; for he and Lois had been making plans. At first they were vague – how nice it would be to have a café somewhere in or around Silbridge, how essential it was for Dick to have an object in life, not to spend his whole life, like her father, working for someone else . . . And then, after his mother's death, the plans became much more clear-cut.

They were dressing by the fire when she brought out the plan. Not, of course, explicitly.

"Dick," she said, fastening her skirt, "are you sure you really love me?"

"There's nothing more I can do to prove it at the moment," he said.

"Don't be silly," she said, impatiently. "It was heaven, it really was, Dick, but it's not much fun like this, is it? We shouldn't really – and it's always a risk."

"I wouldn't let you down," he said.

"I know you wouldn't, darling, but it wouldn't be nice for me, would it?" She knelt beside him, her head on his thigh. "We should be married soon, Dick, and then it wouldn't matter if we do have a baby. Listen, darling, and don't be angry with me. Daddy's seen a shop in Tanbury that he thinks would suit us."

"What about my father?"

"He can manage, Dick."

"Can he?" he asked.

But there was an answer to that: Dick's father should sell now whilst the market was good and put something into Dick's business. He'd said he'd help, hadn't he, darling? And Daddy was going to help too. Daddy was near retirement age and he wanted an interest, he'd always fancied a café. . . .

"Father can't be left by himself," Dick said.

"I don't mean that, Dick. He can live with us, there's a house with the shop . . ."

He stroked her bare shoulders. "You'd better put your blouse on," he said.

The subject wasn't mentioned again that evening, but on the following Wednesday evening he inspected the shop with Lois and Lois's father, and the next evening he tackled his father about it. That was the first real quarrel he'd ever had with his father, and at the time he couldn't understand it; his father was as if possessed.

"This is my home and I won't leave it!" he shouted. "I like your bloody cheek planning my life behind my back! Never asked me to see the bloody shop, did you?"

"You can come any time, Dad," Dick said. "It's a damned good business. We all thought so."

"We? Who's we? A twenty-year-old girl and you and Matty Rinchett. I've met him. Carries his money in a purse, that's the sort of man he is. And he thinks he knows it all, same as you do . . . I know what's in his head: he'd put in about one-tenth what you needed and expect five-tenths of the profits—"

"That's not worked out yet."

His father laughed and mimicked the dry enunciation of Lois's father. "The details, Richard – aaah, we can work them out latah to our satisfaction, Ai'm suah . . ." He made a gesture of spitting. "I can just see him now, grinning all over that parchment face of his . . . And old Muggins here" – he tapped his chest – "he's going to sell up and give you the lot and live on your charity and Lois's and Matty Rinchett's – what the hell do you take me for?"

"I'm only trying to help—"

"Trying to help?" His father raised his fist. "You cheeky young devil, I've a damned good mind to give you a hiding, big though you are!"

"You'd better not try," Dick said quietly. He'd pushed away his plate, the sour taste of bile in his mouth.

"Trouble with you is you're spoiled rotten," his father said. "Your sister's worth ten of you and she's always been given the dirty end of the stick and you've had everything. And your brother – he's a real man, he's had the guts to do something with his life. But you – you're waiting for dead men's shoes, and you can't even wait until I'm dead. All you care about is driving the car hell for leather – and that bloody fiancée of yours."

"Leave her alone."

"You want to watch her," his father said, his voice quieter now. "I'm just trying to save you sorrow." He put his face close to Dick's; his breath smelled of beer. "I've seen her having coffee at the Co-op with your pal, Tom. I've seen the way she looks at him . . . Tom's doing a bit better than you now, you know."

"Of course I know about her having coffee with Tom," Dick

said, forcing himself to be calm. "They met by chance. No harm in that."

His father took a cheroot and lit it, but didn't offer Dick one.

"Just by chance," he said contemptuously. "He'll give her a baby just by chance, one of these days."

Dick leapt up, taking hold of his father's lapels. "I'll break your bloody neck!" he shouted. "Take that back!"

His father made no answer and no resistance; suddenly he seemed to have shrunk, his eyes bleary and puzzled, his face without hope. He was hurt and lonely and old and, Dick could see from his plate, hadn't even begun his tea. And he had made the meal too, for what it was, and had waited until Dick came in from work to begin – suddenly Dick couldn't be angry with him any more, but he couldn't stay in the same room with him either.

He rammed the gears of the Morris through viciously into top, cursing as they jammed going into third. He was three miles out of Silbridge and the speedometer was touching sixty before he realised that he not only didn't know where he was going but there was nowhere he wanted to go. When he reached Tanbury he found his spirits lifting a little; it wasn't much of a city but it *was* a city, with bright lights and people on the streets, and it would serve as a destination. But after he'd parked the Morris in a side street by the Town Hall, he discovered that he'd been mistaken; the only difference between Tanbury and Silbridge was that Tanbury had more lights and more shops. And he'd already seen all he wanted to see of the shops on week-end visits with Lois; and in any case it wasn't possible to wander round the streets of Tanbury at night for longer than half an hour without a copper moving you on. He passed a fish-and-chip shop and became aware of his missed tea; he hesitated at the open doorway and then walked on in the direction of the Raynton Hotel.

A cold wind from the flat treeless plain south of the city swept down the street; he jammed his hands into his pockets and wished that he'd had the sense to bring his overcoat. He ran up the steps of the Raynton and went straight into the cloakroom. When he'd washed his face and hands and put a dollop of Brylcreem from the wall dispenser on his hair he began to feel a little more cheerful;

he looked at himself in the mirror and saw that his cheeks after the cold and the rub with the rough towel were pink and his eyes were shining. He gave the attendant a shilling and strolled into the lounge. He looked for an empty corner-seat, wondering why a corner-seat was so important when by oneself, thought with a definite pleasure of sandwiches and beer, then looked at the man and woman at the table in the far corner again. It was Tom and Lois. It was Tom and Lois, Tom his best friend who owed him a hundred pounds and Lois, his beloved, his dear one, who was at night-school brushing up her French, who'd asked him especially not to bring her home from Tanbury Tech. because I don't like that cough, darling, and you must *promise* to go straight to bed . . .

The woman's back was towards him; but he knew that yellow hair, that short curly hair; and he knew Tom's face. Tom hadn't seen him yet; he was looking at Lois too intently. Dick strode over to the table and sat down beside them. "O.K., Tom," he said, his voice trembling. "This is it" – then saw that it wasn't Lois at all but a woman at least ten years older, with a hard, carefully made-up face.

Tom smiled at Dick. "Hello, old boy. Grand to see you." He nodded in the direction of the woman. "This is Mrs. Warklock, Dick. Dick Corvey, Mrs. Warklock. She and I and Mr. Warklock are thinking of doing some business together."

"I won't intrude," Dick said and rose from the chair, the woman's faintly amused eyes on him.

"Don't be daft," Tom said. "What you drinking?"

"It's all right, Tom, I'll leave you to your business." He felt angry with himself for having jumped to conclusions so quickly and, queerly enough, a little angry with Tom for having behaved so well.

"We've finished our business," Tom said. "Sybil and Ossie are just having one for the road. Here's Ossie."

Ossie Warklock, who emerged from the telephone booth in the entrance at that moment, was a heavily-built man of about fifty with a thick red neck bulging out from a stiff white collar. He was smoking an oval Turkish cigarette.

"I know you, lad," he said, "though you don't know me. Tom

mentioned your name tonight. I was in the Duke of York's with your father. Just mention me to him – he'll remember me. Ask him if he remembers that little lass in Amiens – but don't tell your mother!" He winked.

"My mother's dead."

"I'm sorry," he pulled the corners of his mouth down quickly. "I'm sorry, lad. There's no-one like your mother, lad. I know I'm old enough to be your father – well, of course I am – but I'm not ashamed to tell you I still miss my mother myself. You only have one mother, when all's said and done . . ." He turned towards Tom. "I've phoned him," he said. "It's O.K."

Tom nodded. The smile returned to Warklock's face and he slapped Tom's hand. Tom slapped it in return. "That's fixed it then," he said. "Skipton-fashion, eh? Well, time waits for no man." He pressed the bell on the wall. "The waiter'll get you lads whatever you want," he said. "Come on, Sybil." The next moment they had gone. Tom grinned at Dick.

"Glad you came," he said. "My nerve was beginning to crack. I've practically lived with those bastards for two weeks."

"Who are they?"

Tom snapped his fingers at a passing waiter. "Two double whiskies, please," he said. "And bring a syphon." He leaned back in the basket-work chair and stretched his legs with a sigh of relief. "They're not people, really," he said. "They're Landle and Marco's Stores. Don't ask me what happened to Landle and Marco, because I don't know. Anyway – but keep this under your hat – they're going to sell our new line." He took a note from his wallet as the waiter approached. The waiter shook his head. "Special instructions from Mr. Warklock, sir. You're his guest."

Tom shrugged, and after a second's pause, gave the waiter a shilling.

"He seems a nice chap."

"Ossie? Ossie, a nice chap? Listen, Dick, if you were his best friend, or come to that, his brother, and you were starving, he wouldn't lend you as much as sixpence for a cup of tea and a slice of bread. God, he wouldn't even give you a drink of cold water. But if he thought he could make sixpence profit out of you – why, then, he'd give you everything you wanted. Particularly everything you wanted to drink. Remember Byker?"

"The chap who blew his brains out?"

"He did business with Ossie. Landle and Marco's trick's always the same, you see. Bigger and bigger orders every time; so you expand, so you don't, so you can't, bother about any other customers but them. Then one fine day there *are* no other customers, and they withdraw their order." He drank his whisky and snapped his fingers again. "But I'm not falling for that one, Dick. I put up a front, a bloody good front. Got hold of that Triumph – can't really say I bought it, because I couldn't even afford a kiddy-car cash – got a new suit – hell, I'm dressed new from top to toe. Ossie wanted to make it a big order and God knows we need a big order, but I said no, sorry, Ossie, our order book's full. Export, Ossie. America's crying out for the stuff. I've engaged extra staff but there's only a week's work for them. Every bloody thing's on credit, and I owe a packet—" He laughed. It was a singularly care-free laugh. "I know what you're thinking. You're thinking what a fine time I'm having in my Triumph Razor-Edge and you're wondering if you'll ever see your hundred pounds again. You're sweating, Dicky. So's my bank manager. So are about a hundred other people in Silbridge. So's your future father-in-law; didn't know that, did you? Wants to be a capitalist, does old Matty. My Old Man sold him twenty shares. My clever papa, the Captain of Industry, the only one who never worries." He took out a packet of Rennies. "Not now, anyway. Not since Ossie came, his big mouth wide to welcome the little fishes in . . ."

"I'm not worrying," Dick said.

Tom lit another cigarette and pushed over the open packet to Dick.

"Of course you're not, love. But to hell with business. Let's relax and drink Ossie's whisky. His personal bottle of White Horse. How come you're on your own tonight?"

"She's at night-school."

"When are you getting married?"

"Difficult to say. We were thinking of buying a shop, in Tanbury. Father could live with us. He won't wear it, though."

"What?" Tom sat bolt upright in his chair. "The bloody old fool! Excuse me, Dick, but he is. You tell him to get rid of that shop pretty quick."

"Why?"

"Dick, you'll die poor. Just take my word for it, will you?"

Somehow or other that warning had passed him by; he'd been silly enough again, yet again, to feel sorry for Tom and, because of his relief in discovering that Lois hadn't after all done the dirty on him, he'd drunk rather too much whisky, and then, at Tom's home afterwards, eaten rather too much supper. When he returned at half past eleven to discover his father sitting at the table almost, it seemed, as he'd left him, amongst the still unwashed tea-things, he'd cleared the table and washed up without a word and then said, "I'm sorry, Dad."

"It's me that should be sorry," his father said. "You've been very good, and I know you meant it all for the best. But I was mad at you – you seemed to take too much upon yourself." He swallowed. "I've not been myself lately, Dick. I'd been drinking, I expect you guessed."

"That's all right, Dad. I've seen drunken men before."

"Aye, but not me. I've always liked my glass, but I could always hold it. Well, I'm sorry. That's all I can say."

Dick put his hand on his father's shoulder. "Forget it, Dad."

"You want some supper?"

"I had some at Tom's. I'd like a cup of tea, though."

"What did you have at Tom's?"

"Home-made meat pie and chips and beetroot."

"That's more like it. You hardly had any tea. You mustn't neglect your meals, Dick." And then he started crying; and between comforting him and making tea and persuading him to drink a glass of rum and seeing to it that he himself held down four double whiskies and meat pie and chips and beetroot there hadn't been the opportunity to tell him about Tom's warning; and when winter started he had his own troubles to think about. With the first fogs – and they came early that year – Rita decided to live with him twenty-four hours of the day. For a while he staved her off by cutting down his smoking; but even that, even the great panacea, made no difference. Then one January morning he found himself kneeling by the bath spitting blood. His face wasn't dry and the smell of Palmolive blended with the taste of blood. He dragged himself upright and drank a glass of cold water. He turned on the tap and swilled away the blood – it occurred to him as he looked at it that it couldn't possibly be blood, it was too gaily coloured, just the right shade for a model fire-engine. He brushed his teeth and rinsed his mouth gingerly, not looking at the wash-basin, but keeping the tap running. Then he heard his father rattling the bathroom door. "What is it, Dick? Are you all right?" And he opened it and, when he saw his father looking at him white-faced and staring-eyed, told him the lie which, when he came to think of it, his mother must often have told him, emerging from the same white-tiled Gethsemane.

"I'm all right," he said, gently as if reassuring a child. "Don't worry, Father." And then the cough started again and he tried to suppress it but couldn't and he wanted to be sick but there was nothing on his stomach to bring up, nothing but dark-coloured blood, not half so bright as the blood recently washed away down the bath. And he let himself go, he let himself fall into his father's arms; it was unconditional surrender, he'd stopped fighting, the nerve was broken, the sword snapped across the knees.

Then there was the doctor, loveable beetle-browed old Mifton, the family doctor, telling him that he'd had every symptom except irregular and scanty periods and why the devil hadn't he seen him before, but with these new drugs they'd soon have him better, never fear; and, of course, his loving fiancée Lois, kissing him and saying she wasn't frightened of catching it and putting his hand inside her blouse and then baring her breast – *Oh, my dear one, I've never loved you so much before, you really need me now*—

Dick put his fist in his mouth and bit the first two fingers. He looked at the red marks and then bit the fingers again, worrying them like a dog. "The mucky little bitch," he said, under his breath. "The lying little bitch." *I'll wait for you, my darling, I'll wait for you . . .*

Yes, my darling, I'll wait for you, as long as it's convenient, as long as you remain solvent . . .

He heard footsteps in the passage; he knew that it couldn't be Nurse Mallaton but until the very moment that Nurse Dinston came into the cubicle, pretended that it was.

"Put that bloody light out," Nurse Dinston said. "Want to get me sacked?"

"I'll keep it on if you don't bring me some tea," Dick said.

"I'll think about it. Lie down now, you restless devil."

Dick grinned at him. "You still haven't brought me a nice young virgin."

"Wait and see what God sends you," Nurse Dinston said, leaning over the bed to switch off the bedside lamp. "Goodnight, lad."

"Goodnight," Dick said.

The rain had stopped now and the wind had diminished to a breeze striking fresh and cool on his face. There was a cup of tea coming, he thought, and he could only, after all, die once. His fingers were aching where he'd bitten them; he put his hand against the cool linen sheet. His mother was dead, and no-one could make her die again; Lois had gone and nothing could bring her back. And his father had been right about Tom; the week after Lois had broken off the engagement they were seen together in Tanbury, going into the Raynton, of course. And he'd written a letter to Tom which had, he hoped, penetrated even that thick skin. And now all that remained was to wait for his cup of tea and listen to the rain dripping from the eaves and to think about Nurse Mallaton. "I never cross my heart," she'd said. "You'll just have to take my word." Well, the promise had been easy enough for her to give; she knew she'd never have to honour it. She was sorry for him, he thought savagely, she wasn't thinking of him as a man at all. The anger inside him grew; but this time he realised it wasn't directed at anyone else. It was anger with himself. He understood now what Sergeant Barlby had felt that day he'd lagged behind in the march on the wrong side of the Chindwin. He could still feel the sharp slap across the face, still hear the contempt in that hoarse voice. "One warning, you f—g little nance. You fall behind again and I'll blow your f—g brains out. Now get on!" And he did lag behind again – he was asleep on his feet – but every time he did that hard hand would lash out, that hoarse voice would pour out insults and threats.

That was it then; Corvey, that whining failure, Corvey, had to be driven on, and it didn't matter how it was done. His reason told him that it was hopeless; he was surrounded this time by a worse enemy than the Imperial Army. But he could only drive himself on towards that destination he'd chosen two days ago; and even if he never reached it, at least he'd be going towards a destination he himself had chosen. And that was a beginning, that was something to build upon.

14

THE rattling of the bathroom door rose to a crescendo and Evelyn heard Nurse Fendigo shouting: "Oh do hurry up, Mallaton, you selfish pig."

"Won't be a minute," she shouted back. "I'm not dry yet."

"You've been half-an-hour—" The door began to rattle again. Evelyn sighed and climbed out of the bath. The Nurses' Home had once belonged to the Nedham family: one of its most pleasant features was that one could imagine oneself – whilst in the bathroom anyway – living in a private house. The bath was cast-iron and high-sided, set on a dais, as was the w.c., and the tiled floor and walls were decorated with red and yellow and blue flowers. It wasn't exactly beautiful, and for some reason the hospital authorities hadn't fitted it with a radiator, but at least it wasn't institutional. Or wasn't so until she heard that would-be refined, all-girls-together voice of Fendigo. No, not Fendigo, she thought as she hastily rubbed herself dry: Betty. She'd be damned if she'd go in for that matey, hearty sexless form of address. She was a woman and she wasn't going to pretend otherwise. She looked at herself in the bathroom mirror – B cup and fast approaching C if she didn't cut down on the starches, and very soon a girdle wouldn't be something to hold her stockings up but her belly in . . .

She put on her dressing-gown and walked out of the door past Nurse Fendigo, who stuck her tongue out at her as she passed. Alone in her room, she took off her dressing-gown, powdered herself with French Fern talcum, and lay down on the narrow bed with the white iron frame. She took a Player's from the white deal bedside table and inhaled deeply. Cigarettes, the nurses' friend, together with cups of tea and egg and chips, and probably in later years, snuff. It was very warm in the little room with the plain but bright furnishings; she looked at the orange chintz curtains on the window, the red chintz curtains of the built-in wardrobe, the orange rug, the three cream bookshelves, the cream floorboards with very real hatred. *O chintzy chintzy cheeriness, Half-dead and half-alive* . . . That was very neat; that hit it off exactly.

It was no use feeling sorry for herself, though; she'd have to take a job nearer civilisation. One had to pay for one's romantic impulses: and the desire to help T.B. patients had been all too romantic. So, in the first place, had been the desire to be a nurse. In consequence here she was, unmarried, unengaged, lying pink and floppily naked all by herself to all intents and purposes, wondering whether to keep a date which she knew very well she'd keep because there weren't, as far as she could see, any other men in the district. She could put on her dressing-gown, make a 'phone call, and then she didn't have to see Harry. And the whole wonderful evening would be open to her – a trip to the village pub or tea and buns and TV. in the Staffroom. *All dressed up and nowhere to go*: it was frustrating enough to powder and perfume yourself for a man you'd no intention of letting anywhere near the very places you'd taken the most care with, but it was a hundred times worse to have done it for the benefit, if you could call it that, of your own sex.

It was very warm in the little room with the matchwood partition, a portion of some senior servants' room a hundred years ago: she reached out and opened the window a little, feeling the cool moist air on her naked body. For a moment there was nothing but pleasure, warmth and coolness exactly balancing, her body free and unconstricted; and then she jumped off the bed and began to dress, haunted by a sense of guilt. When finally she was fully dressed and putting on her lipstick she suddenly perceived, cursing herself for it, the reason for her guilt. It wasn't fair for a young woman to lie naked on a bed a few hundred yards away from all those hungry, lost male faces, from men like Dick Corvey. It was cheap of her, she was being not just a tease, but an invisible tease. It was as if she were hitting him in the face as he lay there helpless.

She brought up her lower lip on to the lipsticked upper one and smoothed the outlines of the lipstick with her little finger. That was it. She needn't deceive herself. It wasn't the other men in the sanatorium whose lust bothered her, only Dick, with those ferociously hungry brown eyes – like some family pet's gone mad – and those hands with the long tapering fingers which, if only he were hers, she'd let go wherever they wanted. Just as she wouldn't mind what those hungry brown eyes saw of her.

She bit her lip. It was the sanatorium atmosphere, that queer closed-in atmosphere you got nowhere else in the world, working on her at last. It always caught up with you in the end. She stood up and, squinting over her shoulder, put the seams of her stockings straight. That was it; she hadn't been her usual self ever since that day she'd touched Dick's hand, had started to think of him as a person. Why should the incident stick in her mind a full forty-eight hours afterwards?

It stuck in her mind because – she might as well be honest about it – she was glad it had happened. She was sorry only that there'd never be anything more between them. She found to her irritation that her eyes were moistening. They'd never eat that dinner; the fact of his extracting the promise from her was sufficient proof of its impossibility. She'd seen it before; at the very last, with, at the longest, six months to live, they believed that they were going to recover, they started to make plans for the future, and their masculinity flared up again. She needn't be flattered by his interest: any young woman would serve the same purpose for him. He didn't care about her, Eve Mallaton, as a person, as a human being; his mind was with that bitch of a fiancée of his, who'd ditched him as soon as she found out he wasn't going to recover.

And that was yet another feature of sanatorium life which she felt she wasn't going to be able to take much longer – the betrayals, the lack of love, the broken engagements and the divorces, the kicking of men already down. But most men hadn't Dick's capacity for being hurt, most men wouldn't allow a woman to hurt them so deeply. He was living in the past all the time now;

those large brown eyes were seeing only what had happened in the past. But, she reminded herself, he hadn't been looking in the past the morning he'd quoted that poem . . .

Angrily, she lit another cigarette. It proved nothing except that she was frightened of becoming an old maid; and that Dick Corvey, like most men, wouldn't lose interest in women until the lid of his coffin was screwed down.

She heard the sound of a car engine from the drive; that would be him, dead on time as usual. She took out her best coat, the Harris tweed which had cost her a month's salary, and gathered up her handbag.

As she went down the long corridor to the staircase, walking slowly because the worn coconut matting was apt to catch high heels, she saw Nurse Fendigo emerging from the bathroom, her round cheeks rosy.

"Is it Harry again?" Nurse Fendigo asked.

"There's no-one else," Evelyn said.

"You're lucky," Nurse Fendigo said. "I can never find a man in Nedham."

"You can have Harry if you like," Evelyn said.

Nurse Fendigo giggled. "I may take you up on it," she said as Evelyn turned away. "Good men are scarce."

The words were still in Evelyn's head when she was sitting beside Harry in the car: *good men are scarce.* She glanced at the tall narrow outline of Block M2 and found herself wondering what Dick Corvey was thinking about at this moment. And she was surprised at the vehemence of the feeling – she hoped that it wasn't about that fiancée of his, that sensible girl who hadn't wanted to throw her life away on a sick man. She hoped that he was thinking of her instead; she couldn't get those eyes, those hungry brown eyes, and those white listless hands out of her mind. For no good reason, she felt a sense of betrayal; she had no business to be riding beside Harry, dressed to kill and smelling of French Fern. It was as if she were on the side of Dick's ex-fiancée, among the strong and healthy and sensible members of the pack, running happily ahead.

Harry's voice broke into her thoughts. "Penny for 'em, old girl."

She took her mind away from Dick with an effort.

"Good men are scarce," she said, and saw him grin.

"That's worth sixpence," he said, and handed her the coin. He turned into the London Road and the car gathered speed instantly.

"Lovely engine," he said. "I'm going to tune it up one day and give some of these blighters in M.G.'s a shock. Light me a cigarette, will you, Eve? They're in my pocket."

She took out the packet of Player's and lit one for him, feeling that it wasn't his kind of gesture; it was the sort of thing which Tyrone Power was always doing in white tie and tails before the war. Harry was the pipe-smoking Jack Hawkins type, or at least would be if only his face were less cheerfully smooth and immature, smooth and immature despite the heavy chin and big nose and hard pale eyes.

"I'm ravenous," she said.

"We'll have to do something about that," he said. "How about a bite in Leeds?"

"It's too far, Harry. You won't have enough petrol."

"No trouble," he said. "Bought two old heaps today. Just junk really, a '28 Chrysler and a '27 Essex. But I'll draw a ration for each of 'em."

"I fancy the Raynton," she said.

"Bit near home."

"Why should that matter?" she said sharply.

"Don't be silly, old girl. Just thought you'd fancy a little drive out, that's all. Tanbury's not a very gay place."

She put a hand on his knee. "I'm terribly hungry, Harry, and it's the nearest place. But you needn't take me there if you don't want to."

"Anything you want, midear. But don't blame me if you don't like your dinner. Place has gone downhill lately." He drove on in silence, his big red hands and the mat of black hairs – looking at them she again remembered those beautiful ineffectual white hands back at Nedham – holding the steering wheel with surprising delicacy.

When they had passed the Darton Parish Church and the car was climbing towards Mapplewell, the apocalyptic glare of the coke furnaces on their right the only warmth in the cold blackness around them, she was seized with a terrible sterile loneliness. Harry, giving only a perfunctory glance to his left, turned the car to the right, its brakes screaming; and the harsh metallic sound, as if beings of another species whom one couldn't possibly help, were being made to suffer because of someone's sheer callousness, helped to accentuate that loneliness. And the way in which Harry had received her suggestion of the Raynton for dinner helped to give her a sort of emotional hysterectomy too; it didn't and it never should matter where they ate together.

It wouldn't for instance matter if Dick Corvey were driving that car tonight instead of Harry. He'd be delighted to take her anywhere, anywhere at all, and be proud of her into the bargain. It wouldn't matter, she thought as Harry put his foot down again driving through Sandal, if Dick hadn't even got a car, if they were changing buses again for the third time, holding hands on the rackety bus, not just worrying about how they'd reach the Raynton but how they'd get back. If she'd been with Dick, it would have been a question of two people out together; now it was a question of a machine, which might or might not break down – though she knew very well that it wouldn't – and herself and Harry. And Harry – the car stopped with a jerk by the Chantry Bridge and then nosed left – wasn't out *together* with her. He wanted her mouth and her newly-washed hair and her breasts and her ankles and no doubt even more; but he didn't really want Evelyn Mallaton. Within five minutes, if not less, she'd become as far as he was concerned, merely another lump of easily-bought flesh. And she was something better than that, she thought resentfully, looking at his face, now turned positively babyish by a faint scowl and a pushed-out upper lip.

It was warm in the car; she slipped the tweed coat from her shoulders and saw his glance flicker sideways at her nylon blouse.

"That's very pretty," he said.

"You don't miss much," she said.

He grinned, his good humour regained. "It's a public menace," he said. "I'm not looking where I'm going any more."

"I'll put my coat on again," she said.

"No, no. I'll just peek at you when we're on well-lit stretches."

He put out his left arm and squeezed her shoulders. "Pity the car can't drive itself," he said, and guffawed. He put back his arm almost immediately; but her shoulders still seemed to bear its weight even when she entered the hotel twenty minutes later. And the trouble was, she admitted to herself, that she'd enjoyed it, that for two pins she'd have made some excuse for him to stop the car.

When they took their seats in the dining-room it was evident that Harry had been to the Raynton before: the waiter took their order immediately, disregarding another couple at the next table. "It's so nice to see you again, sir," he said breathily. "We've some nice pâté, I can thoroughly recommend it . . . And there's a beautiful piece of undercut . . ." He went through the menu with Harry, his eyes having slid over Evelyn with a faint contempt. Suddenly the big room felt stuffy: there was too much food and drink there and too much talk about food and drink. Harry was altogether too fussy about it, showing off a bit too much choosing the wines. "I think we'll have that Beaune, Sillson, though I know the lady would rather have something sweeter . . . Yes, and the Liebfraumilch, and don't for God's sake freeze it . . ." And he was nearly as bad when the Beaune came, sending it back because it was too cold and then when it came back, taking a sip and saying testily that he hadn't asked them to mull it. He was quite right, she knew; of course the waiters should be made to do their job properly, of course the red wine should be at room temperature and the white wine cool; but she found it difficult to enjoy either the food or wine as much as she'd imagined she would. But she ate it all, nevertheless, to Harry's approval – "Like to see a girl enjoy her meals, Eve. Can't bear waste. Some girls just pick at their food – silly bitches think it's ladylike." He pushed back his chair. "We'll have coffee in the lounge, Sillson. And I'll have a large brandy – Hennessy if you've got it. And the lady" – the waiter looked at her inquiringly but Eve saw again that faint twist of the mouth which indicated that the waiter knew very well what she was and it wasn't a lady – "will have a Cointreau – that was the final choice, wasn't it, Eve?"

"I thought you said the place had gone downhill lately," she said as she sipped her Cointreau in the lounge.

Harry laughed, a little thickly; he had drunk most of the wine. "You know how it is," he said. "You've a hard day at the mill, you eat a meal here feeling out of sorts to begin with, something's not just to your liking, so you're prejudiced forever afterwards. Mind you, I'm fond of this place; it used to be one of my brother Keith's favourite stalking-grounds." He looked around the room, beginning with the maroon fitted carpeting and ending with the glass chandelier, as if it were a room in his own home; his face for a second crumpled into a grotesque sadness. "Poor old Keith, poor old Keith . . ."

"Your brother?"

"Yes, I told you, didn't I?"

"You did, Harry. I wasn't thinking."

He brought the edge of his hand down on the table. "Out like a light," he said. "Just like that. The Old Man had just died, and Keith had the whole burden to carry, and he simply wasn't strong enough. And now" – he looked at Evelyn as if she were a deputation he were calling to order – "the burden's on my shoulders. It's no easy one, Evie, it's no easy one—" He wagged his head solemnly.

A young man walked over and slapped him between the shoulders. "Harry Thirleton!" he said. "What a surprise, eh? You're as fat and boozy as ever, Harry." He stood over them, swaying slightly.

"Sit down, Vernon," Harry said. "You make me feel dizzy."

"Can't, old man, got a girl with me. My intended, actually."

"Bring her over," Harry said. "Let me buy you a drink to celebrate."

"I see she's on her way," the young man said. "She's not the sort of girl to sit on her tod for long." His eyes wandered over Evelyn's body, finally stopping at the cleft between her breasts. "You still haven't any manners, Harry. Introduce me."

"Evelyn Mallaton," Harry said. "Vernon Lunkett. And rapidly approaching us to see what Vernon's up to, Molly Stridd."

He leapt up and took hold of the hands of the girl approaching the table. "She's mad. Marrying Vernon, just imagine. Well, sit down both of you, for God's sake, and let's have something to drink."

He was happy and expansive amongst his own kind, the tall young man with the barathea blazer and the gold wrist watch, the rather cold-eyed girl with the Paris dress and the real pearls; and she wasn't one of their kind. Beside the girl she felt a little flustered and disarranged, the peekaboo blouse which had seemed such a good idea originally now seemed vulgar, a barmaid's uniform; she received surreptitious glances for the rest of the evening from both the men but there was neither admiration nor envy in the girl's face; she was perfectly polite, but she looked at her much as the waiter had done.

When Harry stopped the car on the lane off the London Road where he always stopped it, she felt an enormous boredom and disgust with him and herself.

The boredom and disgust extended to the car in which she'd been so often glad to sit these last three months; it was warm and comfortable, it would take you anywhere you wanted, but what if there were nowhere you wanted to go? And just now it was no more than a stuffy little room in some house of assignation, a stuffy little room where a naughty little girl who wore peekaboo blouses paid for the dinner the kind gentleman had given her.

Harry said abruptly and in a half-embarrassed tone: "You were the best-looking girl there tonight. The nicest too."

She was enormously touched; instantly the car became a car again, and she and he were human beings.

"You're sweet, Harry," she said and twisted round in the seat to put out her arm, stroking the nape of his neck gently, feeling with a premonition of pleasure the crisp shaven hair.

"Used to like girls like Molly," he said. "But they're so stupid – they haven't an idea in their heads but clothes and dancing and new watches and cigarette-lighters and rings – hell, if she'd showed off that bloody Dunhill just once more I'd have walked out."

He leaned towards her and kissed her. And, despairingly almost, she found herself enjoying it; there was so much of him, his hands were so hard and now that he was excited she could smell what was far better than any after-shave lotion or cologne, his sweat, harsh and male. After a while his hand moved to her breast, passed over it lightly, then moved under her skirt. Her whole body became lax and soft despite herself; then a car passed on the London Road and its headlights momentarily revealed his flushed face with the sweat gleaming on it and her skirt rucked up to the stocking stops. She saw herself suddenly through his eyes: the nurse I'm going around with, wonderful little bit of stuff once she's warmed up. Cost me four quid for her dinner at the Raynton, but it was worth every penny . . .

She sat up, pulling her skirt down.

"The back seat's more comfortable," Harry said thickly.

"No," she said. "Take me back to the hospital, will you?"

Without a word he started the car and turned into London Road again. She could see that he was angry and felt half-sorry for him. He had, to do him justice, behaved better than she had; the time for her to stop him had been the moment he put his hand under her skirt, not ninety slow seconds after. And he hadn't protested about having been led on, he hadn't pointed out how much money he'd spent on her, he hadn't tried to either wheedle or force her into submission.

The car purred up the hospital drive; she felt disarranged, unwashed despite her bath, and draggingly tired. She had had a good dinner, she'd been given a taste of luxury, she'd wanted to escape the atmosphere of the sanatorium for an evening and she'd done so. And she hadn't done anything that she'd regret, she hadn't been taken in again as she had been with Hicknall. And she wasn't happy, she wasn't satisfied and she felt so lonely that she could have wept then and there.

She stood at the door of the Nurses' Home for a minute after Harry's car had gone out of sight, her hands thrust deep in her pockets. It was cold for March; winter stayed late in the hills around Nedham. The air tasted clean and fresh after being in the car and the hotel, she took deep gulps of it gratefully.

"I'll phone you," Harry had said when he left her; she knew what that meant. And she didn't care. Unbidden, instantly categorised as silly and sentimental, there came to her the thought: *if he doesn't want me, I know who does.*

The light over the big arched doorway went out; she ran inside and walked quickly down the corridor, her feet tapping the black lino in almost a skipping rhythm.

15

Rock put his hand on Basil's bare chest. "What a lovely pair," he said. "Just like a woman's."

"Chuck it," Basil said. "It's too damned hot."

He folded his arms across his chest, then had to take his hand away to mop the sweat from his forehead. He sat down on the wooden bench against the wall and squirmed. "Even the damned bench's hot," he grumbled.

Rock paced the drab little green-distempered room restlessly, his crêpe-soled suède shoes, mangy like the skin of an old tiger, hitting the grey concrete floor with a curiously irritating softness, the rubber detaching itself with a sound on the verge of a hiss. He stopped finally beside Stevie Kidanski, slumped forward on the brown varnished bench in a long-sleeved woollen vest, and shouted at him. "We wait, Stevie, we wait. Eh?"

"Me not like X-rays," Stevie said. "Doctor say: You are stupid. Me not like X-rays still."

Rock made as if to cuff him, then took another half-dozen steps up and down the room. "You hear that?" he said. "Mr. Kidanski doesn't like X-rays."

He pulled a handkerchief from his pocket and with it a half-crown which dropped on the floor. He stooped to pick it up; when he straightened his back he grunted with pain. "That bloody P. P.," he said. "Redroe put two thousand in me this morning, I'll swear he did."

"He's dead rough," Peter said. He pointed to the patch of dried blood on his belly.

Stevie looked at him with frightened eyes. "Me no like needles," he said.

Tom Dellable, a Woodbine held in his cupped hand, suddenly guffawed. "You've come to the wrong place then," he said. "They haven't even started with you yet, Stevie."

"We wait," Rock said. "We bloody well wait. They send us here in the hell of a flap, and then when we get here the radiologist hasn't come."

"You've plenty of time," Basil said. He had folded his arms over his chest again; he had folded his shirt and vest and jacket and put them behind him to act as a cushion; he now appeared perfectly cool and at ease, a solid citizen drowsing in a comfortable armchair.

"You look like some fat old Buddha there," Rock said.

"You're probably quite right," Basil said. "He's here now anyway. I know his walk."

Tom Dellable hastily snuffed his cigarette and waved his shirt to dispel the smoke. The radiologist, a pale young man with short bristling hair and a pink bow tie, walked into the Screening Room without looking at the five men.

Hard on his heels, Nurse Kanley pushed in Dick's wheelchair.

"Hello, you stinkers," Dick said. He was wearing a new dressing-gown in navy-blue wool with white pipings and a blue polka-dot rayon scarf. "Basil, you're revoltingly fat."

"I'm going to have another op," Basil said.

"They'll never be able to cut through all that blubber, man." He turned to Rock. "By the way, what about that game of chess you promised me?"

"Thought you'd lost interest," Rock said.

"Well, I haven't. Come over this afternoon." His eyes were very bright, he radiated a febrile energy; and the new dressing-gown and the neatly-folded scarf gave him a drawing-room comedy smartness.

"How you doing anyway?" Rock asked.

"I'm saying goodbye to the bedpan tomorrow," Dick said. "But they're sticking to the letter of the law, so this big lummox still has to push me around as if I were a cripple. Does him good; he's nearly as fat and flabby as you, Basil."

"I'll bash you when you're a Taskman, Corvey," Kanley said in his high tenor voice.

The radiologist came to the door of the Screening Room and gestured towards Dick.

"There you are," Kanley said. "You get priority, mate. You'll be sorry when you haven't me to look after you." He pushed the wheelchair towards the Screening Room, automatically lowering his shaggy head as he went through the door.

"Dick looks better," Tom Dellable said, lowering his voice.

"When we were on M2 with him he was up an hour each day," Rock said. "He ebbs and flows with the seasons, does Dick."

"Shut up," Basil said. "He'll hear you."

There was an uneasy silence over the room until Dick emerged, still cheerful. "That's about my hundredth since I got the Bug," he said. "I'll be shining in the dark soon . . ."

"Stop yattering," Nurse Kanley said. "Come on, your car's waiting."

When they emerged into the sunlight, Dick saw Nurse Fendigo approach them from the Administration Block. She was walking jauntily, a half-smile on her face as if contemplating her own attractions – her black springy hair, her round bosom, her rosy face. Dick put his finger in the corner of his mouth and whistled. "Hey! Are there any more at home like you?" he shouted.

She didn't answer, but she winked; Dick, in an unconscious preening gesture, ran his hand over his hair and adjusted his scarf. Nurse Kanley abruptly pushed him up the let-down tailboard of the ambulance; when he'd fastened it again and closed the door he shook his fist at Dick.

"Leave her alone, you dwarfish Casanova," he said. "That's my girl. I'll have 'em put bromide in your tea if you try that on again."

He was smiling as he said it; but Dick detected the note of jealousy in his voice.

"I can't help it if I'm better looking than you," he said, looking through the blue-tinted window of the ambulance with a mounting exultance. He didn't really care about Nurse Fendigo; but her wink and that unmistakable jealousy of Kanley's meant a lot: it was as if negotiations were afoot, negotiations with the object of giving him back his manhood.

16

"MATE," Dick said.

"No," Rock said.

"It is, you clot. Look again."

"It's a fluke," Rock said. "You didn't know what you were doing."

"I always know exactly what I'm doing," Dick said. "You should have gone after my bishop, not my rook." He yawned and stretched himself; the sheets had been changed that morning and their smooth, cool freshly-ironed texture hadn't yet completely worn off; they added to his sensation of well-being in much the same way as his victory with that absolutely inspired sacrifice of his rook had done. He brought out a box of Terry's All Gold from his locker.

"Have a chocolate," he said. "Better for you than cigarettes."

"My father doesn't have a sweet shop," Rock said. "I can't get a quarter a day."

Dick laughed. "Mine won't have a sweet shop so much longer," he said. "He's scheduled for redevelopment."

"So what?" Rock said. "You bloody shopkeepers are always all right."

"My Old Man's not," Dick said. "Someone's leaked the details of the redevelopment plan – mind you, someone's been leaking the details for long enough – so the property's not worth more than a hundred now."

"Ah, come off it," Rock said disgustedly. "You're always the same. Made a fortune during the war and you're still making one – you can't expect it to last forever, mate."

Dick felt his enjoyment of the afternoon, of the fresh sheets, of his victory at chess, even the taste of the chocolate in his mouth, diminish. He hadn't really thought about the shop lately; he'd thought that at least that particular bruise – the last kick in the ribs to the fallen man – had healed.

And Rock's attitude – almost as if he were glad that his father would soon lose his livelihood – made it no easier to bear. He looked at Rock coldly. "Listen," he said. "The Council's got a redevelopment plan. They're pulling down all the buildings in that area. My father's ruined. What the bloody hell d'you mean he's alright?"

Rock shifted uneasily in his chair. "Ah, forget it, Dicky. I'm sorry." He lit a cigarette. "Finished with this *Lilliput*?"

"Yes, you scrounging sod."

Rock sat for a minute in silence, leafing through the photographs. "Hell, look at this," he said. "They just print these damned things to torment poor devils like us . . ." He put the magazine down. "There's no point in working yourself up about it, Dick," he said. "Those Councils – they just do whatever they like with you. Nothing can alter 'em. They're like the bloody Government – whichever lot's in power it's all the same in the end. Somebody'll make a packet out of it." He picked up the magazine and went out. "I'll give you a trouncing tomorrow," he said.

"That's what you think," Dick said, grinning; but he had to force the grin. It was the old story again: pity, patronising, sickly, rotten pity. No-one would even argue with him properly, not even Rock, the most argumentative man in the hospital; they didn't want to hurt the feelings of a dying man. Whoever the Vodi had put its mark upon was sacred, a being apart.

He felt the old familiar hopelessness descend upon him; he opened the lid of the sputum cup and spat the chocolate into it. Even if he got his discharge, what was there for him to go home to? The shop was going downhill anyway; he knew that when his father sold the Morris. And probably the fact of his having the Bug had helped to shove it downhill quicker. People weren't keen on buying sweets from a place where a consumptive had lived.

Then he saw Nurse Mallaton pass; he didn't push away the hopelessness by an act of will, but felt it lift despite himself.

"Evelyn!" he shouted.

She put her finger to her lips and came to his bedside. "Don't call me Evelyn when there's anybody about," she said. "Matron's awfully sticky about it." She smiled at him. "I'm not sure whether I'm friends with you any more," she said. "You've been making eyes at Nurse Fendigo."

"*She* made eyes at me. It's my new dressing-gown; I'm irresistible."

"That's no excuse. I'm very jealous. You do it just once more, Dick, and our dinner date's off." Her voice was gentle but there was no hint of pity in it. She was looking at him as a man; and once she'd reached that point, he knew that she couldn't return.

"I've gained six pounds," he said. "Let's work out that dinner menu now."

"When you've gained eight pounds more, we'll work out what we're going to eat," she said. "And when you've gained another stone, we'll decide what we're going to drink." She leaned over him to look at the chess-board on the bed-table. "Who won?"

"Me."

She pointed to the black king's knight. "If he'd moved that you'd have been in trouble." She straightened her back; as she did so his fingers brushed her bare forearm. He saw her shiver and bite her lip.

"Sorry," he said quickly.

She smiled again. "What are you sorry about, silly?" She leaned over the chess-board again.

"I've got three brothers," she said. "They were all mad about chess, so I had to learn too." He looked at her forearm, the golden down on it gleaming in the sun; gently and deliberately he stroked it. She took it away slowly. "I must go now," she said. She stopped at the doorway. "That's nice after-shave lotion you're using now," she said. He gaped at her and then to his surprise, her amused eyes upon him, found his face reddening.

17

Waiting in the queue outside the Examination Room in the hall of Block A Dick felt the usual tension in the pit of his stomach. It was raining again; the steady drumming accentuated his nervousness.

"They're the hell of a time with Rock," he said peevishly to Basil.

Basil brought his eyes away from a girl who was running, a bright red plastic mackintosh over her head, over to the Administration Block. "The new typist," he said. "Took my pension form over there yesterday and caught her fastening her stocking. Lovely legs she has."

"You're over-hormoned," Dick said impatiently.

"Can't help it if I am," Basil said. His mouth twisted as if holding back a smile. "How's Nurse Mallaton, by the way?"

"You mean Evelyn," the Schoolmaster said. He put his finger to the knot of his Royal Artillery tie. "Evelyn's fine; she told me so herself. Clever girl, that. Had a chat with her when I had my refill yesterday."

"I hope it goes down into your southern regions next time," Dick said.

"Naughty, naughty," the Schoolmaster said. It occurred to Dick as he looked at him that he looked rather like Tom, except that his features were more regular. In fact, he was so proud of his profile that he turned his head sideways far more often than was strictly necessary. He was doing it now, looking at the Administration Block, his head tilted slightly upwards.

"What are you looking at, Chas?" he asked. "You'll get your neck jammed in that position if you're not careful."

"Don't be so ridiculous," the Schoolmaster snapped, jerking his head to the front. Dick's jealousy suddenly evaporated; to jeer at the Schoolmaster's pet vanity was like peering at a little boy in his cowboy outfit.

"There's nothing there, Chas," he said. "That's what I mean. No need to be huffy."

He looked gloomily through the plate-glass swing-door, and then, for the third time that morning, at the notice-board. "It's done nothing but rain since I got put on Six Hours," he said. "When I was on Absolute, the sun seemed to be cracking the flagstones every day."

"There you are," Basil said. "You should have stayed where you were. Absolute Rest, warm and cosy, with Nurse Mallaton to fetch bedpans and bottles for you. And now she's far away in M2. You were too eager to transfer, boy."

The door of the Examination Room opened, and Rock came

out. He gave the thumbs-up sign. "Two months from today, and I'll be a free man!" he shouted, and started shaking hands with the others. "Eighteen months' hard that'll be. God, when I look back, I can't think how I stood it."

"Back to the old job then?" Dick asked.

"I've not worked that out yet. Hinstock's not keen on it." The cheerfulness vanished from his face. "I'll find something. Plenty of time to worry about that." There was a brief silence. It was like leaving school, Dick thought; you wanted to do nothing else from the moment you first went there, but as the day approached, the outside world seemed colder and colder. He saw Rock's eyes flicker round the hall with its lime-green distempered walls and parquet floor, green baize notice board and vase of carnations on the ledge above the radiator and fancied that he detected regret in them.

But that wasn't his own worry at the moment; he was thinking about the post-war settlement instead of the campaign itself. Hinstock had seemed doubtful about giving him that six hours; he was notorious for his cautiousness and had no scruples about putting anyone back on Absolute from even eight. And there was that damned X-ray, that last deep X-ray; the old devil would be gleefully spotting fresh patches at this very moment . . .

When Sister Lardress called him into the Examination Room he went in as if to a court martial, holding himself rigidly so that he wouldn't tremble. The green baize blinds were drawn and Dr. Hinstock was peering at an X-ray plate on the frame on the desk. There was a smell of iodoform and surgical spirits and, emanating from Hinstock himself, a smell of cigars. Sister Lardress was standing by the desk with a dossier which Dick saw was his own; Redroe was sitting beside Dr. Hinstock, his face frowning and intent. "You see," Hinstock said. "Absolutely unmistakable. Couldn't be worse." He looked up at Dick. "Sit down, Mr. Corvey. What have I told you hundreds of times, eh? Never stand when you can sit." He scratched his head with extraordinary energy and said resentfully: "I'm very pleased with you, Mr. Corvey. You've done very well! Yes, you've done very well!" He scratched his head again. "I don't often say it, you know – it's a most vague way of expressing oneself – but you've made wonderful progress. I've just looked at some of your earlier X-rays – only twelve months ago – and the difference is incredible. Particularly since you're allergic to drugs."

Redroe in a brisk A.D.C. tone said: "Surely, sir, it's easy to understand. Trudeau's treatment's still the best. If you stick to the rules. You've said so often yourself."

"Ah, yes, Mr. Corvey obviously has stuck to the rules. Rest, a balanced diet and fresh air. Splendid."

"How much nearer am I to my discharge?" Dick asked.

Hinstock looked shocked. "We won't talk about that yet," he said. "It'll be a long time before you get on that Tuesday morning bus" – he pronounced the s of bus as if it were z, a mispronunciation which was oddly touching – "a long time indeed. We must proceed with care, Mr. Corvey. Still, are you ready for all day?"

"Any time, Doctor."

Hinstock scribbled a note on the card beside the X-ray holder. "Right. As from tomorrow, Mr. Corvey. Walk, not run. And keep on building your weight up. Good-day, Mr. Corvey."

When Dick had gone Hinstock pulled at his upper lip thoughtfully. "Some would say I was rushing him," he said. "He's come a long way in five months. But I know I'm right. I'm still puzzled, though."

Redroe said. "Surely it's a classic case? You know the boy's background? He got T.B. because his W.T.L. – will to live, I mean – was broken; his W.T.L. reasserted itself and then it was broken again. And now for some reason it's reasserted itself. It happened recently in America—"

"I read the *Lancet* too, Dr. Redroe," Hinstock said. "It was a pretty little story. Highly romantic." He smiled at Sister Lardress. "You know Corvey's case very well, Sister. Would you agree with Dr. Redroe?"

"Yes, Dr. Hinstock. Definitely I would."

"Ah, you don't think that this magnificent fibrosis here and here" – he pulled out another X-ray plate – "is the result of his P.P.? Or of rest, a balanced diet and fresh air?"

"They're very important, Doctor. But I still think that it's the will to live that counts. It's been awakened—" She stopped.

Hinstock wagged a bony finger at her. "Sister, do I detect a trace of embarrassment? Have you stimulated this young man's W.T.L.? I'm surprised at you; you know what Matron says to all the new nurses . . ."

He laughed. "Well, who knows? It's a very queer disease. Bring in Rinkler, will you, Sister?"

Evelyn was entering up the Ward Supply Returns when Dick went into the Sister's office on the top floor of Ward M2. He gave her his news like an expensive present.

"That's wonderful," she said. "Absolutely wonderful. I'm so glad for you, Dick."

"Nelly must be relenting," he said unthinkingly.

"Nelly?"

"Forget it. It's just a game Tom and I used to play when we were kids. My *friend* Tom."

"Tell me," she said.

"It'd take too long. I haven't thought about it lately." He wanted to add *Not since I met you*; but an odd shyness held him back.

"Don't be so mean," she said. "Tell me, please, Dick." To her disgust her voice was taking on a wheedling, sugary note; she was never in control of herself when she met Dick, she was always the Little Woman, almost the Pretty Little Nursie of masculine folklore. And the worst of it was that she didn't mind; he was so undisputably masculine, those large brown eyes always looked at her properly.

"Nelly runs the Vodi," Dick said. "That's all."

The word made her shiver; it seemed somehow to contradict the even healthy colour in his cheeks, the air of suppressed energy which he had about him lately.

"It isn't all," she said.

Dick looked away from her through the bow window at the dark dripping pines which bordered the Circle.

"Some people do everything that they should," he said. "Never do anyone any harm, and they're always unlucky. Everything goes wrong for them—" There was a note of self-pity in his voice now that she didn't like; his masculinity was diminished by it, became no more real masculinity than the red crinkled paper in the fireplace of the office was a real fire. He paused. "You know that, don't you, Eve? The decent people always get it in the neck. And the real swine, the selfish ones, always have good luck. They're favoured always. Well, it isn't an accident."

"You didn't work all this out when you were children."

"No, I don't suppose we did," he said with surprise. "We just had this idea of the horrible fat old woman and the gang. All of them looking exactly the same – little ferret-faced men with eyes that shone in the dark. I told you, it was only a kid's game. We never thought it was real, I don't now." He grinned at her, and suddenly his masculinity was real again, the fire was blazing away. "I'm not dippy, Eve."

"I know you're not. But you feel things too much, Dick."

Yes, she thought, and isn't that a good way to be? She remembered other men she'd known – the clever empty ones, the animal empty ones, all of them in their own way calculating and mean, with no warmth to give any other human being.

She looked at her watch. "Oh Lord," she said. "Only five minutes to Rest. You'll have to hurry to get back to A Block."

"I'll see you again," he said.

"Oh, yes," she said. "I'll see you again."

He put his cap on and turned up the collar of his trench-coat. "Eve," he said, "I've never told anyone about the Vodi before."

She sat still for a moment, happily bemused.

She sighed, and took the big brass handbell from the desk. Standing at the open door she rang it vigorously. The phrase *Bell, book and candle* ran through her mind; she rang as if to exorcise Nelly but also to celebrate the fact that he'd told her, and no-one else, told her, she realised because he knew she'd understand. So there weren't five hundred people in the hospital now: there were only two. She returned to her desk and finished the returns quickly, then returned to her happy bemusement, her pen in her hand and the folder open so that it wouldn't be too obvious that she wasn't working.

When Sister Lardress came in, she didn't look up; her mind was still with Dick.

"Anything to report, Nurse?"

"No – no, I think not," Evelyn said in confusion. "I've finished the Returns."

Sister Lardress hung up her wet cape and stood by the empty fireplace.

"You don't *think* there's nothing to report, Nurse," she said. "There's either nothing to report or something to report."

"There's nothing to report, Sister."

"Good." She sat down heavily. "My poor feet. I'll really have to go on a diet. In sanatoriums you always eat too much. It's the monotony."

She looked down. "You wouldn't think there was a doormat here," she said. "After poor Jackie spent a full hour polishing the floor, too. Have you been having visitors from Block A?"

"Dick Corvey said hello," Evelyn said. With any other Sister she'd have told a lie; but Sister Lardress, unlike so many of her kind, wasn't a bitch. And because she wasn't a bitch, even a white lie would have been insulting to her.

"I thought he'd tell you his news," Sister Lardress said in a neutral tone. "He's done marvellously well in five months."

"Hasn't he? I was terribly pleased."

"Doctor Hinstock can't really understand it. After all the trouble he had with drugs there didn't seem much hope. And now – it's not very far from a miracle. That's what Dr. Hinstock doesn't like. So I left him talking about the psychosomatic element in T.B."

"It's always there, Sister."

"Yes," Sister Lardress said, "but behind the word there's people. In the case of men, it's women." She rose with an effort. "I'd better see what's happening in the kitchen," she said. "You'd do well to remember one thing, Evelyn dear; it's as easy to fall in love with a healthy man as a sick man. I know." Her voice turned harsh. "I shouldn't say it, of course I shouldn't say it – but do you want to be a nurse *all* your life? An unpaid nurse?"

18

"It was nice of you to send that card," Harry said as the V8 climbed out of Mapplewell towards Wakefield.

She looked at him with affection. Any other man would have seen through the device; short of her writing him to say she was sorry – and she couldn't very well say that she was sorry – it had been her only way of getting him back.

"I always remember birthdays," she said.

"Don't know how you do it. I only remember Mummy's birthday" – the childish diminutive dropped easily from his lips – "and even then I make entries in my diary weeks beforehand so I won't forget."

She stretched out her legs, hearing with pleasure the rustle of her stiff petticoats. Suddenly the worry of the last few weeks had lifted, she wasn't faced with choices any longer, she knew exactly what she would try to do. She'd been on the point of committing herself to Dick, and to all the complications of a hospital love affair – the letters in place of conversations, the meetings – if you were lucky – in an empty cubicle but more often on the ward, virtually in public; and even then you had to be careful; there were always other eyes upon you, you couldn't even risk an endearment or the squeeze of a hand. And both of you were jealous, jealous of the staff, jealous of other patients; and the man couldn't bear to see you go out of the hospital into a world he couldn't share; and when you went out you weren't free any more, you were, you might say, neither maid, wife nor widow. And if it did come to anything in the end then, as Sister Lardress pointed out, you remained a nurse, you remained a nurse all your life.

She put her hand on Harry's shoulder, feeling the bulge of muscle under the smooth cloth. He shouldn't really wear a checked suit with his figure, she thought – but then why should he attempt to disguise his bigness?

"It's lovely to be out with you again," she said.

"Lovely to be with you," he said. "By God, you're what my old

Nanny used to call a bobby-dazzler in that dress. Did you buy it in my honour?"

"Don't ask questions," she said. "And keep your eyes on the road."

"You're always telling me that," he said, changing down to pass a Deira Services bus. "Where shall we go this afternoon anyway? Tanbury and tea at the Raynton, then a flick?"

"No, not the Raynton," she said. "I'm not all that fond of it." For a moment the sun seemed to shine too brightly, the boats on Wintersett Lake seemed too gaily coloured, Harry seemed too large and breezy and pinkly smooth-shaven; it was as if some crack regiment were marching to war against a handful of children with tin swords. "Let's go to Wakefield," she said. "I love the market there."

"Wakefield? Fine. We'll have a drink at the Castle first. About time you tried a Pimm's." He started to sing in a surprisingly tuneful baritone voice. *"Sur le pont d'Avignon . . ."*

"I didn't know you could sing," she said. "In French too!"

He gave her a quick malicious glance. "We woolmen aren't quite illiterate, you know. Thirleton's has an associate in France." He grinned complacently; he had scored one over her. And, she thought, he was so healthy, so self-confident, so triumphantly justified in his harmless conceit, that she didn't mind at all.

At the end of the day when they were driving to Tanbury she said to him out of a sudden impulse of fairness:

"I'm glad your birthday's in August. I don't know what I'd have done if it hadn't been."

"You needn't tell me," he said. "I'm not as dumb as I look." His voice was pleased.

It's as easy to fall in love with a healthy man as a sick man; the words came back to her. "It was all my fault," she said. "I shouldn't have let things go so far."

He didn't answer but his eyes scanned the road from left to right. He pulled into a narrow lane and stopped by a gap in the drystone wall. He opened the door, walked round to the other side, and held out his hand to Evelyn. She took it gratefully; the strength for the moment seemed to have gone out of her legs. The ground was rough – stones and short harsh turf – and Harry put his arm round her waist.

"Thought I remembered the place," he said. "Haven't been here for years." He jumped through the gap, landing noiselessly, then helped her through it. The field sloped down gradually, then levelled out and before them they saw the lights of Tanbury on the ridge.

"It's not much in the daytime," Harry said. "Too many pitheads and mills. But I like to see the lights. You'd never think it was such a damned ugly place when you saw those lights in the valley."

She put her arms round his neck, feeling free and cool and weightless in the taffeta dress, a breeze from the hills flurrying her skirt and petticoats.

"It's been wonderful today, Harry," she said. "I can't remember when I enjoyed myself so much."

"I did, too," he said. "Can't think what we'll do with all those things we bought at the Market, though." He kissed her. She pressed herself against him, putting her tongue between his lips; his arms tightened round her and then released as he put a hand to her breast. She drew herself away from him, then took his hand, held it tightly to her breast for a moment and kissed it.

"It's cold now, Harry," she said. "I promised Father and Mother to be home early – it's not often I get a weekend leave."

"All right," he said. He put his arm around her waist and kissed her on the cheek. "Let's look at the lights just one minute more."

"Only one minute," she said. "It's not always easy for me to be good with you." She could tell from his smile that she'd said the right thing; she knew that she'd done the right thing, but why, why did she feel like a whore?

19

Tom, since he'd last seen him, had put on a lot of weight; the bottom button of his red flowered waistcoat was, to judge from the tightness of the material, left unfastened not because that was the correct thing to do, but because he hadn't any option. He stood at the door of the cubicle, shifting his weight uneasily from foot to foot.

"Happened to be in your part of the world," he said. "So I thought I'd drop in. You needn't see me if you don't want to."

"It's been a long time," Dick said.

"A year now." Tom came up to the bed. "Mind if I sit down?"

"Help yourself," Dick said. He looked up at Tom calmly; after the first incredulity at seeing him there at the door of the cubicle had passed, he'd expected to be wildly angry. But he felt nothing whatever; perhaps he'd hated Tom too much the last twelve months, killed or beaten him up too many times in his imagination; all his bitterness was spent long ago. Tom looked so affluent in his new suit – a long cry from the sort of clothes he used to wear – that he almost wished that he could hate him. He had good reason to; but he hadn't even been able to hate him – or anybody – recently.

"You're looking really fit," Tom said. "Changed your quarters since I last saw you, too."

"M2's for under four hours," Dick explained. "A's for six hours and upwards."

"So you've got promotion," Tom said. He shivered. "No weather for brass monkeys."

"Soft devil," Dick said. "It's only October." He took off the red day blanket he'd had round his legs and gave it to Tom.

"Thanks," Tom said, and tucked it under him. He ran his hand over its smooth bulk. "Bit of good stuff, Dick."

"The long-service men get the new ones," Dick said.

"The cunning old bastards like you, you mean." He shivered again. "Christ, it's cold here." He opened a silver cigarette-case. "Have one?"

Dick hesitated. "Just this once," he said. The first mouthful made him cough, but after that he enjoyed it, needed it too, because though he still wasn't angry, he was disturbed in a way he couldn't quite analyse. The cigarette was long and thick, and instead of a maker's name had stamped on it in gold SOOPADOOPA INC and after that a black facsimile of Tom's small neat signature. "You're doing bloody well for yourself, aren't you?" he asked.

"Doesn't cost anything," Tom said. "Advertising. Legitimate expense, old boy." He opened his brief-case and pulled out a bundle of paper-backs, a hundred carton of Player's, a honeycomb in a wooden container, and a large pie on a tin plate.

"One of Ma's meat pies," he said. "She remembered how you liked them. And a pot of her strawberry jam, and some new-laid eggs" – he winked – "half a bottle of Gordon's best. I know it's against the rules, but it must be death to a boozy beggar like you to go T.T." He winked. "You'll note I've put it in a lemonade bottle. You'll be able to be pickled all day tomorrow and no-one'll ever know it." He took out a thermos flask. "Give me your cup," he said.

He uncorked the flask; the cloud of steam from its neck had a faint spirituous smell. Dick's hand was reaching out for the cup on his locker; he brought it back to his side.

"How's Lois?" he asked.

Tom filled his cup with tea before he answered. "I don't really know," he said. "I haven't seen her for six months."

Dick leaped off the bed. "You're a bloody liar!" he shouted.

Tom sipped his tea. "I haven't been out with her for six months," he said. "That's all. If I see her I don't spit in her eye. I say hello and she says hello and we go on our ways. You've a mind like a tuppenny novelette, Dick. Give me your cup or I'll drink the bloody lot myself."

Dick took the cup from his locker. "You've been out with her just the same," he said.

"I was a shoulder for her to cry on, that's all. I don't mind admitting I always had a lech for her, I don't mind admitting I took her out. But she didn't break off the engagement because of me."

The tea was unsweetened; Dick went to his locker and took out the sugar tin. "No," he said. "She broke it off because I hadn't any money. That's why. The dirty filthy rotten whoring little bitch."

"Lois isn't a bitch," Tom said. "Why should she marry you if she didn't want to?"

"She left me at a fine moment." The bitterness was coming back now; if she'd been in the cubicle at that moment he knew that he'd have spat in her face and then kicked her out of the room.

"Better now than later," Tom said. "You're lucky."

"Yes, I'm lucky. No job, no future, no woman."

"You make me sick," Tom said. "You're so wet. Hell, you're alive, aren't you?"

"If you can call it that." He looked round the cubicle, almost the exact duplicate of his cubicle in Block M2 except for its green colour scheme. It had seemed even cosy when Tom had come in the cubicle to remind him of the outside world, to remind him of the past, to remind him even of Evelyn's V8 boy-friend who'd now reappeared and seemed to be taking her out almost every other night . . . "I'm alive," he said. "There's some spider that stings insects but doesn't kill them; just paralyses them so they'll keep fresh. When she's hungry she eats them alive . . ." He drained his teacup, unfastened the cap of the bottle of gin, and took the neat spirit at one gulp.

"Steady on," Tom said.

"Ah, don't be a bloody old granny," Dick said. "All I'm trying to say is this: some are born lucky and some unlucky. I'm unlucky, that's all."

"Nonsense. Everything that's happened to you has been your own fault."

The wind suddenly rose, bringing a flurry of dust and cold air into the cubicle; Tom wrapped the day-blanket more tightly round his legs, and poured himself another cup of tea-and-rum. "All your own fault," he repeated. "Don't blame anyone or anything else."

"So T.B.'s my own fault?"

"Of course. You should have taken more care of your health."

Dick started to laugh uncontrollably, near hysterics. Finally he pulled himself together. "Well, thank you very much," he said. "Come to see me again. You cheer me up, you do really. Come and see me again when Lois lets you. Please. Please, my dear." He poured himself another gin, aware that he was behaving foolishly, aware that when Tom had gone he was probably going to finish off the gin and become very drunk and be thrown out of the hospital and make his life even more complicated than it was, but not caring, because he needed the immediate exit from reality, he needed something to help him contradict, even if from the false premises of a common bio-chemical reaction, Tom's bland superiority, his unshakeable common sense.

Tom poured himself a full cup of gin. "All sickroom visitors do it," he said. "If I'd brought you grapes I'd have eaten them . . . Dick, you don't have to believe me, but I've never gone the full way with Lois, she wouldn't let me."

"I have no words to express my sorrow with," Dick said. "You must have gone through hell."

"I suppose she was saving herself for her wedding-night," Tom said. He stubbed out his cigarette and lit another one. Blowing his usual series of perfect smoke-rings he said moodily: "Nothing wrong in that. But she was too interested in Soopadoopa Inc. You know we were walking a tightrope until lately; she walked it with me. She was too damned pleased when things went well and too heartbroken when they didn't. I know a girl's got to take care of herself; there's no sense in marrying a bankrupt. But there's a limit. She used to give me the feeling that if we were married and I made just one mistake in business – and, believe me, one mistake and the others'll tear your throat out – she'd be off double-quick. Mental cruelty. Well, I expect it'd have kept me on my toes; but a man doesn't want to be on his toes all the time. So that's it. You're lucky, honestly you are."

"I'll change places with you," Dick said. Lois didn't seem to matter any more now; he'd rid himself now of all feeling for her, as one would spit out the last fragment of an extracted tooth. There'd be a twinge from time to time, but soon he'd entirely forget her.

"You'd be very sorry," Tom said. "Barney's last line was a winner, but all that means is more tax to pay and more problems we never had when we were running on a shoestring."

"I remember you when you'd just pulled off that deal with Ossie Warklock," Dick said. "You had *real* problems then."

Tom smiled. "I remember. I remember a certain distrustful friend of mine who hadn't any faith in my business ability, but who lent me a hundred pounds. I've never known anyone who'd do as much for me before or since. Mind you, I've never known anyone who'd be so bloody rude as not to thank me for returning it so promptly. With full interest too."

"I was angry with you at the time," Dick said. He felt something of the old affection return.

"It's ancient history now," Tom said. "Look, Dick, what are you doing when you leave here?"

"I don't quite know," Dick said. "I doubt if I'll go back to Larton's."

"I'd do with someone in Sales," Tom said. "You might bear it in mind."

"Thanks," Dick said, feeling strangely embarrassed. There was an awkward silence then, without quite knowing why, he asked: "How's Lorna?"

"She's fine," Tom said. "She's fine."

The Rest Bell rang: Tom jumped and then settled down in his chair, the thick blanket tightly round his legs. As he sat there in the tepid afternoon light Dick had the impression that it wasn't a man sitting there but an expensive worsted suit and made-to-measure silk shirt and a pair of manicured wax hands – ten pink shiny nails, ten white half-moons – awaiting an owner.

20

DICK watched Old Farvill climb on the operating table. Doctor Redroe took the long needle in his hand; holding it above Old Farvill's belly, he took careful aim. "We'll give him a thousand this time, Nurse," he said to Kanley. "A big fat man like him should be able to stand it. O.K. we're coming in on the beam, Mr. Farvill." The needle plunged down, the rubber tubing attached to it quivering a little; there was no change in Old Farvill's expression, except that when the needle penetrated the flesh, he closed his eyes.

The glittering green and white walls of the Operating Theatre, the dry warmth which pervaded it, the curiously neutral quality of the light coming in through the high-set glass windows, made Dick feel curiously unwashed and untidy: he felt unclean because of his human condition, because he could never be clean in the way that chromium and glass and tile and rubber composition flooring could be. And, as always, waiting to go next, he was frightened, not so much because of the pain of the needle but because, whatever they might say, something could go wrong.

"O.K. Mr. Farvill," Doctor Redroe said. "Next week, same time, same place." He looked at Dick. "Come on lad. Next for shaving." As Dick climbed on the table, he scowled at him. "And don't hold your private parts this time, as if you were trying to save yourself from a fate worse than death. I'll stick the needle through your hand if you do."

Dick heard Kanley giggle behind his mask. "I don't want anything to happen to them, Doctor," he said.

"Flapdoodle, Mr. Corvey. It's only once in a million years that the air goes the wrong way." He changed the needle. "You wouldn't believe it but you need a longer one than Mr. Farvill," he said. "Anyway, why worry? Nothing wrong with having air-cooled testicles. Keeps your mind on higher things. O.K. Nurse. A whole litre for Mr. Corvey too."

Dick felt the sudden coldness of surgical spirits on his belly and then after what seemed like ten minutes, the prick of the needle. "There you are," Doctor Redroe said. "The air, having entered through your peritoneum, is now forcing its way upwards to support your lungs a little. Just like stitching a gash. And keep that hand where it is, because this isn't the only needle I've got. Nurse Kanley'll swear it's an accident, won't you, Nurse?"

Lying there Dick felt, for no reason that he could ascertain, completely contented. Even the Operating Theatre had no power to intimidate him. The steel table was like a bed; only the withdrawal of the needle prevented him from dozing off. As he tucked his shirt into his trousers he found himself doing it slowly and fumblingly; he didn't want to leave the Operating Theatre, he didn't want to leave anywhere. He was even glad of the slight feeling of constriction in his chest; he would he realised be as uncomfortable without his refill as a fat woman without her corsets. Nurse Dinston's words came back to him as he walked slowly out of the building *My God, tha wor never better looked after in all tha life . . .*

He went in the direction of the Nurses' Home; there was a bend in the path from which part of the South Wing was visible; once Peter claimed to have seen Nurse Fendigo undressing at the third window on the second floor, and since then it was a ritual with all the male patients to slow up at the place where the path was near the slight dip in the ridge which kept the building out of sight of the Track. He stopped for a second, half-ashamedly, ostensibly to fasten his shoelace. But, as usual, there was nothing to see but chintz curtains.

He walked quickly up the hill to Block M2. Then, within sight of it, he stopped suddenly and sat down on the bench on the crest of the hill. Again a curious warm inertia overtook him; the bench had been made with some regard to human anatomy and had a back shaped to fit the curve of the spine, the sun was warm on his face, there was an hour to go until Rest Time, and until then he didn't have to go anywhere or do anything except enjoy the sensation, not yet taken for granted, of good health. Let me face it, he thought; if she'd believed she'd have to honour that promise, she wouldn't have made it. And the likelihood of his weekend leave – if Hinstock gave him one which was unlikely – and hers coinciding was remote. It had been too much to hope for from the first. It was better to sit on the bench and read his paper and enjoy the sun; it was better to admit defeat and leave her to the boy-friend in the V8. He'd often seen him lately; broad-shouldered and ruddy, reeking of money and success, Evelyn sitting smiling by his side.

There had been a time when he dreamed of defeating him; there had even been a time when he didn't see the Ford at all. And that had been the time when they lent each other books, when, in the few moments they had alone together, it seemed to him that only caution prevented them from embracing. And he'd told her about the Vodi; he'd made himself defenceless and naked, once again he'd put himself at the mercy of another human being.

He saw Maureen Tempest and Betty Pulborough come over the crest of the hill. Betty gave him a small prim smile but Maureen stared at him boldly then put out her tongue. She was wearing high-heeled shoes and a pink satin blouse with black corduroy slacks; but, Dick thought, pulling a face at her, that hardly mattered when a girl was only nineteen and had chestnut hair and a white skin which, when you were close to her, made silk look like hessian.

"See you at whist this afternoon!" Maureen yelled over her shoulder in her piping slightly common voice.

"It's a date, love!" he shouted, and returned to his newspaper. That was one thing Basil was right about; consumptives should stick to consumptives. Then you both started from scratch, one wasn't asking a big favour from the other, and the parents, as far as they entered into it, would be only too glad to get the bruised fruit, the damaged stock, off their hands.

But there was only one flaw in his reasoning. He didn't want Maureen or anyone else but Evelyn. He sighed, folded his paper, and stood up. It might be futile, he might be making a fool of himself and, one way or another he was storing up past grief and pain. But he was still going to ask her. He hadn't really any choice, just as his body, he realised gratefully as he half-ran down the hill, had no choice now but health.

21

"ARE you seeing Harry tonight, then?" Evelyn's mother asked.

Evelyn, looking into the mirror over the mantelpiece, frowned. "No," she said. "I wish I were."

"You *are* a silly. Why go out with a man if you don't want to?"

"Oh, Mother, don't be so damned nosey!" Her hand began to tremble; the lipstick slipped and a red line appeared under her lower lip. "Now look what you've made me do!"

She saw her mother's face sadden; she cleared a pile of books from the sofa, sat down beside her, and kissed her.

"I'm sorry," she said. "But I'm only going out with this man tonight because I promised a long time ago."

"Who is he?" her mother asked.

"Dick Corvey. He lives in Silbridge." She poured herself a cup of tea from the hand-painted teapot – one of her father's latest enthusiasms – which stood on the small table by the sofa. When she lifted up the teapot the table wobbled; that, and the two white-painted bookcases, had been earlier enthusiasms.

"I'm going to have an accident with that table," her mother said.

"I'm going to break off one of its legs, chop it up for firewood, and buy a little coffee-table from Woolworth's."

"You wouldn't have the heart," Evelyn said. She stroked the table; her father hadn't put enough coats of varnish on and the deal was beginning to show through.

"It's hard to keep the house tidy with a man like your father," her mother said.

"Never mind," Evelyn said. "It looks lived in." She didn't want to go out at all, she realised, not even with Harry; she wanted simply to sit here on the shabby old leather sofa listening to her mother's soothing voice slowly relishing the old familiar topics – her grandchildren, her husband's untidiness, the fantastic price of meat, the even more fantastic price of coal . . .

And she wanted to be there when her father came in, to see her mother's expression when he came in, her face for a second becoming as smooth and unlined as a young girl's. And always, before he came in, her mother would half-surreptitiously straighten her untidy grey hair in the mirror, and put on a little makeup. The lipstick and rouge seemed to give the large face – almost masculine in its heaviness – not less but more dignity.

This room was what it was – not just lived in but happily lived in – because all her mother's decisions had been taken over thirty years ago, and they'd all been the right ones. But her daughter was going out into the cold outside, to meet those large hungry eyes of Dick's again, to be plagued by the necessity of taking decisions which she could never be sure were right.

"I think I'll phone Dick and tell him I'm ill," she said.

Her mother looked up from her knitting. "That'd be a lie," she said.

Her face was not so much shocked as puzzled.

"It's so awkward," Evelyn said. "When he was very ill, nine months ago, he asked me to go out with him. I promised I would if he gained three stones. I never thought he'd recover and I never thought he'd manage to get weekend leave. But he has. And now I don't know what to do."

"You'll have to keep your promise, that's all," her mother said, her voice unusually sharp.

"But what about Harry? We're going to the Raynton. I know he won't be there because he's away at Warley shooting. But there'll be some of his friends there."

Her mother picked up her knitting again. "Good," she said.

"Oh, Mother, don't be so stupid!"

"I'm not so stupid, dear. And I've lived a lot longer than you," her mother said. "And I went out with other young men before I was engaged to your father. Then I didn't, naturally. But you're not engaged to Harry, are you?"

"I see perfectly well what you're hinting at," Evelyn said with irritation. "You think I should make him jealous. Honestly, that woman's magazine stuff, just the sort of advice these damned aunties give."

"You shouldn't swear so much," her mother said, composedly. "And the women's magazines aren't as silly as you think. But you please yourself, dear; you always do."

Evelyn rose and went to the mirror, dabbing at her chin with a piece of cotton-wool. "I *am* fond of Harry, you know."

"Of course you are," her mother said. "He's a very nice boy too."

"He's not a boy," Evelyn said. "He's a man. Dick's a boy, that's his trouble." She turned to face her mother. "Do you think this is too low-cut?" she said, pointing to the neck of her blue cocktail-dress.

"It's perfectly all right," her mother said. "You've a beautiful figure, Evelyn. It's nothing to be ashamed of. But you've worn that dress when you went out with Harry, haven't you?"

"That's entirely different. Harry hasn't been in hospital for eighteen months."

"No," her mother said. "But I'll tell you something, Evelyn. You don't need all that rouge."

"Don't be stuffy, mother."

"I'm not." Her mother's tone had become faintly mocking, an adult explaining something to a child.

"You don't need it because your cheeks are rosy enough already. I've never seen you look so pretty for Harry."

The grandfather clock by the shiny glass and beech cocktail cabinet (which never yet had held any other alcoholic drink but beer and sherry) whirred for two minutes, emitted a sound like a cough, and struck seven.

"Oh, Lord," Evelyn said. "I'll be late." She took a final glance at herself in the mirror and put her lipstick and compact into her handbag.

"I can't understand why he doesn't call for you. Harry always does."

"Dick wanted to," Evelyn said. "But it wouldn't be fair somehow."

"Evelyn, don't concern yourself about what's fair. You're not engaged to Harry."

"You needn't remind me again," Evelyn snapped.

"All right, dear. I won't. You bear this in mind, though: Harry's a good catch, but that's not enough for a happy marriage."

"There isn't any suggestion of marriage with Dick," Evelyn said, trying to keep down her anger. "I *will* 'phone him if you go on any more about it, Mother, I swear I will."

Her eyes started to moisten.

"Crying won't help you," her mother said. "You might try following your instincts for a change."

Evelyn took a deep breath. "I'm going now, Mother," she said. She gave her mother a brief kiss on the cheek. "Don't wait up for me."

Out in the street waiting for the bus, Evelyn felt her anger mounting again. She had somehow been made to feel not only childish but a little hard; her mother, as usual, had won. And, what was hardest to forgive, had won fairly; she wasn't the Silver Cord type, she'd never been possessive.

The bus, when it arrived some ten chilly minutes later, did nothing to lighten her spirits. Her seat was hard and uncomfortable and didn't seem quite clean; and in the gangway was a little heap of sawdust covering what was, to judge from the smell, the results of someone's travel sickness. The bus driver was evidently a novice or not used to the Tanbury cobbles; the bus pitched and swayed continually and, when it stopped, did so with jarring suddenness.

The road surface changed as they passed Kellogg's Woods and the bus rode more smoothly; though not as smoothly, she reflected, as Harry's new Rover, in which she might be sitting now if she weren't a sentimental fool. She looked at the spiky outlines of the trees on the ridge to the left; the moon made their shadows steel blue. Dick would probably have been walking in those woods today, wallowing in the past, weaving new fantasies about the Vodi. She closed her eyes and then saw before them the face of a fat old woman with four long black teeth; she opened them again instantly.

The smell from the little pile of sawdust on the floor seemed to grow stronger; she put her handkerchief to her nose.

But, against all expectations, when she saw Dick in the foyer of the Raynton the old feeling, the helpless bemused happiness she'd experienced that day he gave her his news of being granted six hours, came back to her. He was wearing a dark grey suit she hadn't seen him wear before; he had a white shirt with the lustre of the filler on it, and his white handkerchief was brand new, too. But that wasn't what made her happy, what drove all thoughts of Harry from her head: it was that wonder-struck expression on his face, the expression of unqualified adoration.

"It's like the old story," she said. "He says *How nice you look in a dress!* and she says *How nice to see you not in pyjamas!*"

"Come now," he said. "You've seen me dressed."

She took his hand. "I've only seen you in that tatty sports coat," she said. "You look so debonair and, well, *civilian* in that suit. I love to see men dressed up."

"Let's have a drink before dinner," he said. "My first in eighteen months if I don't count the noggin I had with Tom last night."

"Be careful," she said. "Doctor Hinstock has spies everywhere."

"He can give me my discharge now if he likes," Dick said. They sat down at a corner table in the lounge. "What would you like to drink?"

"Guinness, please," she said.

"Don't be so daft. Have a short. I've been saving up for months."

"You'll need it all when you leave hospital."

She saw from his expression that she'd said the wrong thing, that she'd hurt his pride; so she allowed him to buy her a sherry and didn't protest later when he ordered wine with their dinner.

When they were drinking their coffee in the lounge she said: "Dick, I can't remember when I enjoyed a meal so much." It was true, she thought; it wasn't the smoked salmon or the tournedos, or the Peach Melba, or the Beaujolais or the Turkish coffee or the Cointreau, but his almost childish delight at being there with her; and it was his slight awkwardness about knives and forks and the choice of wine, too; he wasn't a gourmet, he didn't show off. He looked just a little out of place in an expensive hotel; his place would have been in the living-room of her home—

She stopped herself; the warmth of her feeling towards him was becoming dangerous. Another drink and she'd lose control, she'd clothe the feeling with a word. And it would be a good word, the best of words, but in connection with Dick hopelessly unwise, totally ruinous.

Dick took her hand. "I've wanted to do that for months," he said. "I've never had a better meal either. But with you I'd enjoy sandwiches in a railway refreshment room."

She felt his eyes upon her bosom, and realised with panic, that she enjoyed having him look at her there. For she couldn't detect the furtive sad look of lust in his face; what she saw – she had to use the word – was love. She turned her head away from Dick and saw Vernon Lunkett and Molly Stridd come into the lounge. Why, she thought, this is what I came for; as they came nearer she said in a loud voice: "Hello, you two."

In the taxi Dick sat in silence for a while, and then said in a sulky voice: "I could have done without their company."

"I think they're very nice." Deliberately she kept her voice cold.

"I know them. Vernon's a useless boozy twerp, and Molly's a little tart."

"They happen to be my friends."

"And Harry's too?"

"You get to know everything at the hospital, don't you?" she said bitterly. "Harry's a friend of mine, too. It's none of your business anyway, Dick."

He looked out of the window at Kellogg's Woods. "The Vodi's still operating," he said, half to himself. "Nothing ever changes."

"Please, Dick, don't talk about that. Promise me to forget it."

"Some people have good health," he said, "some have money, some have girls. I've just got the one thing. I'm not going to forget it."

His face was empty now, not angry, which she'd have welcomed, but withdrawn. His face was turned in her direction, but he wasn't looking at her; from his seat in the left-hand corner he was straining forward to see Kellogg's Woods through the nearside window.

He sat back, and still not looking at her said in a low voice: "It doesn't matter very much, but I love you."

"Oh, Dick, it's so hopeless. We don't really know each other—" She saw with relief that the taxi was approaching her home. Another minute, and she was safe; he only had to be less defeated, he only had even to ask one question and she'd be lost.

"I knew it wouldn't be any good," he said. "But I'm glad I took you to dinner."

"I'm glad you did, Dick. I've really enjoyed it. Truly. Thank you very much." She saw that the taxi was approaching Rincart Street; it was safe for her to touch him now, and she squeezed his hand.

"Nothing to thank me for," he said. "Thank *you*. You were sorry for me, weren't you, Eve? Thank you for your charity."

The taxi stopped. As the driver opened the door, Evelyn kissed Dick's hand. "It wasn't charity," she whispered. The door closed after her and Dick saw her run up the steps into the house.

Dick looked at his hand, his face puzzled. He settled himself more comfortably as the taxi drove off towards the Kasbah. Now it was all over, he thought with relief. He couldn't understand why it didn't hurt more; but that would come later. He suddenly remembered Walter Perdwick. He'd often wondered why he'd given himself up so easily; he knew now.

22

"Harry Thirleton won't ever marry you," Dick said. There was a twist about his mouth that Evelyn didn't like; as he stood there in the Sister's office on Ward M2 in his navy-blue donkey jacket and black corduroys he had a look of street-corner violence; he was, quite credibly, the vitriol-throwing type. When he took his right hand from his jacket pocket she flinched instinctively; but it was only a letter he brought out, another of the letters he'd been bringing her daily since their evening at the Raynton, another of the letters which she wouldn't answer because there wasn't any way to answer without hurting him still more.

"I don't want to discuss him," she said.

He came up to the desk. "Neither do I. Frankly, I couldn't care less about him."

The phrase depressed her; it was as if the day – damp and misty, drifting already into darkness at half-past three – had spoken through his lips.

"Don't talk about him, then," she said. "And please don't write me any more letters. I won't answer them, so there's no point in it."

"I expect you to burn them unread. Or laugh over them with the other nurses." He looked at the letter in his hand, then tore it up and, coming over to her side of the desk, threw the pieces into the waste-paper basket. "All right then, you won't be bothered any more. But I'll tell you what I put in the letter; when Harry Thirleton marries, it'll be someone like Molly Stridd. He only wants one thing from you, and if you give him it he'll drive away like the wind and you'll never see him again. Goddamn it, Evelyn, don't you see?" He took hold of her arm and wrenched her closer to him. "I love you. I want to marry you—" He let her arm drop and went back to the other side of the desk. "I'm sorry," he said.

She rubbed her arm. "You're stronger than you look," she said. "But I don't burn your letters and I don't show them to anyone else. You know I wouldn't do that."

His fingers had gripped her hard on the muscle; her arm was throbbing painfully. She didn't want the throbbing to stop and she didn't want him to leave the office; he was angry and alive now.

"I'm sorry," he said. "I should control myself better."

"Ah God no!" she cried. "You're like a car with good brakes but no engine. Dick, listen. What are you going to do about Harry? What can you do? And what can you do about me? When I marry I want to make a full-time job of it. I want to have children. Can you support me?"

The colour went from his face for a moment. "You bitch," he said. "You know damned well that I can't do anything about Harry. You needn't remind me that I'm a feeble weedy consumptive" – he spat the word out – "and that I'm practically a bloody pauper and I haven't even got a job. You just do the sensible thing, pet – try and hook Harry. I won't bother you again." He turned at the doorway. "But don't say I didn't warn you."

She opened her mouth to speak, if only to say No, if only to protest against his diminishing himself; it wasn't his malice that she minded but the weakness behind it. For a moment when he'd gripped her arm he'd been a free man, he'd been fighting; and then a second later he'd brought out the dirty old white flag he always carried about with him. He had surrendered, he had become no-one, his retreating footsteps down the corridor were the footsteps of a ghost.

She stooped to pick up the fragments of his letter; her arm still ached, but the pain was now merely a minor unpleasantness, its meaning had disappeared. She laid the pieces of the letter on the desk. She found herself unable to take in any more than disconnected sentences – *It was worth being ill to meet you . . . I only got better for you . . . I think all the time about marrying you . . .*

Her eyes were blurring with tears, she blinked them back and put the letter in her apron pocket.

In her room that evening she took out the letter again. *When I'm in my cubicle at night I sometimes hear the sound of a car engine from the drive. I can't see the car from my cubicle unless I go to the far end of the balcony and then I sometimes catch a glimpse of its headlights through the trees. Then I go back to bed and wish I had something stronger than tea to drink. And I saw you with him last Saturday afternoon; you were smiling at him and the car seemed to be going very fast. I hated you both so much that I felt sick, physically sick. But it's no use. This was bound to happen. I shouldn't have got better. I shouldn't have cheated Nelly. Some people she likes, some people she doesn't like. I can't fight her, but I can tell you that I love you . . .*

She put the letter down and started to cry. She wasn't crying for him, though she could all too clearly visualise him standing at the end of the balcony watching the car headlights, watching her being carried away into the world outside, then slowly turning to go back to his cubicle, to the narrow bed and the cold sheets and the radio which would be switched off at nine o'clock; she was crying for herself. For somehow he'd involved her in his own defeat; she felt that she was a victim now. And worse than a victim: for the moment, she'd ceased to want anything, there wasn't any future. She'd slapped him across the face that afternoon, dug the spur into his sides; she'd been cruel, she'd been unfair, and he should have been properly angry, he should have yelled at the top of his voice that he'd give her ten children, that he'd give her a house, that he'd get ahead of Harry if it killed him. She wouldn't, couldn't have stopped him if he'd been outrageously stupid and embraced her there and then, if he'd lost her her job: she couldn't argue about what she felt when he touched her; her body was always at home to his hands, always even now when she knew that he was the wrong man for her, didn't merely welcome him but unroll the red carpet down the garden path and send out the trumpeters.

She took off her dressing-gown and looked at her arm. The four marks his fingers had left were still discernible, faintly yellow. She smiled as she looked at them, and then went over to the bedside locker and took out a Biro and a writing-pad.

She pulled a chair up to the locker and wrote – *My dearest.* She put down the pen and stared dreamily at the paper. It was very warm in the room; she felt a pleasant lassitude steal over her, a lassitude which seemed to have a personal presence, to be enumerating, slowly and admiringly, the details of her body; she put her hands to her breasts, half-ashamedly, and felt the nipples harden under the nylon slip. She picked the pen up again, and wrote rapidly. *I want you so much, more than I've ever wanted any man. I'm here by myself, looking at the bruises on my arm. They'll fade soon, but—*

She stopped writing. There was only one picture in her mind; it was brutally specific, and even to make those marks on the writing-paper which would, sooner or later, make that picture real, seemed artificial and irrelevant. Her body was real, the room was real, the heat from the silver-painted radiator was real; and Dick, scarcely three hundred yards away, was real. His hands, his eyes, his mouth were real and they always had been. It wasn't something she could argue about, and never had been, right from the day that she'd just touched Dick's hand. She could change her beliefs, she could make wise or unwise decisions, but she couldn't change her body.

There was a knock at the door; she turned over the writing-pad and put on her dressing-gown. As she unbolted the door she realised that the spell wasn't broken, that she wouldn't be surprised to see Dick standing there; and if only he were, if only the right and proper event wasn't always the impossible event, then all her problems would be solved.

She opened the door slowly and saw Nurse Fendigo in a green tweed suit and high-necked white blouse. The ensemble didn't agree very well with her olive skin and ebullient plumpness; she looked dumpy and hearty, too much the nurse off duty. A sense of futility drifted into the room; Evelyn thought of a photograph she'd once seen, of a medium in a trance, a thin woman in a black chemise dress and black wool stockings with whirls of ectoplasm, grey and sticky-looking, in circles round her body and fastened like fingers in her long white hair.

"The bus is due in ten minutes," Nurse Fendigo said. "Just thought I'd remind you, duckie." There was a packet of cigarettes on the locker. She took one out and lit it. "First cancer stick today," she said. "I keep trying to stop, and then people like you leave temptation in my way."

"I'm staying in," Evelyn said. "I've some letters to write. I might even read a book. You know, those rectangular paper things."

Nurse Fendigo laughed. "You'll read yourself blind one of these days," she said. "Come on to Nedham, kid, and live dangerously. We might even pick up a couple of men at the Seven Flies."

"I've enough trouble with men already," Evelyn said, unthinkingly.

"I know," Nurse Fendigo said. "You've been having quite a few letters lately, haven't you?"

Evelyn went over to the wardrobe recess and took out a skirt and jumper. "I only had one letter last week," she said, slipping hurriedly into the skirt. "From my Aunty Lora in New Zealand."

She put on a pair of brogues. "I'm ready if you are," she said.

"You look lovely like that," Nurse Fendigo said. "And perfectly decent. But they wouldn't understand at the Seven Flies."

Evelyn flushed angrily, the amused brown eyes on her bare shoulders; they seemed to be dwelling unduly on Dick's finger-marks, which now began to embarrass her like an old tattoo. She dived into her jumper; the neck was small and through the wool she heard Nurse Fendigo's voice, slightly muffled.

"Your letters are special delivery. Nedham Hospital G.P.O. Or D.P.O."

Evelyn went to the dressing-table and ran a comb through her hair so roughly that she heard it crackle with static electricity. "They're just a nuisance," she said. "I'm not interested in him. Come on, Betty, let's go."

Nurse Fendigo stubbed out her half-smoked cigarette abruptly, then shredded it into an unsmokeable mess. Looking at the shreds of paper and tobacco, she said, still in the same light tone: "You're a dog in the manger, aren't you, dear?"

"Your genders are wrong," Evelyn said in the same tone. There was no other reply possible, except to say that Nurse Fendigo was welcome to Dick; and that she realised as they ran down the corridor, wasn't quite true. Neither Nurse Fendigo nor any other woman was welcome to Dick. She simply didn't want him to touch anyone else. But marriage with him was impossible; he was already married to someone else, he was a bridegroom of Nelly. From whom, as he'd said to her himself, there was no divorce. She couldn't and wouldn't marry him; but she didn't want anyone else to have him. It was true enough; indeed she was a bitch in the manger. And there seemed no way out of it. Sooner or later he'd leave the hospital, or even take a job there; sooner or later they'd be alone together, and, wherever it was, her body wouldn't say no.

They slowed down to a walk as they reached the main staircase, partly because it was against the rules to run downstairs and partly because the stairs were lethally steep, and arrived at the entrance in time to see the headlights of the bus as it ground slowly up the drive. The rain had come at last and there wasn't going to be any fog; the night was wet not humid, and the cold was the cold of winter, not merely the absence of warmth. She had snatched up her plastic raincoat and hood as she went out of her room; when she first touched them they'd been clammy and cold and now their texture was as familiar as her own skin. The Seven Flies was five minutes' walk from Nedham Market Square; if it was still raining when the bus arrived, she'd unroll the raincoat and hood. The raincoat in particular would unroll a little reluctantly, there'd be a slight stickiness, and that queer inhumanly edible plastic smell, as if one were opening a bag of toffees specially made for well-mannered, well-brought-up robots; and then there'd be the walk across the Market Square and up Poulter Street, just a long enough walk to enjoy the rain on her face and the feeling of freedom, of being away from the hospital.

When they were inside the bus she lit cigarettes for herself and Nurse Fendigo. The bus seemed to wait longer than usual; she deliberately didn't look outside at the Nurses' Home. She'd seen it too often, she knew it too well, she hated even the door lamp above the family arms. She wasn't going anywhere very exciting but she was going away from Dick, from her problems, even if only for a few hours; and she'd be a little nearer Harry's world, the uncomplicated world in which men didn't go to bed at eight o'clock, the world in which men worked for a living and didn't have their temperatures taken twice a day. The bus moved away after what seemed like ten minutes; and as it went slowly down the hill she suddenly realised what she must do. It was so simple; why hadn't she seen it before? It was like the story of the man who was in prison for twenty years and who one day tried the door, found it unlocked, and went out.

She smiled to herself and then deliberately looked out towards

Ward M2 below on the left. There was nothing to be frightened of there, she thought with relief. It couldn't follow her; and soon it and the hospital would be out of sight, rooted there in the rain. She settled back in her seat, still smiling.

23

"I REALLY like this room," Evelyn said. "It's so warm and yet it's so spacious."

Mrs. Thirleton smiled. She was a large woman, nearly as tall and broad as her son, but a plain black dress with what Evelyn guessed would be very expensive corsets underneath made the fact unimportant. Sitting rigidly upright in her high-backed chair, she said: "Harry thinks my taste very old-fashioned. He doesn't like Victoriana."

"There's too much of it here," Harry said. "Good Lord, Mummy, I don't know how another article could be crammed in here. I can't move an inch without knocking into something."

"That's because you're so clumsy," Mrs. Thirleton said. "I bought almost everything in this room at sales, Evelyn. This walnut table here – see how beautiful the inlay is, each tiny little piece done by hand – cost me not seven shillings. And that wing chair in which my son's sprawling as if his back were broken cost me just ten. Even the carpet was a bargain. And those floor tiles – they're exactly the colour of clover honey, aren't they? – are bankrupt stock." She looked at Evelyn's empty cup. "Would you like some more tea, Evelyn?"

"Thank you. It's really delicious. I've never tasted that flavour before."

Mrs. Thirleton looked at her approvingly, just as she had done when she discovered that Evelyn preferred her tea without milk or sugar.

"You have a palate," she said. "That's Orange Pekoe. I've just been able to get hold of some. It's wasted on Harry, though: he likes black Indian tea with sugar and condensed milk. He didn't notice it; but I knew you would."

She didn't add *eventually*: but Evelyn detected reproof, a very mild one, an A minus instead of her usual A plus. She should have said that she noticed it with her first cup; Mrs. Thirleton liked people's reactions to be not only correct but swift. Evelyn glanced downwards: dress over knees, knees together, stockings straight. Harry laughed. "Never you mind, Evie. You still love me, even if I'm a barbarian, don't you?" He appeared unexpectedly slim and dapper in his black shadow-striped suit and white collar: but not too dapper, not too dressed-up. Even when Harry was wearing new clothes, they never looked too glossy, too stiff, just as his sandy hair never either seemed either freshly cut or in need of a cut. She liked that; and she liked the drawing-room with its darkly gleaming furniture and its rose-patterned wallpaper which could have been fussy and claustrophobic in a small room; she liked the pink velvet curtains and approved of the open-fronted Minty case (the only modern piece in the room, since Mrs. Thirleton thought glass-fronted cases vulgar). And though she sometimes felt a sensation of always being set examinations of one kind or another profoundly irritating, she knew that as far as the most important subjects were concerned, she'd already been awarded full marks, she had six Distinctions, she was through with flying colours.

She looked at her watch. "Harry," she said, "we'll be late for the party."

"Plenty of time, darling," he said.

"We really will be late, dear. It's nearly two hours to Warley and the roads are icy."

"Nonsense, girl. Hour and a half at the most. I've done it."

His mother interposed. "You have done it, Harry. In an M.G. for a bet. And you were lucky you weren't killed. Evelyn's quite right."

When they were coming out of Tanbury, Harry said abruptly: "You're a great success with Mummy."

"I'm glad, Harry. I like her very much."

"You know, people are often frightened of Mummy. She's a bit overwhelming but she's a good sort really."

"She'll be lonely in that big house, Harry."

"Needs some grandchildren." He swallowed. "Evie, we've got

five minutes to spare. Anyway, damn the Lamptons." He turned off the road.

"Eve," he said. "What's this Corvey fellow to you?"

"I don't think you've the right to ask that," she said. She was surprised to find her voice perfectly steady.

He lit a cigarette, then stubbed it out after the first puff. "I'm smoking too much," he said. "Drinking too much, as well. Eve, I haven't had a night's sleep since Vernon told me."

She bit back the words and said coldly: "That's not my fault, Harry."

"Evelyn, we've been going out together for six months. Why won't you tell me?"

"I'll go out with whom I like," she said in the same cold tone.

"Oh, will you?" His voice rose to a shout. "You'll just go out with me! You'll not waste your time with bloody consumptive counter-jumpers!"

"Harry, I'm becoming rather bored. If you don't take me home this moment, I'll walk home." She turned the door-handle, reflecting wryly that the shoes she was wearing – eight silver straps, two soles and two six-inch heels – would cut her feet to ribbons in less than a hundred yards.

"Eve, I love you."

She released her grip of the door-handle. The words were more than she could bear: they made Harry real. She put her arms round his neck and then to her own surprise began to weep.

"Stop blubbing," he said. "And close your eyes." She felt him take her left hand; when she opened her eyes a large solitaire diamond ring glittered on her third finger. She looked at it for a moment in silence, then out of the window at the black lifeless hedgerows and the ruts in the lane whitened with ice.

"I'd like to look at the lights with you, Harry," she said, and kissed him.

She saw from his expression that she'd said absolutely the right thing, that she'd passed another test. Looking at him, she felt a faint pity, then more disquietingly, a feeling of anger.

24

Dick gave the brass tap a final rub and stepped back to admire it. "It's like gold," he said to Gordon Hinster, who was mopping the floor. "I'll be able to get a job as a lavatory attendant anywhere."

Gordon squeezed out the mop in the bucket and took out half a cigarette from his pocket. "It's about all they train you for in this bloody place," he said. He had a thin gloomy face which never seemed properly shaven; standing by the pitted, cream distempered wall smoking his cigarette greedily he seemed as if waiting for a firing-squad.

"You've got a trade," Dick said.

"Oh, yes. Painting's wonderful treatment for the lungs. You're starved daft on scaffoldings outside or starved daft inside. The bastards never light a fire for the painter." He walked over to the mouthwashing basin and spat into it. "I wouldn't have had this complaint if I hadn't been a painter. And now I've got it, I can't be a painter again."

"Never mind," Dick said. "You'll be on that nine o'clock bus on Tuesday." He felt a little sad at the thought of Gordon being discharged; he wasn't particularly fond of him, nor was he envious of his being discharged, but he didn't like to see any patient leave the hospital. It spoiled his pattern of the life he'd been building up for himself, since Evelyn had gone, a life run to a strict routine, in which boredom and despair were held at bay by the routine itself and by the fact that you were never alone. There was always someone in the same boat and, once you came to know them, each had some kind of talent, even if it were only for billiards or dirty jokes. When they left, there was a gap, you felt if only for a moment lonely, you had an absurd fear that you'd wake up one morning and hear no sound, that you'd run from ward to ward and find all the beds stripped, that you'd try the dining-hall and the Recreation Rooms and the Ablutions Room and the Operating Theatre and the X-ray room and the Nurses' Home and the Administration Block and finally, in despair, the Morgue and there'd be nobody in the hospital, living or dead, and you'd be totally and finally alone . . .

"Nurse Warvett's leaving on Tuesday, too," Gordon said.

"Hell, soon there'll be no women nurses left. All the nice bits go."

"Or they put them on the Women's Ward," Dick said. He glanced round the Ablutions Room. "Damn, I've missed a tap," he said, and took down the duster and tin of Brasso from the shelf above him again.

"Don't be a clot, man," Gordon said. "It'll be all mucky again tomorrow."

Dick went over to the unpolished tap and rubbed it furiously with polish, hating the damp gutty texture of the duster, but glad to have an excuse to occupy his hands. "I like to do a job properly," he said.

Gordon rummaged through his pockets and found another half cigarette. "I'd like to do Nurse Warvett properly," he said. He grinned. "I remember when I was on Total in M2. She gave me a bed bath. When she reached the Equator she handed me the cloth and asked me if I'd like to finish myself off. No, I said, I'm too weak. Well, she didn't turn a hair." He lit his cigarette from the stub of his first. "She'll know what it's for, that one."

Dick rubbed the tap still harder. It suddenly occurred to him that Evelyn had been on M2 when Gordon was on Total Rest. He put down the duster and polish and mopped his forehead with his handkerchief. He couldn't quite give a name to what he felt: it might have been jealousy, it might have been lust, it might have been regret. A picture was there in his mind, brutally direct; he thought about stories he'd heard when he first came to Nedham. They were all the same; and the girl in question had always left the hospital under a cloud. "They all know what it's for," he said. "But I'd have thrown the cloth in your face if I'd been her."

"I wouldn't have asked *you*," Gordon said. "I'm glad I'm leaving, they'll all be male nurses soon."

"I wouldn't take the job unless they put me on the Women's Ward," Dick said. "It's time Hinstock developed a new outlook. If it cheers you up to have a nice young woman look after you, it'd cheer the women up to have a nice young man to look after them."

"Bet you'd be a second mother to the young ones," Gordon said, and guffawed. He blew out a cloud of tobacco smoke; in contrast with the institutional smell of the Ablutions Room – Dettol and metal polish and Vim and carbolic – its bar-room acridity had a warm cheerfulness.

Tom Dellable bounced in, twirling his walking-stick. "Four Circles this morning," he said. "Some people lounge about lavatories smoking and others indulge in healthy invigorating exercise. Excuse me, gentlemen, for using your nice clean bogs, but the cold has attacked my bladder." He ran into the w.c., slamming the door so hard that the draught blew the contents of Gordon's dust-shovel away. Gordon swore and stooped painfully with the sweeping-brush.

"Don't use those wicked words," Dick said. "You shouldn't have left the muck lying around in the first place." Gordon scowled at him and went out to the dustbin. When he returned, Tom Dellable, his back against the radiator, was opening a packet of Churchman's. Gordon snatched one from him and lit it.

"You cheeky devil," Tom said.

"You shouldn't be so stingy. You said you had none this morning."

Dick smiled faintly. The picture of Evelyn and Gordon together had vanished entirely; obscenely improbable though it had been, its vanishing made even these trite exchanges amusing. Contentment came up to him quietly: he'd done his day's work, such as it was, Nurse Dinston was on duty that morning so the cocoa would be hot, it was the Red Cross Library afternoon, and in the evening that film show. And that afternoon a batch of new patients would be arriving; some of them might have new stories, some of them might be able to give him a decent game of chess or bridge. There was only the Schoolmaster left to play chess with now that Basil had been discharged and Rock was on the staff; and their being no longer patients had broken up the bridge foursome too. And in any case it was always pleasant to welcome new entries to the club of which he was now a life member if not honorary president: and it was consoling too, to know that people in the world outside, that superior non-infectious world, still got the Bug.

He looked at his finger-nails; they were black-rimmed. He filled the wash-basin with hot water, noting with a fussy displeasure that the tap-washer leaked and would very quickly mar the polish. Scrubbing his nails energetically, he heard Tom Dellable say: "Nurse Mallaton. Our lovely Nurse Mallaton." He didn't turn round, but continued scrubbing his nails; the dirt underneath them was gritty and obstinate.

"She's done well for herself," Gordon said. "Those bloody Thirletons use five-pound notes for toilet-paper. She looks a smasher in this photo, doesn't she?"

"She hasn't got anything on," Tom said.

"No, it's an evening-dress, you can see the line of it here."

Dick took down his towel and dried his hands slowly. The news wasn't really a surprise; but that didn't make it any easier to bear. The day he'd contemplated was now in ruins, shown up for what it was – a day at the Nedham Orphanage, a day full of little treats to keep the grown-up kiddies happy. He turned to face Tom and Gordon.

"Let's have a look," he said, aware as he spoke that he would just as soon not look at the paper, that he was only torturing himself. He put out his hand for the paper; Tom stuffed it into his pocket, and gave him a cigarette, then lit the cigarette for him and handed him the paper. Dick didn't unfold the paper immediately but smiled at Tom. Tom's face seemed, for all its ruddiness, worn and sagging and wrinkled; Dick suddenly realised that it was the face not only of Tom Dellable, a member of the Nedham Club, but the face of a man well over fifty, old enough to be his father.

He stared at the two photographs; they were unusually clear and sharp, the heads and shoulders of a handsome young man in captain's uniform and a pretty young woman in an off-the-shoulder evening dress which escaped indecency by a hair's-breadth. But her smile, her cold flaunting smile, indicated explicitly enough that she wasn't just anybody's property, that if you wanted to pasture on those magnificent shoulders and breasts and the regions southwards you had to be healthy, you had to be rich, you had to be triumphant, you had, in fact, to be like Harry Thirleton. It seemed to him as if he'd been looking at facsimiles of such engagement photographs all his life; he didn't bother to read the paragraph underneath, but gave the paper back to Tom.

"Good luck to them," he said. He mopped his forehead again. "And to Harry Thirleton. May it drop off."

"I don't know what you mean," Gordon said. "But it won't."

Dick picked up the tin of polish from the shelf over the wash-basin and threw it at the wall. It didn't relieve his feelings; he would have liked to throw it at a mirror or a window, to see and hear something smashed, and he despised himself for his instinctive caution.

"Don't take it out on the poor old wall," Gordon said.

"Shut your bloody trap," Dick said.

Gordon stiffened. "Steady on, chum. I'll not—" He looked at Dick's white savage face and stopped.

Dick lifted his hand as if to hit him, then turned sharply on his left heel as if on parade, and walked out. Through force of habit he turned right in the direction of the Circle and then, with the same military abruptness, turned left and walked past the Administration Block towards the drive. As he passed the Administration Block he saw Rock in his white nurse's coat; he waved and shouted something, but the wind carried his words away.

The drive sloped upwards until it reached Block Z20, then levelled out. He stopped for a moment and rested with his back against a pine tree. He heard the County ambulance pass – there was no mistaking that smooth note of the Daimler engine, so different from the hospital ambulance's spluttering roar – but didn't look up. He looked in the direction of Ward M2 and remembered their last meeting in, of all places, the Sluice. "It's no good, Dick. Of course, I like you enormously, but—" And then he'd asked her why, asked her for one good reason for not marrying him. And then the last blow came: "Dick, you're so sweet. But you don't want anything badly enough. You don't fight hard enough. You dream too much. You'd be wonderful as a lover but no good as a husband."

Her words were more vivid to him now than they had been that morning; he'd been too upset, too hurt to take in any more than the simple fact that she's wouldn't marry him and therefore didn't love him. So after that he'd taken the easy way out: he hadn't visited M2, and he hadn't on the few occasions he'd seen her, spoken to her.

A few patches of ochre showed in the grey sky, as if dirty paint were peeling to show rust, then disappeared again. Dick's teeth began to chatter; he walked on briskly towards the main gate. It was a gate in name only; there were only two mortared scars on the inside of each tall stone column to commemorate what had once stood there.

Dick looked out at the road, his feet an inch behind where the gate had been. The ten o'clock bus to Nedham would pass in a moment.

"It's not Shopping Day today," Rock said.

Dick jumped. "I know it isn't," he said.

"There's nothing for us out there," Rock said. "Those iron gates are still up, double-locked as far as we're concerned." He grinned sourly. "And Evie's double-locked, too. And every bloody woman like her. I told you that once."

"I don't want your advice," Dick said. "I've had enough of this place."

"You'll soon have enough of it outside," Rock said. "What's your hurry, anyway? You'll be discharged in February."

Dick had turned his gaze back to the road. "I can't wait a month," he said. "You'd better go back to your ward, Nursie."

"You'd better come to your senses. What are you going to do when you get home? Beat Thirleton up and carry her off on your shoulder?"

"I want Evelyn. I can't stand this place without her. I'm going to Tanbury—"

"And then what?" Rock asked, his voice very gentle. "Tell me, Dick."

The east wind sprang up again; the fir-trees rustled convulsively. Dick recognised, almost with hatred, the same expression of pity on Rock's face as Tom Dellable's; and as he recognised it, he felt his anger drain from him. "I don't know what I'd do," he said. "I don't know."

"Stop wanting what you can't have," Rock said. "Stay here, mate. You're safe here."

"You're right," Dick said, with surprise. "You're safe here." Why hadn't he grasped it before?

He had only to stop fighting now, to stop wanting anything and he was safe. He wouldn't be safe because Nelly had ceased to dislike him but simply because she'd forget that he existed. Posted missing, presumed dead; but he was alive behind the lines.

"Come on then," Rock said, impatiently. "I'm half-frozen standing here." He stalked off up the hill, his arms swinging; Dick followed him, his jacket collar turned up against the cold.

25

"I'M afraid it wasn't much of a dinner, lad."

"It's fine," Dick said. He put butter on the last potato. "Look," he said, his mouth full. "I've been a good boy and eaten it all up." He smiled at his father. "Can I have my pudding now, Dad?"

His father stared at Dick sadly. "There's some tinned peaches. Tinned soup, tinned meat, tinned peas, tinned peaches – every bloody thing tinned but the potatoes and I didn't boil *them* long enough . . ." He collected the plates and shuffled into the kitchen. Dick watched him with mingled pity and irritation. His father didn't have to drag his feet or let his shoulders sag quite so much; he was a healthy fifty-four and not an ailing ninety . . . He leaned back in his chair and unfastened his waistcoat; he'd eaten that last potato – in fact all that had been put before him – far too quickly. If he hadn't cleared his plate his father would have been both offended and frightened. (*"What's up with it?"* or *"Dick, Dick, don't tell me you're losing your appetite again?"*), but since he had cleared his plate the old fool still had to find some excuse to be miserable, to blame himself, to suffer. An act as commonplace and as necessary as eating had, in his father's eyes, something like the emotional significance of the Last Supper.

It wasn't like eating in the Nurses' Hall at Nedham, where you were free to enjoy your food or to leave it half-eaten or simply to treat it as fuel to be absorbed at regular intervals. He felt a deep longing to be in that large airy room facing the sun, that room in which there were always young women. Even though hospital protocol didn't allow you to sit with them, and particularly not with Betty, they were there, and just to see them and hear them was enough. His father's house was dark and smelled of loneliness now; it was neither dirty nor untidy but there were the unmistakable signs that a woman didn't live there any longer – the Welsh dresser no longer carried a deep polish, it was a full day since the range had been blackleaded, and there was a film of dust over the mantelpiece, the cake-tin was empty, and in the bread-bin there was only a wrapped ready-sliced loaf. And outside the doorsteps weren't yellow-stoned any more and the backyard and pavement weren't ever scrubbed. When his mother was alive he'd often told her what a waste of effort it was to furbish stone which so soon would be dirtied if not by people walking over it then by the black smoke which, rather than oxygen and hydrogen, composed the atmosphere of Silbridge. But her answer had always been the same; a tolerant smile and then, slowly: "My mother always yellow-stoned her doorsteps and scrubbed the backyard and her part of the pavement too. It was a bit slummy where we lived in Leddersford and most of the women in our street didn't bother. But my mother did. And when I was a little girl coming home from school I could always tell which was our house. It looked nice from outside. And if a house looks nice from outside, it'll be nice inside, too . . ."

The fire was burning low; he went over and put on some coal. The grate was low-set and as he straightened his back he felt the litre of air pressing upwards against his lungs change position. He grunted involuntarily; it wasn't a severe pain and didn't last for more than a split second, but it was definitely a pain, like being hit in the solar plexus with a very small but very hard fist.

His father, setting down the bowls of fruit, said to him reproachfully: "I'd have done that if you'd asked me."

Dick slowly poured cream over his peaches, delaying the moment when he would have to eat them. "I'm not a cripple," he said. "You don't have to wait on me hand and foot, Dad."

"You've been very ill," his father said, lugubriously. "You wouldn't still have that damned P.P. otherwise. You might harm yourself very easily bending like that."

"I'm cured," Dick said. "Good God, can't you grasp that? Don't fuss, Dad. You're like an old woman—" He stopped himself; the pain on his father's face was too much to bear.

"You'll understand when you've children of your own," his father said. "You'll worry and fuss over them, especially when they've been near dying."

"I'm sorry," Dick said. "But there's no cause for you to worry now. I'm well looked after at Nedham." As he pronounced the name he once again felt a deep longing to be there; I'll be back this time tomorrow, he thought with guilty relief.

His father lit a cheroot and blew out a cloud of smoke with no apparent pleasure. "It's lucky you're there," he said. "Not that I reckon much to the job, but it's useful work, I suppose."

Dick flushed. "There's nothing else I can do," he said. "I've heard what it's like trying to find a job when you've had T.B. It's like having been in gaol; you can't keep it secret even if you go away from home. God, it's bad enough here – don't think I didn't see the way that bloody char of yours kept her distance from me . . ." His father was on the other side; he hadn't had the Bug, he couldn't understand.

"You know what's best," his father said. "There's nothing for you here, anyway. I'm thinking of giving up the shop soon. Tarkens's new shop has just about taken my best customers away."

Dick felt as if the floor beneath him had suddenly said in a dry matter-of-fact voice that it was going to dissolve into dust immediately. The shop was part of his life, solid as the Pennines, just as his father was part of his life. He thought of the Tarkens and their glossy new branch in Turner Street only two hundred yards away, and felt an enormous bitterness against them. "Those lousy grasping pigs," he said. "Haven't they enough money already?"

"Nay, you can't blame them," his father said. "They'd intended to take that site before the war in any case. That shop's a wedding present for Hubert."

"I wish him joy of it," Dick said. "I bet that area's not scheduled for redevelopment, is it?"

"No," his father smiled wryly. "It's just outside it. There'll be new flats here, and Tarken won't lose any custom; in fact, he'll gain. Well, that's business, lad. Thank your lucky stars to be well out of it."

"What are you going to do?"

"I'll find something. You know, Leonard was talking about buying a shop? He's not very happy where he is. I might go in with him. Joyce'd like me to live with them . . ." His voice trailed away. "I don't know that I'd do that, but I could get a room near them . . ." He rose and took a bottle of beer from the Welsh dresser. "It's no use sitting here waiting for the demolition gang to come." He nodded towards the beer. "Want a sup, Dick?"

"No, thanks." He looked at his watch; he'd have to meet Betty soon. A premonitory tremor of pleasure ran through him; but it wasn't like the keyed-up, almost sick pleasure he used to feel before he took out Lois. And it wasn't hopeless and sad as it had been the one time he'd taken out Evelyn, sitting in this very room wondering whether or not he wasn't making a fool of himself, knowing, as he yearned for her like an adolescent, that nothing would come of it, and then waiting in the foyer of the Raynton, needing a drink badly but afraid to leave the foyer in case she came in and assumed he wasn't there. But he knew he'd see Betty Fendigo and with her would come comfort. That was the word; a pleasant sane word. Comfort and cuddles and shop-talk; to meet her here away from Nedham would be like meeting someone from the same regiment. The sun was very bright now; Dick noticed the patch of dark stubble on his father's neck and, for the first time, the fact that his collar didn't quite match his shirt and that the knot of his tie was frayed. His father had shaved, but not with the same meticulous care as when his wife was alive; his shirt and collar were clean, but he didn't care whether they matched or not; and, of course, he had plenty of ties but he now snatched up the first one that came to hand. His father's head was bowed, his hand holding the untasted glass of beer as if for support; Dick had a desire to comfort him, but didn't know how to.

"I'll have some of that beer after all, Dad," he said, and saw his father's face lose a little of its melancholy. By the time they'd finished the second bottle, he was talking about how much better it would be for his health when he was living at Warley and how he'd take his grandson for walks every day; he even upbraided Dick for not producing grandchildren – "Your brother and sister are well ahead of you, lad. It's high time you found a good girl to look after you. You don't want to be an old dried-up bachelor . . ."

"I haven't had much chance to find a wife lately," Dick said.

"Well, you have now," his father said. "What about all those nurses, eh?" His face was flushed and his eyes bright; he wasn't drunk with beer but drunk with company, drunk because he wasn't having his beer alone.

"I've got one to meet now," Dick said. He drained his glass. "I mustn't keep her waiting."

"You're a deep one," his father said. "Never told me, did you?" He went over to the dresser for another bottle of beer. "I expect it's that Nurse Mallaton that used to be on M2. You were always a bit sweet on her."

"It isn't," Dick said.

"After another, are you? You're a fickle devil, our Dick."

"She's left Nedham. And she's engaged. Didn't you know?"

"I don't know anything, if folk don't tell me." He refilled Dick's glass. "Don't say you can't manage another at your age." He lifted his glass. "Well, here's to the new one, Dick, whoever she is."

Dick muttered Betty's name; for some reason he felt an almost prudish reluctance to do so. But his father scarcely seemed to have heard it; he was talking again about Warley and about the room they'd give him at Joyce's, a sort of bedsitter where he'd be private and not bother them: if he took it, that was, because you could never tell, they might have other children . . .

And that, Dick thought, was the last of his worries solved. When his father left Silbridge there'd be no need for him to visit the place again. It would be as if this house had never existed and as if Tanbury had never existed, nor Kellogg's Woods nor the Kasbah nor the Vodi: his past would be abolished. He rose from the table and picked up his raincoat which was lying on the sofa; that, he thought, was another of the untidinesses which wouldn't have been allowed when his mother was alive, another of the reasons for the house being home no longer.

As he opened the back door his father said: "Wait a moment, Dick," and came over to him and put two pound notes, folded small, into his hand. The action was surreptitiously executed, as if he were passing a betting-slip in the street, and when Dick thanked him he looked almost irritated.

"It's nothing," he said. "It's nothing. Buy your young lady something nice." He went back to the table, shuffling wearily again; as Dick closed the back door he was left with an impression that the room was very big and his father very small.

But by the time he'd reached the bus stop he'd pushed his father from his mind; he had six pounds in his pocket and didn't care if he spent it all; it was a fine spring afternoon and the air was fizzing with sunshine, and he was free. Free of Lois, free of Evelyn, free, now, of Nelly. *Stop wanting what you can't have*, Rock had said to him that day he was going to make an absolute fool of himself. It had worked; for once someone had given him good advice. He might have added: *Enjoy what you can have.* And he had Betty, part of the pleasure of having her, if having was the word, was that he'd always known, since the day he'd had that deep X-ray and he sensed Kanley's jealousy, that she liked him, liked him without complications. And soon, he reminded himself, there wouldn't be the necessity to make these fortnightly visits home, where every person you met discussed your state of health and your illness in a loud ringing voice and where you suspected the landlords of keeping a special glass for you and throwing it away as unfit for human use when you'd left. The last three visits hadn't been much fun; his father had been progressively gloomier each time, the journey was a long and dreary one and, above all, he'd been without a girl.

A Morris Oxford drew up beside him, and Hubert Tarken put his head out of the window. "Where are you off to, Dick?"

"Tanbury. Filper Street."

"I'm going that way. Hop in."

"You're looking terribly fit," Hubert said as he turned into the main road. "Sometimes I think I wouldn't mind a stay at Nedham myself. It's all work and no play for poor old Hubert these days. I haven't seen a football match for a year." He took out a packet of cigarettes and offered Dick one. Dick shook his head.

"Expect you've got to be careful now," Hubert said. "No more boozing and bad-living, eh?"

"In moderation," Dick said. "But you can't afford to do much of either on a nurse's pay."

Hubert belched. "Excuse me," he said. "I like my wife's cooking too much. They say no-one cooks like Mother, but it's a bloody lie . . . So you've given up shopkeeping, then?"

"The Council's made sure I'll give it up."

"I know. My father played hell about it – on principle, he's not affected personally – but what can you do?"

"You can't do anything," Dick said. "A few people'll make a fortune and a lot'll be ruined. That's the way it always works out."

"It won't be as bad as all that," Hubert said. "It's bad enough, I agree, but there'll be alternative accommodation offered." He rolled out the last three words with relish; Dick felt an impulse to argue with him but curbed it. All that mattered now was to be with Betty and away from this bridegroom of Nelly with his sunlamp tan and his gold signet ring and his new Morris Oxford.

"I suppose there will be," he said, flatly. "Anyway, I'm well out of it. There's not much money in nursing, but it's healthy."

"That's right," Hubert said. "Must put your health first. Money's no good without health. My wife was a bit seedy last winter – she'd worked like a black getting the shop ready – so I sent her off to Jersey. Cost a packet but it was worth it."

"You can't be too careful," Dick said. "You can't be too careful."

Hubert left him at the top of Filper Street. "Don't forget, Dick, drop in to see us any time," were his last words. "Any time at all, don't be shy. We'd love to see you."

As Dick walked down the street he smiled to himself; nothing, he knew, would have more dismayed Hubert than for him to accept that invitation. He looked round him with distaste: the road, badly pitted now after years of neglect – was so straight, the red brick houses with their mean little porches so uniform, that it seemed unlikely that in a moment he'd be with Betty. She didn't belong here, any more than he did; every house here was full of strangers.

He quickened his pace, then realised he'd forgotten the number of the house where Betty was staying. He stopped dead, hunting through his pockets for his diary, feeling an enormous disproportionate despair; he'd be here for ever vainly cudgelling his memory with eyes watching him behind curtains or he'd have to ask fifty suspicious house holders for the address of a couple whose name, too, he couldn't remember. The gabardine raincoat which had seemed too light earlier in the day seemed too heavy now and he began to sweat. Then he saw Betty waving at the window of the house opposite and he ran across the road.

He took her in his arms as he closed the front door behind him, staring at her greedily; she was wearing a square-necked red dress he'd never seen before, and her black hair looked as soft and shining as alpaca. She was a good answer to Hubert, he thought, pulling her forward to kiss her. This was the first time they'd embraced in comfort; the last time had been in a shop doorway in a Nedham side-street; it was a cold night and they were so well wrapped-up that it was more like the encounter of two parcels than a man and a woman. Here in this tiny hall crammed with coats and mackintoshes and goloshes and toys it was warm and private; he could sense from the quietness of the house that there was no-one else there. Her plump body was so palpable under her dress that he found himself trembling; he tightened his embrace and forced her lips open with his tongue.

After a moment she pushed him away. "That was nice," she said. "You're a jolly good kisser. Who taught you?"

"You did, darling, just now."

The contrast between those adolescents' words with their flavour of hockey and the classroom and that so obviously mature body, excited him still further; he took hold of her roughly and tried to kiss her again, but she pushed him away, a faint smile on her face.

"You'll want a cup of tea," she said, and pulled him by the hand into the kitchen.

"I don't really," he said. "I had beer with my lunch." He cleared a pile of newspapers and a golliwog and a teddy-bear from an armchair and, sitting down suddenly took her on his knee. She wriggled off and went over to the stove.

"I could smell it," she said. "Tea's much better for you."

He leaned back in his chair and stretched his legs; for what seemed like the first time in his life he felt an absolute contentment. The kitchen was scrupulously clean and the yellow paint on the walls was gleaming, but there were black hand-marks at waist level and long white scars obviously from the handlebars of the child's tricycle that stood in the corner. And there weren't only men's socks and shirts and underwear on the clothes-horse but three pairs of children's pants and three vests and a pink rayon slip and two pairs of stockings. A family lived here; for a moment his contentment was soured by a bitter longing.

"Tea's much better for you," Betty repeated. She came over to him and ruffled his hair, and then half-danced away from him to take down the teapot from the cupboard.

"It eats away the lining of the stomach like acid. Beer builds you up. Queen Elizabeth used to drink it for breakfast."

"It's none of my business, really," she said, her back to him. "I shouldn't tell you what to do. There's nothing men hate more."

He went over to her and put his arm around her waist. "That's all right, honey," he said. "It's a long time since any woman worried about me. I don't mind." He rubbed his cheek against hers and then ran his hand gently over her hair. That was enough, he thought; the happiness he felt now wasn't counterfeit, but it wasn't big, it was the small change of love. He hadn't a wallet full of splendid crinkling fivers, only a few silver threepenny bits, but perhaps they'd be enough to buy what, looking at that small, untidy, warm and impregnable room, he now knew that he wanted.

"I didn't mean that you were a dipso, Dick," she said. "But I've never been out with you when we didn't go into a pub."

"You like a drink yourself," he said, without heat. It was quite true; because it was so long since a woman had worried about him as a person he didn't mind her criticising his habits. In fact, he welcomed her concern; though, he thought, moving his hand down to stroke her back gently, the only possible cause for resentment as far as the owner of such an indisputable collection of endearing young charms was concerned, would be that she didn't take any interest in him.

"I do sometimes," she said. "But I don't want to go to a pub tonight. Or out for tea. It costs too much." She kept her face turned away from him as if she were making some shameful confession; suddenly he felt a horror of her otherness, a fear that once again he was going to be involved too deeply, that once again he was going to put himself at someone's mercy.

"I've plenty of money," he said. "I'd half-arranged to see Tom at the Grey Lion."

She stiffened in his arms, and then said coldly, "Excuse me. The kettle's boiling." She made the tea in silence, her lips compressed, and then rather noisily set out the tea-things.

"I thought of going to the flicks," she said. "Or we could go for a walk, if it keeps fine. We're invited to tea here." Her voice trailed off. She took a packet of cigarettes from her handbag; Dick took the packet from her and put two in his mouth. He lit them and handed one to her and said, "I half-arranged to meet them, Betty. I didn't definitely promise to be there." The cigarette was a brand he'd never cared for, and it tasted of face-powder; it tasted exactly as cigarettes used to do soon after he'd begun to smoke, a harsh adult taste.

"Jim and Mona'll be back at four," she said. "And Barry. He's sweet. Just three. He's mad about cars and bunny-wabbits."

"They mightn't be as keen as all that to have me to tea," he said.

"Mona was in hospital with me. It's not like ordinary people." She paused, her hand on the teapot. "I remember visiting some friends of mine just after I came out of hospital. They have a little boy of five, and when he wanted to kiss me goodbye they wouldn't let him. They said he was too old to kiss people. But he wasn't, you know. That was the first time they'd told him that."

"They must have been reading the bloody N.A.P.T. pamphlet," Dick said. "Sleep alone, don't kiss people, if you're a decent person you don't want to infect anyone . . ."

She poured out the tea.

"Not to worry," she said briskly. "It was a long time ago. It only happened once. I don't know why I told you about it – it hasn't crossed my mind for years." She put her hand on his and squeezed it. "You take everything too much to heart, Dick. You've got to accept things as they are."

He didn't answer, but looked at her fixedly. Her dress was low-cut and she was leaning forward a little; her hand on his was hot and moist.

"You're not listening," she said.

"Looking's enough."

"You mustn't look at me like that. It's *most* impudent." But there was no anger in her voice and her grip on his hand tightened.

As he walked down Minden Street that night he found himself whistling; he felt that he had somehow physically to demonstrate his happiness. The afternoon and the evening had been almost like a return to childhood, or at any rate, adolescence. The comfort and cuddles in the afternoon, the family tea with bacon-and-egg pie and home-made bread and cakes, the holding hands at the cinema in a courting-seat – double-sized with imitation leopard-skin upholstery – in between eating Terry's All Gold and ice-cream, the cup of Bovril in the Italian café next to the Electric Palace, the kiss on the doorstep at Filper Street, and even the ride home alone on the bus afterwards, surreptitiously scrubbing his lips with his handkerchief, had all made the sort of day he used to dream about when he was sixteen. And the comfort and cuddles had amounted to just that; so the fusillade of knocks on the front door and the kitchen-door before Jim and Mona entered, and the heavy-handed witticisms – *Can we come in? Are you decent? Aren't you sorry now?* hadn't left a bad taste in his mouth, and now he was coming home after a day spent with a girl, without considering whether he'd gone too far or not far enough, and without being either hurt and humiliated or so stupidly exultant that he'd have to pay dearly for it later. It wasn't a question of her being cold, of her leading him on, but simply that comfort and cuddles were enough, that all he had wanted was to burrow into her warm softness, to be safe and – that was the word – cosy.

When he went into the living-room there was a smell of gas. The fire had died down to a few embers and the room was cold. His father was sitting at the table, his elbows on it, he seemed to be scrutinising a stain on the pink check tablecloth. When Dick entered he grunted something under his breath; Dick turned from him impatiently and went into the kitchen where an unlit ring was hissing under a full kettle. He opened the kitchen window, gathered up a newspaper and a bundle of firewood from the box underneath the kitchen table and went into the living-room. He felt full of an almost destructive energy, an emissary from a tidier, warmer, younger, more organised world than that represented by his father who now, shivering, had shifted his glance from the table-cloth and was watching him lay the fire.

"We'll be going to bed soon," his father said. "There's no point in lighting the fire again. Coal's dear, our Dick."

"You'll want some supper," Dick said. "I don't want to catch my death even if you do."

His father sighed. "I've just this moment come in. The kettle's on."

"I know it is. And you haven't lit the gas. You might have killed yourself, you damned fool." He raked the grate angrily, coughing a little as the smoke caught his throat.

"You said you were going to the Grey Lion," his father said accusingly.

"I only said I *might*," he said. "Why didn't you go to the club? Or the Dancers?"

"Fancied a change." The voice was blurred. Dick looked at him in surprise. A change was precisely what his father never had fancied; ever since he could remember he'd always been securely and happily handcuffed to his habits, among which the Grey Lion had never been included. His father hadn't gone there because he needed a change but because he was lost, a small figure walking through a black canyon.

He put the image out of his mind, as he laid the fire. His father, like him, had put out the white flag; his troubles would soon be over. He put a match to the fire and with a subdued contentment watched the yellow flames scutter towards the sticks. It didn't matter how much the brave ones sneered; in the end there always had to be the compromise. He wanted, with a vague but real vehemence, the kind of prosperity that Tom and Hubert now enjoyed; he'd wanted the kind of woman that Lois, and even more Evelyn, had represented. And now he had Nedham and, he was fairly sure, Betty. It wasn't what he'd wanted, but it was as much as he was going to get.

He remembered the Bassett-Lowke Flying Scot in Muttle's in Tanbury which he'd longed for at the age of seven, credible in every detail down to the removable lamps and the nameplate; he'd longed for that locomotive and the Pullmans and mail coach that went with it with an increasing keenness as Christmas approached, had taken his father along to see it at least a dozen times, had even prayed that he'd be its possessor; and then, on Christmas morning, what he'd received had been a set of an unknown make. There was an engine – he refused to dignify it by the name of locomotive – with no forward or reverse controls, a non-detachable key, and four wheels naked of cranks or pistons; there were two coaches with the heads and shoulders of idiotically grinning passengers painted on the windows, and a station and a bridge and a circle of track. Choogo was the name; its synthetic coyness in comparison with the massive grandeur of Bassett-Lowke, had made his disappointment all the more painful. But as soon as he'd had breakfast he was playing with it and eventually grew quite fond of it; after all, it was in 1929, and the Choogo was the best his father could afford. And nothing had changed, he thought, as he went into the kitchen; his life was always going to be on the Choogo level.

He stood at the open window for a moment looking out into the backyard and the alley beyond it. The breeze blowing in was cold but had no freshness about it, no flavour of spring; it was cold in an indoor way, cold like an unheated waiting-room. And the darkness beyond the gas-lamps wasn't the same darkness as anywhere else; it had a claustrophobic quality as if a musty black cloth had been thrown over the town. He slammed the window down and lit the gas-ring under the kettle. The gas tap was stiff, as it had been for twenty years. He looked at the oven with a valedictory affection; soon it would be scrap iron, just as the house would soon be rubble. He drew the curtains abruptly as if to dismiss the thought and went back into the living-room. His father was drinking a glass of rum. Again Dick felt uneasy. It wasn't only that his father didn't usually drink spirits at home but that he didn't seem to be enjoying the rum.

"Don't you want any tea?" he asked.

"There's no law to say I can't have both," his father said, refilling his glass.

"You might offer me some."

"I thought you were nearly teetotal now," his father said, going over to the Welsh dresser. There was the suggestion of a sneer in his voice. "Anything with it?"

Dick shook his head. The incident of the unlit gas-ring began to trouble him again; he found it difficult to restrain the words of censure.

He swallowed half the rum at one gulp, coughing a little as the neat spirit hit his throat. He saw his father look at him anxiously.

"I'm all right," he said. "I'm not used to hard liquor now."

"You're better off without it, lad," his father said, heavily. "Much better off without it. But I'm old, you see. Old and worn-out. *Totally*" – he separated the two syllables – "worn-out! Finished." He emptied his glass again, and reached out to refill it. "Learned to like this in the War," he said. "You think you saw something in Burma, Dick, you saw nothing. Sixty thousand, sixty thousand they killed one day at the Somme. They ordered us forward, Dick, they ordered us forward on to the guns and the uncut barbed wire. We wouldn't have done it, Dick, but we were all drunk . . ."

"Never mind about that now," Dick said gently. "It's all over."

"The War to end all wars," his father said in a dreamy voice. "Aye. There was a victory parade in Silbridge. All those swine of councillors and parsons talking about Freedom and Justice and the Supreme Sacrifice . . ." His face contorted with hatred. "They're all the same!" he screamed. "Bloody governments and bloody councils! They're all out for themselves, Dick, they're all out for themselves. They'll get you, Dick, they'll kill you or rob you or both, and there's not a bloody thing you can do about it . . ."

"Don't, Father," Dick said helplessly. "You'll only make yourself ill. Don't think about it. You'll be in Warley with Leonard and Joyce soon" – he felt a pang of irrational jealousy as he pronounced his brother-in-law's name – "and miles away from here. It's a fresh start."

His father stood up, swaying slightly. "I'm off to bed."

Dick caught him by the shoulder. "You are going there, aren't you? Wasn't it all fixed?"

"The charity's all fixed. The charity for the old man."

"I don't understand."

His father came back to his chair. "They don't need me," he said. "How much capital do you think I'm bringing with me?"

"You've had thirty years' experience."

"Aye, with one little shop that's damned near bankrupt." He smiled at Dick and said in an unexpectedly brisk voice, "Just you think about yourself, love. You're all right where you are, you'll always be looked after. As long as you don't fall ill again, I'll be happy. So you needn't worry about me."

Dick put his arm around his father's shoulders. "It'll all work out," he said.

There was a silence; his father looked at him expectantly as if waiting for something else. Then he nodded. "Aye, it'll all work out."

"I'll make the tea," Dick said. He went into the kitchen. Closing the door behind him, busy with teapot and kettle, he stopped thinking for a moment. Then, as he put out the tea-things, he realised what his father had been hoping he would say. He rested his head against the cold stone of the shelf above him, wondering resentfully why events should move so quickly, reminding himself that even if he didn't say what his father hoped he'd say, there'd never be any reproach from him. He pulled himself erect – there wasn't any choice now.

When he took the tray into the living-room his father was staring into the fire, his face set in an expression which, he remembered, had taken over his mother's face when the morphine had softened the pain sufficiently to let her know there was no hope, that she was completely defeated. He put the tray on the table with a bang.

"You soft old devil," he said roughly. "Are we going to give up as easy as that?"

He saw to his delight his father's head jerk up and his face tauten and redden.

26

SMILING fixedly, Old Farvill waved goodbye to the little group standing by the Administration Block. "They're good lads," he said to Dick, stretching his legs out with an air of ease and comfort as if the shabby bus were his own limousine. He unwrapped the parcel which had been pushed into his hand as he stepped into the bus; it was a hundred box of Capstan.

"You'll be able to smoke yourself to death now," Dick said. "They must be fond of you, Bob."

Old Farvill did not answer, but stared at the box of cigarettes, his lips moving as if in prayer. He looked all of his sixty years; the smooth ruddiness which three years of regular meals and fresh air had given him seemed as artificial as rouge. He was no longer Old Farvill, the father of the sanatorium, but simply an old man in a navy gabardine raincoat a size too small for him. "They're good lads," he repeated. "We were a right happy crowd." He started to weep easily and without embarrassment.

Dick turned his gaze from him to Ward M2, just visible through a gap in the pines. A man in a bright blue dressing-gown came out on the verandah and shook his fist playfully in the direction of the bus. Dick smiled sourly; there, he thought, is another one who doesn't know when he's well-off. He shouldn't envy us because we're leaving the hospital this fine May morning with the world smelling of grass and trees and flowers and all the birds singing; he doesn't know what lies ahead of us. The bus smells of stale tobacco and disinfectant and old wood and old metal and we can't hear the birds; Old Farvill is returning to a terrace house in the Kasbah and an old mother who can scarcely look after herself never mind him; and I'm returning to take what my dear sister calls a hare-brained gamble. It had seemed both reasonable and splendid that night; they were going to close the shop down for a week and redecorate it themselves, they even planned the colour scheme – and build up the business again. There wasn't any reason why they shouldn't take some of Hubert's customers away from him. And then they'd look for new premises. They could keep the Minden Street shop going until they got the notice to quit; which mightn't be for two years. Or they could wait and see what kind of alternative premises were offered. If the site were good – If. Or, And, quite inevitably, borrowing money. And snatched meals and ten hours a day on one's feet and the smoky air of Silbridge: why hadn't he thought of all this before?

The bus was on the London Road now, picking up speed on the straight. The river ran parallel to the road until the hospital gates, looped sharply to the left through a gap in the hills, and then looked back to Nedham village. The walk along the river bank had always been one he'd enjoyed; perhaps the only one he'd enjoyed in the whole of his life. There was the arable valley and the wild uplands, the cow and corn country and the sheep and curlew country; from the banks of the river you could see them both. And from his bedroom window, for that matter, he could not only see that, but Roncey Woods to the south and Hardman Woods to the west. Tomorrow morning he'd awake to see the back of Plassey Terrace with the cooling-tower of the electricity works beyond it. The river would be there, the same river he saw now, but he wouldn't see it tomorrow; it went underground at Kellogg's Woods to become part of the drainage system of Tanbury and Silbridge.

The bus turned to the right down Quarry Hill, the steep winding road to the village. The woods on both sides of the road were very thick; one was plunged from a pastel-coloured world into a dark green tunnel. On the left there was a gap in the fence; the white splinters showed up as clearly as suddenly-bare bone. The brakes squealed going into the double bend just ahead; looking at the driver's shoulders, which seemed to be trembling with the effort of holding the bus on the road, Dick found himself thinking, with an almost sexual pleasure, of the various small causes of disaster. A loose nut, a worn cog-wheel, a frayed cable, a fly in the eye, a sneeze or a cough, and the lever would be pulled which would send them all – the driver, the conductress, himself, Old Farvill, the four giggling probationers in the back seat, and the fat old woman and three year old boy who'd just boarded the bus at Tempett Farm – crashing down together into the little stream which ran alongside the road. It was a pretty little stream with steep rocky banks; steep enough, he estimated, to let the bus roll over at least three times. You never knew your luck, of course. A sliver of glass could kill him immediately, could solve all his problems at the cost of a split second of pain, at the first impact; or he might scramble out of the wreckage with no more than a few cuts and bruises.

He felt an elbow in his side. Old Farvill, still weeping, was rummaging in his pockets evidently for a handkerchief. He gave up the attempt and put his hands to his eyes.

"Man crying, Gamma," the little boy said, twisting his head round to stare at Old Farvill.

"Hush, boy, hush," the old woman said.

"Man crying. Why man crying?"

Old Farvill started to blush blotchily, the tears running between his fingers. Dick nudged him and passed him a handkerchief. Old Farvill looked at the handkerchief incredulously – as if, Dick thought, he'd never seen one before – and wiped his eyes.

"Keep the hanky," Dick said.

"Three years," Old Farvill said. "Three years is a long time." His voice was quavering; the voice, Dick thought, with annoyance, of an incompetent actor portraying old age.

"Ah, stop brooding," he said, roughly. "You're not going back, Bob. You're not ever going back. Make the best of things, man."

Old Farvill's face puckered up as if he were going to cry again. "It's all right for you," he said. "You're a young man."

Dick shrugged his shoulders. There was no answer to that, he thought, there never was any answer to the truth. Because he was young, he could only go forward, he couldn't go back. He'd probably be beaten down to his knees very quickly, he probably was as foolish as everyone – Rock, Leonard, Joyce, Matron, Dr. Hinstock, Tom – said he was. Not just foolish, though; mad-headed, selfish, unwise, ill-advised, irresponsible, suicidal. Hardest to bear was Tom's little homily: *You're not really practical . . . You haven't enough push . . . Do you really know what you're taking on?*

"Man no cry now," the little boy said. He was sucking a large lollipop now; there were already purple stains on his white cardigan. He looked at Old Farvill with large unwinking eyes and, leaning over the back of the seat, offered him the lollipop. The old woman snatched the lollipop from the child's hand and pulled him down beside her. Dick scowled; the old cow knows where we come from, he thought. But Old Farvill was smiling at the child, who was wriggling in his grandmother's clasp. "He's a wick 'un, that," he said. "He's a topper."

Suddenly, as the bus turned the corner into the village square, he remembered what Betty had said when he told her he was leaving the hospital. "It's just what she would want you to do, isn't it?" It had passed over his head at the time, but now it seemed enormously important. For he hadn't done what Evelyn would have wanted him to do; he'd done what he himself wanted to do. Somehow he'd won an argument with her. It didn't make any difference now; but she couldn't despise him again, she couldn't take that superior attitude. *Good brakes but no engine*; he smiled viciously.

He stood up to take his suitcase from the rack, trying to dismiss her from his mind. He'd won the argument, but she wasn't going to marry him but Harry Thirleton; she was out of his reach for ever.

"We change here," he said to Old Farvill.

Old Farvill gave him a lost, bewildered look. "We go right through, surely."

Dick laughed. "Only with the visitors' bus. You didn't expect to ride all the way to Silbridge for fourpence, did you?"

He took down Old Farvill's case. "Come on, Bob, I'll look after you."

That's it, he thought, helping Old Farvill out of the bus. You can't have everything. She isn't for me, she never was for me. Then he stopped. "I'm a fool," he said. "She's not married yet."

"What's that?" Old Farvill said querulously.

"Nothing," Dick said. "Just thinking aloud."

He took Old Farvill's arm as they walked across the square to the Silbridge bus stop.

NEW AND FORTHCOMING TITLES FROM VALANCOURT BOOKS

Francis King	To the Dark Tower
	Never Again
	An Air That Kills
	The Dividing Stream
	The Dark Glasses
	The Man on the Rock
C.H.B. Kitchin	Ten Pollitt Place
	The Book of Life
Hilda Lewis	The Witch and the Priest
Kenneth Martin	Aubade
	Waiting for the Sky to Fall
Michael Nelson	Knock or Ring
	A Room in Chelsea Square
Beverley Nichols	Crazy Pavements
Oliver Onions	The Hand of Kornelius Voyt
Dennis Parry	Sea of Glass
J.B. Priestley	Benighted
	The Other Place
	The Magicians
Peter Prince	Play Things
Piers Paul Read	Monk Dawson
Forrest Reid	The Garden God
	Following Darkness
	The Spring Song
	Brian Westby
	The Tom Barber Trilogy
	Denis Bracknel
David Storey	Radcliffe
	Pasmore
	Saville
Russell Thorndike	The Slype
	The Master of the Macabre
John Trevena	Sleeping Waters
John Wain	Hurry on Down
	The Smaller Sky
Keith Waterhouse	There is a Happy Land
	Billy Liar
Colin Wilson	Ritual in the Dark
	Man Without a Shadow
	The World of Violence
	The Philosopher's Stone
	The God of the Labyrinth

* 9 7 8 1 9 3 9 1 4 0 4 0 1 *